Kindest
Regards...

[signature]

To Face The Fire
The 5 Boroughs Series: Book 1

What matters most
is how well you walk
through the fire

ISBN: 978-0-9974946-1-7

First Published 11-April-2016

Tattoo Artwork Copyright © 2016 Eric Lao
darkbishop@gmail.com
(serious requests for artwork and tattoos only)

Cover layout by Lisa Stout

<u>Disclaimer</u>:

This is a work of <u>fiction</u>. Names, characters, businesses, events, and incidents are either the products of the author's imagination or used in a fictitious manner. Any resemblance to actual events is purely coincidental.

All of the towns and cities mentioned in the book, do, obviously exist; as do many locations such as parks, train stations, airports, beaches, and even some businesses. You should go check them out! You can even take this book with you and read it in one of those various places! You can even take a selfie while reading the book in one of the various places and share it with me on Facebook- fb.com/NicolaNobleAuthor and/or on Instagram- @nicolanobleauthor or use #tofacethefire

This book does contain subject matter of a mature nature (ie – sex and violence, though not together). It has quite a few four letter words, like "work", "love", "book", and "this". It also contains some other four letter words that are generally bleeped out on the radio and prime time television. And, it also contains words and/or sentences in a variety of languages other than English. If you are easily offended by anything mentioned within this paragraph, this book may not be for you.

Be sure to see the Notes from the Author section and the Book 2 Preview at the end of this book (after the Special Thanks section. They are there and not here because ... hellooo, spoilers!

"But we mustn't, my love," Bianca said breathlessly, her breasts straining against her tight corset.

"I know, but I cannot contain myself," replied Reginald, accentuating each word with a kiss down her ivory neck. "I must have you now!"

"But my father, what will he ..." her words ending on a gasp of pleasure as his hand roamed under her right breast. Even through the layers of fabric and her corset, her nipple went taught at his touch.

"I don't care what you father says or who he thinks you should marry! You are mine! You always will be!" he demanded as he pressed his hips into hers so she could feel the meaning of his words.

While pulling his face down to hers, Bianca reaches for

...

I roll my eyes.

It's probably better than gouging them out with one of the pens scattered on my desk. I love my job, I really do, but some days I really wish I'd taken up Accounting or Marine Biology. Hell, I'd settle for Underwater Basket Weaving instead of editing ANOTHER horrible "romance novel".

Yes, I use quotes. When speaking to people I even use air-quotes. These stories aren't even long enough to be novellas! And don't even get me started on the predictable plots and one-dimensional characters. I haven't even gotten past the heaving bosoms and quivering member scene and I already know that these two soulless characters will either be caught in the act or in the "after-glow" by either her father or betrothed.

I reach for my tea to put off editing this "novel" for another moment. Then I try not to spit it out as I realize it has gone cold. On the bright side, I now have an excuse to leave my desk (and the abysmal story line) and head to the break room. I make it about two steps before the phone at my desk starts ringing.

"Miller and Hemmet Publishing. This is Donna."

"Hey Donna! I was wondering what you were doing tonight. I'm on my way home from my post chemo follow up and think we should celebrate!" I can hear her smile over the line and it makes me smile too.

I chuckle and say "Count me in!"

It's been a long hard road for Anna. After being diagnosed with Stage III(A) uterine sarcoma, her doctor, who had the bedside manner of a wet sock, immediately followed the diagnosis with "You'll need a hysterectomy. Be sure to see the nurse on the way out and have that scheduled." He didn't even give her time to process the diagnosis or even discuss what type of cancer it is and treatment options.

She left his office and before she could get over the initial shock, she called her fiancé Jerry to tell him what the doctor said. An hour later when she got home, Jerry wasn't there. The bastard left her a note saying that he wanted to be a father and since she couldn't have kids what was the point of being together.

Sitting in my apartment in the middle of a "Resident Evil" marathon my cell phone buzzed. *"Get here now".* One tiny text message and I was up off the couch. I threw a hoodie over my cami, swapped my ratty old bunny slippers for sneakers, and was out the door. Fifteen minutes later, and a bike ride that Lance Armstrong would envy, I was locking my bike to the stoop and running into Anna's building.

I didn't know what to expect when I unlocked the door, but it wasn't my best friend lying on the floor. Her entire face was red and streaked with tears. There was vomit on the floor not a foot from her. In a rush to get to her I tripped over a shoe and went flying. Anna made a sound between a laugh and a sob. Ok, she's not unconscious. That's good, right? I tried to sit her up but she told me to leave her there.

"Anna, what happened?!" I half shout.

This was not like her at all. She started crying again. The kind of crying where you think you're all cried out, but somehow there's more. It had to be bad, very bad. With a shaky hand she pointed to something on the other side of the puddle of vomit. I pick it up to look at it, but it's just a ShopRite receipt. I scan the list of items. I don't get it. I'm missing something but what? Then I flipped it over. A fucking "Dear John" letter? On a receipt?? Really?! And even the note itself isn't making sense. What does he mean she can't have kids?

I put the note on the coffee table in the living room and head to the kitchen. Grabbing a bottle of water, box of tissues, and a damp hand towel, I go back out to the hall. Bending down to pick up Anna my back pops. Geez! I'm only 28! At 140, it should be easy to pick her up and carry her the 10 feet to the couch but she's gone dead weight again.

After setting her on the couch as gently as I can, I use the hand towel to wipe off her face, open the bottle of water and tell her to drink, then replace the bottle with the box of tissues and sit down next to her.

"Anna?" She doesn't even look up. "Anna? What happened?" Nothing.

"Anna Banana Fo Fanna?" I chimed.

My lame attempt for a chuckle had her glance up at least, but the look in her eyes was just dead; like the world was ripped out from under her and she was a hollow shell. I choked on my next attempt to coax it out of her. I took her hand in mine and sat on the couch in silence.

"I'm going to die". It was barely a whisper and I almost missed it because of the noise in my own head trying to figure out what the hell happened.

I turned and looked at Anna. "Jerry leaving is not the end of you," I said and squeezed her hand as a show of strength.

She sat there shaking her head. I could tell she was having a hard time getting the words out so I waited some more. She stopped shaking her head, looked up, and whispered "Cancer".

~*~

A few hours later, Anna walks into the office with two boxes of doughnuts from the bakery on the corner. "I'm not officially back yet, just stopping in to share the news. My last chemo treatment was last week!" Her face lights up. Joan Marie jumps up and gives her a hug.

"Congratulations, dear! I've missed you!"

Joan Marie is like the office den mother. She is older than all of us and has been with the company since before half of us were born. She calls all of us "dear" and makes us each a tin of cookies for our birthdays. Just shy of 5 feet tall, she's slim without looking fragile and wears her silver hair in a bun that collects various pens and pencils throughout the day.

"I've missed you too! It feels great to be here. Just walking through the door I feel like I haven't been gone as long as I was."

Opening the top box of doughnuts, Anna grabs the blueberry one, places it on a napkin, and heads down the short hall to our boss's office. Sitting at my desk I try to tip my head down so no one can see my face as I try to suppress a chuckle. Fifteen minutes later, she's got her hip on my desk, leans down, and says "Ready to blow this popsicle stand?"

Even without the blueberry doughnut, our boss Max would have let Anna talk him into letting me go early. If she'd asked, he'd have let her take the entire department out of the office early. Don't get me wrong, he's a tough boss; at times infuriatingly so. He also has a soft spot for each of us.

After Anna was diagnosed, I convinced her to get a new doctor. Not for a second opinion, but for a doctor that had a team of caring people working for him. Once her treatment options were explained and after a night of us polishing off a few bottles of wine, she went into work the next day and in the privacy of his office asked Max for a leave of absence. When she came out of his office, she slipped off to the ladies' room. Five minutes later when Max walked out of his office to get lunch his eyes were still a little red.

I save what I'm working on and grab my briefcase. "So, where are we off to?"

~*~

"Would anyone care for dessert?" our waiter asks as he clears away our dinner.

"No thank you" Anna says the same time I say "What do you have?" I look at her sternly. "You are having dessert! We're celebrating, damn it!"

Turning to the waiter I ask what they have that's decadent or chocolate or both. I order a slice of the triple chocolate layer cake, a slice of raspberry cheesecake, a cannoli, and a bottle of Prosecco.

The waiter's left eyebrow hitches up the slightest bit, but he doesn't say anything. Anna however, thinks I'm insane. "After three courses, all of which we couldn't finish I might add, you STILL want dessert?"

"We're here to celebrate! What's a celebration without cake?"

"And cheesecake. And a cannoli. And a full bottle of Prosecco!"

I reach across the table and take her hand. "Anna. There's a time to be sensible and there's a time to be impractical. Let's gorge on decadent treats and champagne and worry about tomorrow when it gets here. After all you've been through, all the highs and lows. Let's celebrate all of it!"

The waiter arrives with our desserts and as we eat and drank we laugh about all the things we couldn't (or shouldn't have) over the course of the past 10 months. The only thing we never talk about is the day she was diagnosed. Not then, not now, and likely not ever.

After refusing to go halves, I pay the tab and we head out of the restaurant. It's still too bright out to be called night and too dark to be called day. We've missed the 9-5 crowd rushing out of the office to the bus, subway, or wherever it is they are trying to go. This is my favorite time of the day. It's when the City really seems to come alive. People shed their office selves and it's time to be out and about. It's the end of May but has a hint of the balmy summer weather to come minus the summer Friday grid lock with people venturing out of the City for the weekend. The only thing that tops this is in the Fall with the crunch of leaves underfoot, just before the cold starts to settle in. Oh! And Bryant Park when the ice skating rink is set up! I love getting out of work, grabbing a cup of coffee, and watching the skaters go around.

"Subway or cab?" I ask Anna.

"Cab. Definitely. I don't know if it's the amount of food or the amount of wine, but I'm exhausted!"

I put my thumb and middle finger between my lips and blow. It's an ear piercing whistle, the kind you would expect to hear at Citi Field. (Yes, I'm a New Yorker. Yes, I'm a Mets fan. Yes, I dislike the Stankees. Deal with it!) The whistle turns a few heads, but it also gets us a cab.

"Where to?" the driver asks.

"Brooklyn. 763 Ocean Parkway. Thanks."

Before we even get downtown, Anna's head is on my shoulder and she's sound asleep. It could be the overeating. It could be the wine. Or it could be that for the first time in 10 months she doesn't have to worry about the next chemo appointment. I take a long slow breath through my nose and then slowly let it out. All that's left are her follow up doctor visits. I try not to think about her chemo and the radiation implant just before surgery. I try not to think about how nervous she was before the surgery, worried that something could go wrong, while also mourning the children she always wanted and now couldn't have. I try not to think about how her "we got all the cancer out" happiness bubble burst when the results came back from the pelvic wash saying that although they surgically removed the cancerous tissue, there were still cancer cells found in the fluid. I try not to think about the chemo that followed which somehow seemed worse than before her surgery. I try not to think about the tears in my eyes trying to escape. And trying not to think makes me think more about how close I came to losing not just my best friend but the person who is the sister I never had growing up.

The cab pulls up in front of my building and as I'm taking Anna out I hand the cabbie $40 for a $28 fare and close the door. I don't care about the change; I just want to get far away from the cab and all the thinking.

I get Anna into the building. She's still half asleep and I'm thankful that somewhere during the building's 80+ year history someone was smart and added an elevator. There's no way I could get my klutzy self and a sleepy Anna up the stairs to the third floor. One or both of us would end up hurt.

I somehow manage to get us both through my door with the only injury being the door knob in my spine. Dumping her purse and my briefcase on the desk, I get her down the hall and onto the bed. I manage to get her wig off before she flops down on the pillow. I take it over to the antique hat stand in the corner of the room and put it on top of a baseball cap. It's the best I can do without a mannequin head like she uses at home. I get her sneakers off and toss a blanket over her. As an afterthought I go back down the hall and get her phone out of her purse; plugging it in to the charger on the night stand.

"Goodnight, Anna," I whisper as I turn out the light and leave the room.

Grabbing a spare pillow and blanket from the hall closet, I head to the living room and set up the futon. Then I head to the kitchen and grab a pint of Cherry Garcia and a spoon. After all we just ate at the restaurant I shouldn't, but I do, I totally do.

02

On Saturday, Anna gets up and goes home to shower and change before heading to her nephew's birthday party. Over coffee she kept trying to convince me to go with her. I already RSVP'ed that I couldn't make it, ordered a pair of Sponge Bob pajamas and slippers and five Dr. Seuss books, and had it shipped to Anna's brother Yuri. Don't get me wrong, I adore Anna's family, but I can only handle Yuri's wife Becca for so long. She's a very nice woman and all, but she's too sweet; not like sugar or honey, but like molasses; so sweet it's suffocating.

I toss on a pair of denim shorts, a T-Shirt, my comfiest pair of Chucks and grab my back pack. Instead of riding my bike to the Subway and going three stops, I decide to just ride my bike the whole way to LaLinda's. After last night's celebratory calorie binge, I could use the extra riding.

It's still early, but by the time I get there two stations are already occupied; each by a little old lady sitting with perm rods all over her head. I don't see Linda, so I head for the back room. They all know me here, so no one stops me from going into an area of the salon that's clearly marked "Employees Only". Not only have I known Linda since second grade, but I helped her scrape, paint, and paper the shop when she bought it. Just thinking about it has me chuckling. We were both so excited when she bought it. Even though it was back breaking and gross, the more we worked, the giddier we got. We finally both ended up on the floor laughing so hard our sides hurt when I stepped off the ladder, tripped over my own feet, and went ass first into a tray of paint.

I find Linda in the back unpacking a large cardboard box of hair dyes. The dye is tempting, but I just don't want to feel stuck inside for that long today. "Hey Chica!"

"Hey Momma, what's shakin'?"

She's always called me Momma. I've always called her Chica. Funny how she's the one with kids and I don't even want to think about my lack of kids or my last boyfriend. Damn, too late! Just thinking of trying not to think of Ralph makes me I grimace and flare my nostrils. I'm so not going there.

Linda comes over and grabs my hand. "You ok, Momma? You've got a look on your face like you're downwind of Jersey."

"What? Oh. It's nothing," I say shaking my head "My mind wandered to the last time I had a date. Don't ask, I have no idea why it went there."

"Ooooo, girl. You know what that means, right?"

"I'm not playing make over today. No. Seriously. I'm not. I was only coming in to get my brows waxed and then I'm headed down to Coney Island. And quit it with the smirk. No matter what you say it's only a brow waxing." I cross my arms over my chest for emphasis.

"Wiry. Grey. Hairs."

She knows me too well. I drop my arms and my chin in defeat and follow her to her station. I have one naturally pure white streak in the front which looks really good, like I spent a lot of time and money to make it look that good. However, in the middle of the top of my head are a bunch of wiry grey hairs that stick out all over the place that I have to cement down.

Two hours later, Linda has worked her magic again. She dyes all but my white streak a deep wine color and has cut it in long layers without cutting a lot off the bottom. My brows have been waxed into submission but I put a stop to the bikini wax. The only two people that even see that area right now are myself and my OB-GYN. That and "hello, McFly", I rode a bike here and am now headed straight to the beach. No thanks!

With a hug and a promise to drop off a loaf of my homemade bread and a half tray of lasagna tomorrow night in exchange for her salon wizardry, I am out the door and headed to the Subway. It's a pain in the ass carrying my bike up the stairs to the platform, but Coney Island is seven stops from LaLinda's. With all Linda just did, I don't want to toss my hat back on but I also don't want to look like a wild beast which would be the result of biking that kind of distance without my hair tamed. Besides, I can always bike the whole way home and only scare my cat; and possibly Molly, the old lady whose apartment is by the front door of the building.

When the weather is nice she calls the Super and he carries a folding chair out for her. When it's cold, she stays inside by her window. She says it's the arthritis in her hip that keeps her indoors. I think it's because ten years ago her husband Harry went to dig the car out after two days of repeatedly being plowed in and while he was out there he had a heart attack. The Super found him about half an hour later when he went out to shovel the sidewalk. Harry was already gone. Ever since then Molly doesn't go out in the winter. If her son can't stop by with groceries, she has them delivered.

Molly actually met her husband because of her hip. She was a USO girl during WWII (seriously ... how cool is that!). One night she was on stage dancing and singing. Her friend's high heel snapped off and as she fell she knocked down Molly too. Molly started going head first off the stage, her hip banging the edge, and just before she hit the ground there was Harry. He had jumped up onto his chair in the second row, over the shoulder of the guy in the row in front of him, and scooped her up just before she hit the ground. The rest, they say, is history.

~*~

Coney Island is one of my all-time favorite places to ride my bike for fun. It's relaxing down here by the water. Even when the Boardwalk is crowded, it's still got a relaxed vibe.

I lazily ride my bike around Coney Island without going any further west than the Cyclone's Stadium. I can't bring myself to go by the spot that used to be the Boardwalk Community Garden. Rat bastard greedy corporations and their slimy ways, they had the garden bulldozed in the middle of the night. Nothing says sneaky underhanded crooks like having workers show up at 4am to demo something that meant so much to so many people, to make way for a $53 million amphitheatre Manny Horowitz wanted. Decades of blood, sweat, and tears ended in the fresh vegetables destroyed, all the chickens tossed into cramped cat carriers, and all the garden cats tossed out into the street. Our Borough President is a dick!

As I ride along Asser Levy Park, my stomach starts grumbling. Weaving in and out of families headed to the Aquarium, I make my way to Tom's Coney Island. When most people think of food and Coney Island, they think of Nathan's. As much as I love the fries there, I don't eat hotdogs. When I think of food and Coney Island, it's Tom's. Chaining my bike to the rail outside the door, I head in and order a Brooklyn wrap, fries, and a vanilla Coke to go. When it's ready and bagged up, I hop back on my bike and ride along the boardwalk looking for a relatively quiet bit of beach.

Once I find a fairly unoccupied bit of sand, I chain up my bike and head to stake my claim. Pulling an old twin sheet out of my backpack, I set up a nice peaceful spot to watch the waves and enjoy my late lunch. Leaning back on my elbows, I take a deep breath and let it out slowly. A sense of calm washes over me. Long before Ralph, this stretch of beach had an effect on me. Here I can always find my center. Here is where I feel the closest to whole.

Before tearing into the bag of food, I unearth my Kindle and decade old iPod. I toss on a playlist at random and smile as The Cure comes on. I'm half way through lunch by the time I've checked my texts, email, Facebook, and Instagram; before opening one of my new favorite books set in an alternate universe. It's 2014 there too, but SO far advanced compared to here. The main character

Korben, is in Central Park walking around looking for a place to sit and finds a bench on the edge of some trees. It's doesn't look like the rest of the ones in the park. It's weather beaten. Most of the paint has worn off, and it looks like when it was fresh and new that it was lovingly carved by hand. It's also the only available bench, so it's that or the ground. He sits down to relax and falls asleep (no surprise here). When he wakes up he's still on the same bench but in the alternate universe. It's got a slow start but I'm glad I stuck with it. The story really starts picking up in the fourth chapter when he ....

"What the flying fuu- uudge?" I yell, remembering at the last minute there are some small kids playing in the sand nearby. Rubbing the side of my head I look down and there's a bright red Frisbee in the sand next to me.

"Whoa. Oh my god, are you okay?"

I look up and there's this guy jogging my way. I can't quite place the accent. It sounds like a mix of British and American with a dash of something else, possibly Australian. It would be drool worthy if it wasn't for the fact that I just got beaned with his Frisbee. He's muscular without being a total meathead, hair that's too long to be short, but too short to be long with the douchey little bit longer in the front, toothpaste commercial white teeth, rich frat boy dress down clothes, and he's barefoot. I half expect to hear him say "whoa, duuude". He comes to an abrupt stop right next to the Frisbee and sand flies into my French fries.

He drops to his knees at the edge of the sheet and puts his hand over mine where I'm holding it on the throbbing spot on my head. I go full on panic in two-point-five seconds. My Kindle, iPod, and sandwich go flying as I jump up, putting a good five feet of space between us, and go hyper drive into defense mode.

"Yo, buddy, back the fuck up!" Sorry little kids within earshot! "I don't know what the people are like where YOU come from, but here we don't think we can start touching perfect strangers!" I start tossing everything in my bag without bothering to shake the sand out first. I toss the now wasted food in the plastic bag from the restaurant, then bending down and picking up the Frisbee I aim it at the water and let it fly. "Fuckin tourists," I mutter as I head toward the nearest trash can.

"Hey! Wait!" he calls after me and I start walking a little faster towards my bike. "Let me at least buy you another lunch!"

I just get the lock off my bike and hop on when he jogs up. As I wrap my hands around the handle bars, he places his hand on my arm and I jerk my arm back instinctively almost falling off my bike. I don't like being touched by people I don't know, and even some that I do know.

"Whoops, steady there," he says as he reaches out to keep me from falling.

I try to pull away and we both go tumbling into the sand; the side of the bike pedal scraping down my leg. I suck in a breath through tightly clenched teeth as I feel it scrape off a few layers of skin. That's going to leave a mark; a very sand filled mark. Lovely.

I try to untangle myself from my bike and this guy that I'm now half sprawled over. I'm too mortified to panic over it either. To make matters worse, my shoe lace is stuck in the chain. Shoot me now. With a grunt I push myself up and try to extricate myself from the wreck in the sand. I manage to scoot myself off the guy and start working on getting my shoe lace unstuck. Out of the corner of my eye, I see him sit up and give himself a shake. As I free my footwear from the bike chain, he knee-walks over.

"Are you okay?" he asks.

"Yeah. Sure. Fine. I gotta go," I reply as I start pulling myself and my bike up out of the sand.

"That's a nasty scrape." Taking my elbow, he helps give me a boost up.

"It's nothing." Oh my god, it burns like a mutha!

"No, seriously," he says, placing a hand on the side of my face and slowly turning me towards him. "Are you okay?"

He looks at me as if he's trying to look through my eyes and down to my soul. Something flashes in his eyes.

"I gotta go," I squeak before breaking contact, hopping on my bike and pedaling away as fast as I can.

What the hell was that?!

03

On Sunday I run the lasagna and bread to Linda as promised. With the extra dough I made a Stromboli which is cooling on my kitchen table waiting for me to get home, cut, and wrap into individual portions. Then I'll toss it all in a large brown bag with a few paper plates and some oranges. When I get out of work tomorrow I'll hand it over to Leo, the homeless kid that sits in the Subway between 5th and 6th at Bryant Park. He's only 17. He came to "the big City" from some little West Virginia town I've never heard of with two friends to try to make it big in the club scene, with dreams of hitting the big time. They ran out of money after 8 months and have been living hand to mouth ever since. I met him about 6 months ago. What got my attention was that he wasn't asking for money. He was asking if anyone had any food they could spare or some warm clothes. I stopped and gave him a bottle of water.

"Will you be here tomorrow?" I heard myself asking.

The next day instead of just stopping, I sat down next to him and handed him a bag with an apple, two peanut butter sandwiches, a bottle of water, and a wool hat. There was just something that felt right about it. Maybe it was kismet, I don't know. But for some reason my usual aversion to strangers was nonexistent.

So, tomorrow he'll get a bag with Stromboli and a few oranges. He'll split it with the other guys and with any luck, they'll get enough loose change and singles over the next week or so from people that go by to rent a room for a night so they can wash what clothes they have, shower, and have a safe place to sleep.

Leaving work on Monday I stop to get a cup of coffee from the cart on the corner. "Helloooh, my sweetheart!"

"Hey Dada ji! Hey Nani ji!" Even though they've told me their names years ago, I can't help using the Punjabi words for Grandpa and Grandma because they remind me so much of my friend Ranii's grandparents. "One coffee, please."

I don't even have to ask; they already know I like my coffee "regular". I pay and as I'm turning to walk away, some ass hat comes barreling around the corner and straight into me. I get a quick glance at navy blue lapels before I realize the steaming hot cup of coffee has been crushed between us. Most of it goes down the front of my cream colored silk blouse. What hasn't spilled down the front of me or managed to stay in the cup has soaked the brown bag of food for Leo and the bottom gives out. The portions of Stromboli hit the pavement with a splat and the oranges try to roll away. Nani ji is able to grab all but one lonely orange that tries to make a run for it down 2nd Avenue and gets squashed in the intersection by a FedEx truck.

"Holy Mother Fucker Shit Balls!!" I can hear my own Grandmother's voice telling me that's not very lady like, but holy hell this coffee is scalding! A giant wad of paper napkins is headed straight for my chest and it isn't Nani ji trying to help. It's the guy in the suit! What the hell?!

"Back off, asshole!" I yell as I take a step back.

Six months of self-defense classes that my Uncle insisted on and my mind goes blank. Instinctively though, all those years of growing up with three brothers kicks in and before I realize it, my fist makes contact with his stomach and he bends forward.

My jaw drops. Pitched forward like this I get a good look at his face. It's Frisbee guy! "You?!" I shout.

Reaching around him, I grab the salvaged food Dada ji has rebagged for me, and walk away as quickly as I can. On the way to the Subway, I text Anna. "Yellowtail Moscato, chilled. Skip the glasses. I'm on my way." I find Leo and with a "dude, don't ask", I hand him the bag of food and head to the train.

~*~

"Seriously, what did I do to piss Karma off?" I ask Anna as I take another sip of wine straight from the bottle.

"I can't believe you sucker punched him!"

"I didn't sucker punch him. I, albeit unintentionally, punched a sucker. Which is the mildest of terms to describe that whole ass."

I cast a glance at the kitchen sink where my favorite shirt has been soaking for 10 minute intervals. It's a futile attempt. Nothing has worked so far. I sigh and take another sip of wine.

"Don't know mean 'asshole'?" Anna giggles. "Maybe you've had enough wine for one evening."

"No, I meant whole ass. Asshole is just one small part. This guy is all the junk in the trunk, not just a small hole. I swear, if I ever see him again, I'm going to force feed him my ruined shirt and dub him Sir Gluteus Maximus!" Ok, maybe I have had a bit more wine than I should.

By Thursday I can't it anymore. I've avoided leaving the office during the day and each night I leave via the loading dock and take a different route to the train for fear of getting mowed down by a dipshit. First it was a knock to the head and a massive sand filled scrape down my leg, the second time it was getting burned by boiling hot coffee; I'm not willing to risk life and limb on a third encounter.

Unfortunately, I forgot to bring in a new box of tea this morning and the coffee in the break room looks and tastes like someone dumped cheap coffee flavoring into the Hudson. I'm caffeine-less, cranky as hell, and ready to climb the walls. I give up! I stand up, slam my briefcase onto my desk, fish out my phone and wallet, and out the door I go. Stupid friggin tea! Stupid friggin Bianca and her heaving tatas! Stupid friggin Reginald and his quivering member! Stupid friggin douchey assholes! Stupid, stupid, stupid!

"Helloooh, my swee-," Dada ji stops short. "Oh my. You look very, very, unhappy. I will make you a large coffee today. This will make you very, very, happy." He hands me a white daisy and gives Nani ji a wink. She giggles. What was that all about?

There's a small light blue piece of paper wrapped around the stem and tied with a piece of twine. It'll have to wait until I get back to my desk since I now have my wallet, phone, and the flower in one hand and the cup of coffee in another. Before I even step away from the cart I look both ways. Turning 180° on the spot, I head back to the office.

"Woohooo. You leave in a huff and come back with cup of coffee and a flower. Who's the lucky guy?" Joan Marie says as she bumps her elbow into my arm and winks.

"Ha! As if. I got both from the couple with the coffee cart on the corner."

I walk over to my desk and set the coffee down far away from the keyboard. I've already learned that lesson. Twice. I have to use scissors to cut the twine it's tied on so tight that I can't undo the knot. Unrolling it reminds me of those horoscope scrolls we used to get out of the vending machine when I was a kid along with stickers and temporary tattoos.

Please accept this
as a peace offering
~K

I head over to Joan Marie's desk and hold the note up in front of me for her to see. All she can offer is a shrug. "Maybe the K is for Krishna and it's a Hare Krishna thing?"

I'm not sure, but I highly doubt it. I shrug and head to the break room to get a plastic cup of water to put the flower in.

Getting back to work I can't help but smile at the silly daisy. It looks so out of place poking its head out of clear plastic cup, all nonsensical in a very practical looking office. That, and it's a nice distraction from the plight of the now banished Bianca and her chained in the dungeon Reginald. (Seriously, who comes up with this crap?!).

At 5:00 on the dot, I save up what I'm working on, save a copy to the thumb drive since tomorrow I'm working from home, and pack up my brief case. As I go to grab the daisy I knock the top of the cup, spilling the water onto my keyboard. If Max thought two keyboards in the past three years was bad, I wonder what he'll think of a third. I turn the keyboard upside-down, give it a shake; then leaving it upside down, lay it on some paper towel and hope for the best come Monday.

Bee-bee-beep! Bee-bee-beep! Bee-bee-beep!

Rolling over, I open the drawer of my nightstand and brush my phone in before closing it again. It's nice to have a day to work from home and not have to get up at 6:30, but that doesn't mean it's any easier to get out of bed at 9.

The smell of coffee brewing gets me out of bed though. I'm so glad Anna talked me into getting a coffeepot with a timer. On autopilot, I shuffle into the kitchen to make myself a cup before setting up my laptop in the living room. Yeah, I have a desk at home. But when I work from home the last thing I want to do is sit at a desk. Heading back into the kitchen sipping my coffee, I toss a bagel in the toaster. Between the smell of coffee and the bagel I'm slowly becoming more human.

Buzz! Buzz! Buuuuuuuuzzzz!

Who the hell is hitting my buzzer this early? Anna is getting here at 10 and she's got a key.

I pick up the phone in the hall that connects to the lobby "Yeah, whadda you want?"

"Is that anyway to talk to your baby brother?"

I reply with a yes, buzz Nico in, and unlock my door. Two minutes later he walks in all "Donna! My favorite sister!" and pulls me in for a bear hug.

"I'm your ONLY sister Nico. What do you want?" Nico is the quintessential Italian family baby boy — everybody adores him and he can do no wrong.

My parents were married for two years when my oldest brother Carmine was born. Two and a half years later, Marco was born. I was born fifteen months after Marco. My parents tried and tried for more, but nothing happened. The doctors said there was no reason why they shouldn't be able to conceive; though years of trying and nothing.

It wasn't until they resigned themselves to the fact that they wouldn't get the huge family they always wanted that Ma found out she was pregnant with Nico. I was 8 when he was born. He was two months early. There were complications. Those first few days we weren't sure if my mother and brother would make it. Carmine, Marco, and I stayed at Nana and Nonno's house. My father was at the hospital and never left my mother's side. The only time they were apart was when the nurses wheeled her down to surgery; which she only agreed to on the condition that my father went home to shower and eat.

Growing up, there wasn't much Nico couldn't get away with. He'd flash an innocent smile and blink his baby blue eyes a few times and like magic he'd get what he wanted. I think part of that was knowing that we almost lost him. The other part is all him. Even as a little kid he was Mr. Personality Plus.

"Who says I want anything?"

"Ok. What did you do?"

"Aaah, come on, Donna. It's not like that. I was just passing by and Ma said you were working from home today. I thought I'd join you for breakfast on the way to class."

"Ah, ha! I knew it was something! And you can drop the innocent look, Nico. That stopped working for you over a decade ago. What did Ma send you over to spy on or get information on?"

"Ah-ight, fine," he whines, putting his hands up in surrender. "I'm supposed to find out if you're bringing a date to the anniversary party; somebody that's NOT Anna."

"I can't bring somebody as a date that's already invited to the party, stupid. You can tell Ma that I am most definitely NOT bringing a date and that next time she can just call and ask me herself."

"Sure thing," he says as he reaches over the table, grabs my bagel, and heads out the door. Little thievin' bastard! That was my last bagel! I go get my phone from the drawer of my night stand and text Anna. "Bring Carbs!"

Half an hour later there's a plate with bagels, muffins, and assorted pastries on the coffee table. I decided to just bring the coffee pot into the living room and set it up on the end table with the sugar bowl and a small pitcher of milk.

"Which one are you working on now?" I ask Anna.

She may not be back in the office yet, but Max has allowed her to work from home. He was able to get her the leave of absence for 6 months. We all thought she'd be back after she healed up from the surgery anyway. At the end of the six months, the insurance company said that if she wasn't back to work, they'd have to drop her coverage. So, Max let her set up at home and work remotely.

"Biography. Nikola Tesla." I'm so jealous. "Are you still on that crap historical romance?" I hang my head and nod. "Wanna swap for an hour?" I jump off the couch and hop from foot to foot.

"Oh please, oh please, oh please! I'll be your best friend!"

Laughing, Anna hands me her laptop and I fork over mine. Well over an hour later I call a time out for lunch. As much as I don't want to stop working on the Biography, I can tell by the sigh of relief coming from Anna that she can't wait to switch back. I can't say that I blame her. If I get anything else by this Sahteen person (I kid you not, a one name moniker that's a play on the word satin) I'm going to throw myself at Max's feet and beg for mercy. I'll latch my hands around one of his ankles and plead as he drags me around the office until he finally caves. The mental image is so funny that I share it with Anna.

"I'd pay to see that," she laughs and heads to the fridge for some more iced tea. "Hey, what's with the flower in coffee cup?"

"I didn't want to put it in a plastic cup. I tried that at the office and knocked over the cup full of water. I figured a coffee mug has more weight and won't tip as easily." (I really hope that keyboard is functional on Monday!) "Ooo," I say as I get up from the table "what do you make of this?"

I take the note off the fridge and hand it to Anna the note before filling her in on the story. Her left eyebrow dips a bit, a telltale sign that she's trying to come up with an answer, but none of them make sense. "Joan Marie thought it might be a Hare Krishna thing because of the K".

"Hmmmm. What if that's not really a K? I mean, that's assuming this line is a dash and the K stands for something. What if the dash is part of the K and it's a symbol for something?" We finish lunch and then waste half an hour looking for something that could be a symbol and come up with nothing. "Dun dun duuuuun. The plot thickens!"

I smack Anna with a throw pillow. "What if it's not a dash K? What if it's not a symbol? What if we're reading into this more than we should and it was something as simple as someone gave it to one of them and Dada ji thought I could use it as a cheering up?"

"You're probably right. It's the only thing we've come up with that actually makes sense."

On Saturday I head over to my cousin Susanna's apartment. It's our last chance to get the center pieces done and the favors wrapped for her parent's anniversary party next weekend. Since her sister Cristina isn't flying in from Italy until Thursday, it's up to me to take her place seeing as Zia Pina and Zio Massimo are my godparents. While bashing her brothers and how bullshit it is that, being males, they are somehow allowed to escape all the planning and prep yet get an equal share in the credit, we're wrapping Jordan almonds in Tulle circles. If I ever see another one of these stupid almonds again after next weekend, I may lose my marbles.

Sunday I decide to leave my cell phone in my apartment and head outside for a few hours to watch all the old Russian men from the surrounding buildings meet up to play Chess out on Ocean Parkway. I have no idea how to play Chess. I've tried learning but it's a futile effort. Even though I have no idea what's going on in the game, and only catch about a quarter of the words being said, I'm having a great time. I haven't done this is so long, I've forgotten what it was like to take a day to unplug, relax, and enjoy my neighborhood. I really need to go back to doing this; I've missed it.

Monday morning, Max calls me into his office. He wants to set up a meeting with the author to discuss the edits.

"I've got a question and I need an honest answer. This book ... is publishing it a favor to someone or did someone lose a bet or something?"

He raises an eyebrow. "Or something."

"I thought so," I sigh. Leaning back in the chair, I put my hand on my forehead trying to come up with the words to convey just HOW bad it is. "Does this 'or something' involve you directly?" Max, being Max, waits until I open my eyes and shakes his head no. "Good, because this book is so horrible I can't even come up with words to describe just how bad it is, Max. It's so bad it's like an insult to whoever reads it once it's published." He raises his eyebrow again. "You have no idea how many times I've contemplated having my eyeballs removed so I never had to look at it again."

That gets a laugh out of Max. "That bad, huh?"

I tell him my begging and pleading visual from Friday.

"Ok, ok, I won't force you to be a part of the meeting then. Since the author is the original Hemmet's great granddaughter it's probably best you aren't there. If it's that bad, you might not be able to hold back on your verbal assessment of the book."

"Thank you! Thank you! Thank you!"

"Have it done by Wednesday morning. I'll set up the meeting for Friday and give you another work from home day. However, I also expect some kind of baked goodies in exchange. Homemade baked goodies. Do we have a deal?"

"Aye, aye, captain!" With a broad smile, I turn and leave his office.

~*~

After work, I run into the CVS on the corner for a loaf of bread and a jar of peanut butter. I snagged a few plastic knives from my desk drawer on the way out and the bananas I'd bought from the fruit guy down the block on the way into work this morning. I make my way to the Subway and meet up with Leo. Sitting down next to him, I apologize for the drop and run last week.

"No worries," he laughs. "You didn't look like you were in the mood to hangout anyway." We sit in silence for a few minutes while he eats a banana. "Hey, the guys and I want to thank you for all the food these past few months. Weekend before last we were able to get a room for the night and get cleaned up. We kind of feel bad though that you're spending your money on us and we have nothing to give back."

"When you guys make it big, dedicate your first album to me and we'll call it even." We laugh.

Leo bumps my shoulder and leans in a little. "Time to move," he whispers. I raise an eye brow. "Same suit walked by three times looking at us out of the corner of his eye. He might be a detective or something. After next week, I don't care if I get stopped. But until then, I'm under 18 and they'll send me back home."

His parents were drunks who liked to use fists instead of words and his uncle was sleazy in the touchy feely sort of way. I understand why he doesn't want to go back.

"Or, he's some kind of nut job," he continues. Either way, I'm walking you to the train. Don't give me that look. It's safer that way, for both of us. If he was eyeing me, I blend in better walking with you. If he was eyeing you, you're not walking by yourself."

The D train shows up first, and when the doors open, Leo gives me a shove in. "This isn't even my train." He tells me to shush. "Ok, a reroute it is", I mutter.

At DeKalb, I transfer to the Q and Leo hops on the D back up to the park. I make a mental note to bake some cupcakes on Saturday for Leo's birthday next week and hope that he hasn't been picked up by then.

Wednesday morning, I show up to work an hour early. Seeing as I'm not a morning person, it was one hell of a feat managing it. But I had ten more pages of the decrepit book left to go over and I wanted to make sure that the pastries I baked for Max were on his desk when he got here.

By quarter after nine, I've got the edits finished up and emailed off to Max. "Booyah!" I yell to no one in particular and do a little victory dance in my seat. Bu-bye, Bianca. Bu-bye, Reginald. Don't let the door hit you on the asses on the way out! Ecstatic to finally be finished, I grab my wallet and head out for some coffee.

"Hey Nani ji! Medium, regular. And, toss in some kind of pastry that isn't blueberry."

"Ah, somebody is very, very, happy this morning." I can't help but smile more at her smile. "$4, please." I hand off a 5 and tell her to keep the change. "This is for you," she says handing me the coffee; "and this is for you," as she passes me a brown bag with a mystery pastry inside. "Oh! And this is for you too!" She hands me a bright orange tulip. This one has yellow paper and twine.

"Thanks," I say not sure what to make of the flower or her giggle. Any other woman in her 60s would look ridiculous giggling like a little girl. On Nani ji it's really sweet. I wave to her and Dada ji who is off to the side having an animated conversation on his phone and head back to the office.

Ten minutes later I'm frowning down at my desk when Joan Marie comes over. "I thought you'd be overjoyed to be finished with that last project."

"Oh I am! Believe me I am. It's just this," I say as I hand her the paper from the tulip.

"Ooo, a secret admirer," Joan Marie says with a wink.

I laugh it off and she hands me back the note as she heads back to her desk. She might think the idea of a secret admirer is romantic. I think it's psycho stalker creepy.

~*~

"I get that you think it's weird and all, but have you even thought to ask who is giving them the flowers?"

"Duh, Anna." I stop applying eyeliner long enough to look at her in the mirror and stick my tongue out at her. "Whenever I ask, she just giggles and he smiles so wide you can count all his teeth."

Walking away from the vanity mirror, Anna heads over to the closet door and takes her dress off the hanger. I watch her reflection as she crosses the room and steps into her dress. I bite down on my back teeth trying not to cry. In only a bra, underwear, and pantyhose she looks so frail. She's dropped thirty pounds since the day she was diagnosed. She used to joke that a lot of the weight loss was her hair which used to be down to her waist; any attempt to lighten the mood back then.

"Just do it," I remember her saying as we stood in her bathroom.

"Are you sure? 110% sure?"

"Yes. I'm going to lose it anyway. I'm sick of having to wash it after I puke because it hurts to tie it back when I'm at my worst. I may not have control over anything else that's going on with my body right now, but this one is up to me. Just do it".

My eyes meet hers in the mirror. The steely determination in her eyes has me nod. I gently pull her hair back from her face so it's all flowing down her back. Holding it loosely between her shoulder blades, I bring my shaking hand up and cut. I put the scissors down and tie a rubber band around the end. I'll call Linda tomorrow and ask if she knows a place that can turn Anna's own hair into a wig for her. I turn to head to the kitchen for a zip top bag.

"Keep cutting," Anna says. I cut it so that it's chin length.

She opens the cabinet and pulls out a disposable razor. "We're not done until we've used this," she says placing it on the side of the sink.

She isn't crying, isn't sad, isn't nervous; she doesn't even look defeated. She looks brave. I draw from that, and with hands a little less shaky I start cutting chunks until it is short enough to shave. Taking a dry wash cloth from the shelf, I brush away the strands that didn't fall to the floor.

"Ok. Ready?"

She reaches behind the shower curtain and pulls out a can of shave gel. "Ready!"

I take a slow deep breath and get to work. I have to drain and refill the sink four times before she's completely bald. I grab a fresh towel, wipe off the remaining foam, and say "Sinead O'Rebellion! Shock me shock me shock me with that deviant behaviour!"

We burst out laughing.

Snap! Snap!

"Donna! Hello? Anyone home?"

I blink a few times and the memory fades to the background. "Oh, sorry, spaced a bit there, huh?"

"Uh, yeah. Zip me up. And you better get a move on, or we're going to be late."

06

The anniversary party was a success! It was great getting to see everyone. Though, to be honest, I could have done without constantly hearing "Where'sa you boy-a-frend? When you gonna getta a new boy-a-frend? How you eva gonna getta married witoutta da boy-a-frend?" I evaded all the questioning as best as I could.

I made sure to get in a dance with Zio Giovanni. Since I was a little girl, whenever there's a family gathering I always make sure to get in a dance with him. It was something that somehow just became our thing over the years. His ice blue eyes always sparkle with mischief and I've never seen him without a smile on his face.

I remember once when I was 6, I was sitting on top of the kitchen table over at his house. He was teaching me how to cut fruit with a paring knife, then tip it and eat said fruit off the back of the knife. When Ma and Zia Grazia got back from shopping and walked in I couldn't tell who was holding who up. Both their mouths looked like fish gasping for air. He put his hands up like a shrug and said "Oops".

My aunt walked over and slapped him on the shoulder. Ma pulled me down from the table and dumped me in a chair. "You know better!" they both yelled, pointing at each of us. I looked at my uncle. As he turned to look at me, we both started laughing.

~*~

I spend most of Monday working through a cookbook. They tend to be pretty straightforward when it comes to editing unless there are stories along with the recipes. This one is all on cooking your way through the Mediterranean and looks promising. It might even be one to pick up once it's out.

When 5 o'clock rolls around, I go get the cupcakes I baked last night to drop to Leo along with some napkins, a few bottles of iced tea, and three T-shirts I picked up from a thrift store; a present for each of them. I'm a little nervous though because I've been wondering if Leo got picked up by the cops. But when I see him sitting reading his book, I smile.

"Happy Birthday, kiddo," I say as I plop down next to him.

He laughs as he takes out a cupcake. "You're awesome!" He bites in, then laughs in surprise when he realizes the frosting is on the inside of the cupcake.

"Less mess that way," I say, "and you won't lose the frosting this way either. Here, check this bag". I hand him the second bag. He looks dumbfounded when he pulls out the T-shirts. "One for each of you."

"You so rock!" He jumps up, pulls off his grubby flannel, and puts on a T-shirt. "Like Manna from the heavens." He flops back down and takes another cupcake out of the bag. "These are seriously good! Where'd you get them from?"

"I made them. From scratch."

"You made these?! Oh my god, you have to marry me! Please! Don't make me beg!" We burst out laughing.

"I know they are for your birthday, but make sure there's some left for the other guys, ok?" I say as I get up to head to the train. "See you next week kiddo!"

~*~

A few days later there's another flower waiting for me when I get a cup of coffee; an Iris this time. As usual, I get a giggle and a toothy grin. I change tactics. "Ok, what can you tell me about the person leaving the flowers?"

"Nice man. Nice man."

"Very, very, handsome!" adds Nani ji

"What do you mean he is handsome? You are my wife! MY wife! You should not be looking at other men like that!"

Nani ji just rolls her eyes and winks at me.

"How do you forgive someone you don't know for something you have no idea what they did?"

"Your guess is as good as mine, Anna. But I don't like it, this is just too creepy."

I pour some wine into the sauce pan, give it a flick, and set the white clam sauce on fire. Jiggling the pan a little as the flames die down, I toss the linguini in the boiling water, add salt, and give it a stir.

Anna stops cutting up a cucumber and looks up at me. "Think you should show this to your Uncle Nino?" My uncle is a detective in the NYPD.

"I've thought about it more than once. You know that if I tell my uncle though, I may as well tell the whole family. If this keeps going or gets any creepier than yeah, I'll give in and call my uncle. But enough of that tonight, let's finish getting everything set up before everyone gets here."

I turn the sauce to low, give the pasta a stir, and check the trays in the oven before going to the hall closet and lugging out the folding table. After getting it set up in the living room, I quickly cover it with a table cloth and head back to the kitchen to start bringing out the food. While I get that set up, Anna sets up a make shift bar at my desk in the office alcove.

Since Anna got sick, we go out to the clubs less, and have friends over more. The get-togethers are always at my place that way if Anna starts getting run-down she can always head home instead of trying to keep up with a house full.

Half an hour later, people have started filing in. There are friends everywhere in small groups around the living room, my office alcove, and especially in the kitchen. I'm working my way through the pile of pots and pans to get them done and out of the way. When I'm done here, I'll can head to the living room to grab a plate of food and hang out before getting out all the desserts. I also know that if I don't take care of them now, there's no way I'm doing them after everyone leaves. That's the thing about these once a month get-togethers, people come and go for the better part of five hours. When the last of guests has left, all I want to do is lock my door and go pass out. Once all the pots and pans are in the dish rack, I open the fridge to get out another bottle of Moscato.

"Anything I can do to help?"

"No, I've got it," I say as I back out of the fridge.

My jaw drops when I stand up. There on the other side of my refrigerator door is Sir Gluteus Maximus himself! The bottle of wine slips through my fingers, hits the floor, and shatters. Stunned, I take a step back and my left heel comes down on a piece of glass.

"*Madre stronzo puttana!*" I yell as Anna comes running into the kitchen.

I'm standing in my kitchen on one leg, my left foot dripping blood into the river of wine and glass on the floor. "What the hell happened in here?" Anna asks.

"Get me the broom and a towel. I need to sweep this glass out of the way. Then I'm going to cover it with the towel so it doesn't slide back and I've got a clear path to hop to the bathroom to take care of the glass in my foot."

Before Anna can move, "Gluteus Maximus" reaches over the glass, picks me up, tosses me over his shoulder, and heads down the hall to the bathroom. I've now added "Neanderthal" to his list of traits after douche canoe and whole ass. I may even add wrecking ball to the list because EVERY time I run into him, he causes bodily harm.

Reaching up, he grabs the hand held shower head before setting me down on the edge of the tub. Then he turns the water on and sprays my feet. The water is freezing cold!

"What the fuck is wrong with you?!" I shriek as I make a grab for the sprayer. I turn it and the water off being careful not to bang my heel on the bottom of the tub. "Are you TRYING to kill me? What are you even doing here?"

"I came with Matt & Nicole," he says as he starts rummaging through my medicine cabinet. Ok, make that pre-Neanderthal, as I'm pretty sure that the Neanderthals understood the concept of boundaries and personal space; concepts this guy clearly doesn't understand. "Here. Give me your foot."

I can't help it, I laugh, albeit sarcastically. "You're kidding, right? Every time you're around, something happens that results in me being injured. No thanks!"

I reach over to the sink where the tweezers are looped on the mug I use as a toothbrush holder; and for the first time in years I'm very grateful that the bathroom is small.

Flipping my foot over I get my first real look at the damage. It's not as bad as I thought, but somehow it's worse. I felt the large hunk of glass that thankfully didn't go in as far as I thought but didn't notice the tiny shards.

Turning on the tap, I let the tub fill with a few inches of warm water as I start getting the shards out. I drop them by the tub drain because I'm not willing to risk putting them on the edge of the tub and knocking them to the floor. After getting a few pieces pulled out, I swish my foot in the end of the tub farthest from the drain to clear away the blood and loose glass; then go back to using the tweezers. When all the tiny pieces are gone, I take the tweezers and give the hunk of glass a wiggle. It's loose enough to pull out on my own. I was worried about having to make trip to the ER to get it out.

There's now a shadow blocking my view. "I really wish you'd let me help you." The shadow sounds despondent, but I'm in too much pain to give it a second though.

"I really wish you'd stop trying to maim me! Now back out of the light and let me get to this." Slowly I ease the hunk of glass out of my foot. When it's finally free, I release the breath I didn't notice I was holding. "Anna!" I yell through the open door and open the tub drain.

"Hey. How's it going in here?" It's a tight squeeze with Mr. Caveman in here but she manages to get between us.

"I think I got it all out." I turn the tap back on and give my foot another rinse. Slowly I run my thumbs over my throbbing foot. "Nope, one more." I yank it out and hold my foot up to Anna for inspection. In an old-timey Western drawl I say, "I dunno Doc. You think I'm gonna make it?"

I laugh. She laughs. Mr. Caveman doesn't laugh.

"Anna, can you get the coffee going? I'll be out in a few minutes to set up the dessert trays. And don't touch the mess on the kitchen floor."

She nods and heads to the kitchen. I grab the bottle of peroxide from the edge of the tub and gritting my teeth, dump it on the bottom of my foot. Holy fuck balls that hurts! I squeeze my eyes shut, gripping the side of the tub tightly as I wait for the burning to pass.

Mr. Caveman walks over and sits on the edge of the tub next to me, placing a hand over my white knuckled grip of the tub. "Let me at least bandage that up for you," he offers quietly.

Opening my eyes, I glance over at him. He looks nervous. "I think you've done enough already." I slide my hand out from under his. With a look of defeat, he gets up and walks away. Stopping at the door, he whispers "sorry" and is gone.

Twenty minutes later, I have my foot bandaged up and the squishy pair of house slippers Ma gave me last Christmas. Even with the extra padding, each step is excruciating. I enlist Nicole to clean up the glass and wine. Her friend; her mess.

"Coop did this?!" she says as she's surveying my kitchen floor. Coop? The name makes me think of that TV show from way back about the basketball coach.

"And this." I pop my bandaged foot out of the slipper. It's already showing a few dots of blood through all the extra gauze.

I flop down in a chair at the kitchen table, propping my injured foot up on another, and dig into the plate of food Anna brought in for me. I could easily join the crowd in the living room, but the kitchen is closer to the bathroom so it's less walking. It has nothing whatsoever to do with keeping away from that guy Coop. Visions of tossing him out the fire escape window; watching him bounce down the stairs all the way to the courtyard puts a smile on my face.

Anna comes in with a glass of soda. "I figured after all this, the last thing you wanted to do was look at wine."

"You're the best, Anna!"

She heads back out to the living room with a tray of assorted cookies and then comes back for the cheesecake. On her next trip in, she's followed by Matt who is helping carry in any empty plates and glasses. Apparently she feels the same way I do. They brought the guy; they can fill in for me as clean-up crew.

"Geez, Donna! What happened?"

"Coop," Nicole says sounding astonished, glancing up from the floor.

"So, he did all this and then just left? That doesn't sound like him at all," Matt says as he reaches into the fridge for a beer.

He left? With a sigh of relief, I know I'll live to make it through until morning.

Not only did I survive the rest of Saturday night, I made it through Sunday without a scratch. I spent most of the day on the couch and only had to rewrap my foot twice. The commute on Monday was killer, but I was at least able to find an open seat on the subway for the whole ride in.

"I'm headed out to lunch. Do you want me to bring you anything?"

"You're a lifesaver, Joan Marie! Where are you headed?"

"Paddy O'Fadden's. So you have your pick from their menu or the place next door. Text me when you know what you want."

"No need. If it's Paddy's, I already know. Bring me back an order of fish and chips. I'd love a Harp's draft to go with it, but seeing as that's impossible just grab me a coffee."

Forty-five minutes later I can smell my lunch before Joan Marie even comes through the door. I'm already pulling my wallet out of my briefcase by the time she gets to my desk.

"One order of fish and chips. One cup of coffee. One gorgeous flower."

"You keep the flower. How much do I owe you for the lunch?" Back and forth we argue about her not wanting my money and me wanting to pay her.

"I'll take $10, only if you take the flower." She's got me cornered.

Resigned I hand her a ten and take the interesting looking purple flower. As she walks away, I pop my head over the top of my cubicle. "No note this time?"

She makes her way back to my desk. "No. No note this time. Sometimes the flower can speak for itself." She turns on her heel and leaves.

I half expect the damn thing to burst into song like the singing bush in the movie "Three Amigos". I decide to give in and google it. I have no idea what kind of flower it is though, so I pick up the phone at my desk and call Joan Marie's desk.

"It's a hyacinth, dear."

So this is what a hyacinth looks like. Interesting. Opening up a new browser window, I type in "meaning of purple hyacinth". HYACINTH, Purple - I Am Sorry; Please Forgive Me; Sorrow

A few hours later, I head out of the office and stand in line for the bus. There's no way I'm walking all the way to the park today. When I see Leo, I hand him the bag of food. "Sorry, can't hang out today."

Reaching into the bag, he pulls out the hyacinth. "Hey, what's with the flower?" I hear him shout as I'm headed to my train. Even if I stopped to hang out I couldn't give him an answer since I don't even know the answer myself.

~*~

Feet propped on the coffee table, Anna and I are watching the first DVD of Masterpiece Theatre's Jane Eyre as we feast on take-out from Asia King. One of my favorites restaurants in the whole five boroughs, they serve both Chinese and Japanese food, and they also have a few items from Korea, Vietnam, and Thailand. Their Kimchi is out of this world!

When the first DVD ends, I want to jump up and toss in the second. Seeing as each DVD is about two hours long and it's already 10 I shouldn't. But .. helloooooo! Toby Stephens as Rochester! Nothing more needs to be said!

Anna clears away the various containers and puts the leftovers in the fridge. From the couch it almost sounds like she's humming. I could be imaging it; it's hard to tell from here. She only hums when she's happy. It's been a long time since I've heard her hum. Hobbling my way to the kitchen, I lean in the door frame. She IS humming! And she's smiling!

"Spill it, sister," I say with a laugh. She tries to hide the smile and act all innocent. "You're not fooling me, lady. It's just been so long since I've seen you this happy", I say as pull her into a hug.

Pulling back a little, she says "I have a date tomorrow night."

"You can't not tell me now, missy!"

We sit down at the kitchen table over tea and she tells me about Tim. She saw him a few times at the hospital when she would go in for her chemo. It turns out that his sister in law Betty had the same treatment times as Anna, and when her husband couldn't meet her afterwards, Tim would pick her up from the hospital. Anna didn't talk to Betty every session since she seemed to prefer to draw in her sketchpad or pop in her headphones and lay there with her eyes closed. They knew each other's names and what they were getting chemo for. Anna knew Betty was an artist. Betty knew that Anna was an editor. Sometimes they would talk about whatever sketch Betty was working on, but they never got into major details about themselves outside of therapy.

On Anna's last day of chemo, Betty had her eyes closed and her headphones in, so she left her a note with her phone number to keep in touch. A few days later she got a text from Tim saying that he's sorry he didn't get to see her that last day but was really glad she left her number with Betty. Over the past few weeks they've texted back and forth a bit. He let her know that Betty had a showing at a gallery downtown and thought she'd like to go see her. She teased him about it being a date and he responded "so should I pick you up at 7 then and officially make it a date?"

I squeal. She squeals. Who cares if it's predictably girlie.

Late Sunday afternoon Anna comes over for early dinner, the second half of Jane Eyre, and of course to tell me all about her date. She had a fantastic time. Tim seems like a genuinely nice guy. Pausing the DVD, she hands me her phone and we go through the pictures she took at the gallery.

"Betty looked stunning. I'm a little jealous. No way I'd have the guts to go out without my wig, let alone rock the look!"

The next few pictures are of her paintings, then one of Betty and Anna. I flip through a few more of Betty's art. "Pardon me while I wipe the drool from my chin! Who is that?!"

Anna leans over and flips to the next picture and there's Mr. Hottie kissing her on the cheek. "That's Tim," she says with a big smile on her face.

After the movie is over, Anna heads home. Tomorrow is a big day, her first back in the office. Max was willing to let her continue to work from home until she had her follow up appointment with the doctor, but she said she just wanted to get back to the office and back to her normal life.

Her first three days back went really well. I didn't realize how much I missed having Anna in the office until she came back. On Thursday we grab some sandwiches and head up to the park in Tudor City.

"I think I'm going to have to cancel my date tomorrow night. I didn't think being back in the office would take this much out of me. I'm totally exhausted!"

"Understandable. I mean, you were getting up at 9. Now you have to be up and in the office by 8. When you were home you could take a nap if you were feeling run down. There isn't enough space under your desk for a nap. You could try though when we go back." I wink and nudge her shoulder.

"I could," she laughs. "Or I can ask Max for a work from home Friday. Then maybe I won't have to cancel with Tim." She blushes.

I laugh. "I like your thought process. Just don't overdo it, okay? If you have to cancel with Tim, then you do. I'm sure he would totally understand."

On our way back to the office, we stop for coffee. "What in the world?!"

Nani ji steps out from the cart and hands me three long stems that have really pretty flowers running down them. I hand them to Anna. "Here, you carry them. I'll carry the coffee."

When we get back upstairs I show Joan Marie. "Ooo, they're lovely!"

"Yeah, but what are they?" I ask.

"Gladiolas of course, dear."

Back at my desk I open a new browser and the recently bookmarked "Language of Flowers" website. "Gladiolus - Give Me a Break. I'm Really Sincere; Flower of the Gladiators". Instead of the usual note and twine, there's a small envelope. Inside there's a note and a ticket to a new Off Broadway show that just opened last week.

Pffft, like hell I will. I grab a piece of paper out of the printer, scribble a quick note, and head back to corner.

"Back so soon, sweetheart?"

"Ok, so for some reason you two think the flower thing is funny. I don't. I find it creepy and infuriating. When this nut job comes back, give him this." I hand Dada ji the note and stomp back to the office.

Instead of ripping the ticket in half, I decide to give it to Max. His wife is out of town visiting her mother, so I thought he'd enjoy a night out. Though I make him swear that if any weirdos ask, he bought the ticket at the box office. He raises an eyebrow, but doesn't ask.

The following week there are no flowers and no notes. And that makes me happy.

08

"What's shakin', bacon?" I hand Leo a bag of food and have a seat.

"Hey, thanks for letting me borrow that book. I needed something new to read." He reaches into the bag and pulls out an apple. "Mike got a sort of job. $30 a day. He basically walks back and forth on Broadway between 43rd and 46th with a sign around his neck for the little electronics store on 7th. We split the wages that way Mike isn't holding all the cash just in case something happens. We're going to live off what Todd and I get pan handling until Mike makes enough to rent a room for a month. Then we'll have an address, a real address that we can put on job applications!"

"That's awesome! I wonder if there's another place that'll let you or Todd be a sign holder. You'd get a place even faster."

"I doubt it. Most businesses tell us to get away from their store if we're begging. The little old lady at the electronics store felt bad for Mike and gave him the job." He gets up and starts putting stuff in his backpack. "Walk with me, talk with me."

I get up and start following him down the hall towards the trains. As we get towards the stairs he starts running. "Come on, quick!" We get to the platform just in time to jump in before the doors close.

"A Queens bound M? Really, Leo?"

"Don't worry, wifey, I'll make sure you get home," he winks and I laugh. When we get to Court Street we transfer to a Brooklyn bound G train. "See, easy peasy," he says as we snag two seats.

"Ok, so, what was that all about?"

"That suit again. Listen, I think we need to switch things up; different day or maybe a different spot."

"Leo. Are you in some sort of trouble?"

"No! Honest! I swear! But paying attention to things out of the ordinary, like a guy that walks passed a few times, is what keeps people like me safe. And it's the same guy. Something's not right. Time to move."

By the time the train gets to Bergen, we've decided to meet up on Wednesdays starting next week at Herald Square. We both get off the train and he heads for the Manhattan bound F while I wait for the one headed to Coney Island. When he gets to the platform on the other side we make faces at each other until my train shows up. As it pulls away, I give a wave and hope that he's going to be ok.

~*~

"I was coming to see if you wanted to go to lunch, but I can see you're busy," Anna says as she comes over to my desk.

"Not busy, so much as trying to give myself a lobotomy with a letter opener."

"Do I even want to know why?"

I toss the miniature sword replica letter opener onto the desk and sigh. "It's the only way I can get through this book. I need to bring myself down to the author's level and the level of her audience."

I'm currently working on an autobiography by Shayna Lorayna. She's some fake tan, fake tittied, big hair, "reality" star. The show only aired a month ago and already she has a book out. It reads like a cross between the diary of an 11 year old girl and the diary of a 50 year old toothless crack whore. For once, can't I just get something normal to work on?

"You need a break. Grab your briefcase and let's go get something to eat."

We grab a couple of burgers from Dag's and head to the Katherine Hepburn Garden. "I think I'm going to talk to Max about cutting back a bit. I'm thinking half day Wednesdays and work from home Fridays. I'm also going to see about moving my follow up appointment up 2 weeks."

"Are you worried something is wrong?" I ask, putting my hand on hers.

"I'm not sure. But I shouldn't feel this run down. I mean, look at Betty. She's still in chemo and not half as run down as I am."

"Maybe it's just different cancer, different stage, different treatment?"

"I'm not sure. But I don't want to wait to find out. I need to get back to normal. I need to get back to me!"

"Anna, you've never been normal." On the way back we stop for coffee. Dada ji hands me a brown bag even though we didn't get any pastries.

"No, no, no!" insists Nani ji, shaking her head and trying to grab the bag, but Dada ji fends her off. I look at Anna and shrug.

When we get back to the office she follows me to my desk. I open the bag and peek inside. It's full of envelopes. I hold the bag up for Anna to look inside. She hitches a shoulder as if to say "beats me".

I dump the bag out onto the desk and begin smoothing out the crumpled envelopes. Noticing that they're dated, I put them in order, then stack them on my desk and stare at them. "They aren't going to open themselves you know."

"Ha ha, wise ass. Go grab and chair and let's dig in." I wait for Anna to come back before opening the first one. Using the letter opener/lobotomizer I break the seal on the first one and read it to Anna.

After you didn't show up to the theatre I was disappointed. To be honest I was a little ticked off.

"Serves the bastard right," I say.

"Shh, get back to reading!"

The next morning, I realized how it must have seemed from your end. For all you know, I could be some stalker. I'm not. But I get that it could seem that way. Or rather I was told it could seem that way when I was telling my sister you were a no-show. She told me I was "an idiot, which is a trait linked to the Y chromosome". I'm sorry if the ticket and invite seemed a little stalker-ish and that's why you didn't show. P.S. – who was the guy at the theatre? He said he bought the ticket at the box office; which I know is a lie.   –K

"Hahaha, good old Max!" The next envelope was two days later.

When I dropped the first letter off to the nice couple at the coffee stand they gave me the note you left for me the day I left you the flowers and ticket. My sister was right. I'll never admit to saying that, but she was. Not only am I an idiot in her eyes, I'm also a "fuckin' psycho looney and need to get a fuckin' life and possibly some meds".

"You didn't!" Anna yells.

"Oh yeah, I totally did."

They also told me that you refuse to take any more flowers or anything else I leave with them. I realize that I went about this the wrong way. I hope that eventually you'll come to realize that I'm truly sorry. I won't know until I drop this note off if you even read the first. I hope you did.   –K

I put the first two letters at the bottom of the pile and wrap them in a rubber band before tucking them in my briefcase. Anna still needs to ask Max about changing things around and it won't look good if he walks out of his office first and sees us sitting here hanging out instead of working. I take one last glance at the letter opener before getting back to Shayna Lorayna and wonder how long before I give in and use it.

After work, Anna and I head to my place so I can make some rugelach for Max (his favorite) to thank him for the theatre and for working with Anna on her hours. I'm rolling out the dough while she reads the next letter.

It looks like you never got my first letter. It kind of caused a bit of an argument between the old couple. She said that because you refuse all flowers and notes that they shouldn't even take them. Her husband thinks they should hold onto them just in case. He had the first one in a brown paper bag when I got there, so I put the second one in and will add this one too if I have to. Honestly, I'm not sure why I decided to write a third time when you won't read any note I leave. But, here I am, at 3am with pen and paper, writing to someone who will never see the letter. Sounds kind of old school black and white movie, huh?

"He's funny".

"Hey, I'm not paying you to comment, I'm paying you to read."

"You aren't even paying me at all!"

I wonder ... do you like old movies? There's this theatre in the West Village from the 1920's that plays classics on Thursday nights and Sunday afternoons. I'd ask if you want to go, but since you'll likely never get this letter it seems a moot point. Still "a guy can dream", right?   –K

"Ooo, smooth. I *like* him. If things don't work out with Tim and you don't want this guy, can I have him?" I throw a pinch of chopped walnuts at her.

Third letter is in the brown bag, so onto the fourth. I think I figured out this whole letter thing. Well, aside from the whole "never going to read them" bit. My sister called me an idiot and, well, you know what you called me. And I realized that maybe if you actually knew something about me, maybe I'd seem less stalker-ish. Well, if you ever bother to read any of the letters that is. So, here are some things about me. I was born in Wellington, New Zealand. My dad is Australian; my mom is American. We moved to America when I was 10. In addition to the sister that thinks I'm an idiot, I have another sister (who probably also thinks I'm an idiot) and three brothers. Yeah, big family. I've never wrestled a crocodile. I don't have a pet Koala. I don't know Frodo Baggins. (Sorry if you don't get that last reference)

Anna snorts. "What? He's funny, ok?"

I roll my eyes. It's either that or flick apricot preserves at her.

I obviously like old movies. I like rugby. I hate creamed spinach. And I'll keep writing in hopes that one day you'll read these and come to realize I'm a halfway decent idiot who isn't a stalker.

–K

When I went to put the fourth letter in the brown bag I noticed it said "Sweetheart" on it. I like it. It fits. So, sweetheart, what else can I tell you about me that will make you realize that although I'm an idiot, I'm not crazy? Well, I've lived here in the City for 5 years now. Before that I lived in Alberta (Canada) for a year. I've also lived in Middletown (New Jersey), North Oxford (England), Clermont (France), and Cairns (Australia). And, if you can't tell, I love travelling. When I was a little kid, I wanted to grow up to be a vet and help sick animals, until I found out that sometimes you have to help sick animals die. When we moved to America, I fell in love with skateboarding and wanted to be a pro like Tony Hawk. That obviously never happened. In high school I wasn't in band or any of the sports teams. I really like pears. I don't like snakes. I play a mean game of tic-tac-toe.

−K

"One more? Or should we leave off here?" Anna asks.

I pop the tray of rugelach in the oven. "Let's do one more while these bake and we decide on dinner."

Hello sweetheart. Long day at work today. Non-stop meetings. Sometimes it sucks being a grown up. Haha. I lucked out and got back to Brooklyn in time to get take out from my favorite place before they closed for the night. I'm not sure if you like Asian cuisine, but if you do you have got to check out Asia King! The Kimchi is out of this world!

"Whoa! What the fuck?! Did he just say Asia King?" I take the letter from Anna and reread that part. Asia King, with the out of this world Kimchi?! My favorite is his favorite?! The buzzer on the oven goes off and we both jump. I pull the tray out, move the rugelach to a cooling rack and sit down at the table. "So, this guy lives somewhere that's close enough to stop by Asia King on the way home from work. He is also up in Midtown somewhere that he can leave letters for me. I had just taken him down half a notch from psycho stalker, but I think maybe he should start moving back up. I think it's time to call Zio Nino," I say reaching for my phone. Anna takes my phone away and puts it in her pocket.

"Stop. Breathe. That's it. In, out, and stop giving me that look. No, stop and listen. I know what you're thinking. This guy isn't your certifiable ex Ralph. Think about it. What do we know about him so far? One – he's from New Zealand. Ralph was born in South Dakota. Two – He loves old movies and likes going out to see them. Ralph would only bother if the movie came on TV or RedBox because it was cheap. Three – this guy knows he screwed up and even admitted he was an idiot. Not only that, but he said that HE was sorry. Ralph was never sorry about anything because he thought he could do no wrong. If something was his fault, he'd twist it around until it was your fault. Four – he lives in Brooklyn and spends time in Manhattan. Ralph is upstate over six hours away. He can't leave letters at the coffee cart. They aren't the same guy, ok?" She takes my hands and gives them a squeeze. "I'll make us some of my mega grilled cheese sandwiches while you finish reading this. If it gets too creepy, I'll even dial Nino's number for you."

She's right. I know she is. Still, there's a part of me that will always go on alert when it comes to guys. I take a deep breath and say to myself "This is not Ralph. This is not Ralph. This is not Ralph."

...The Kimchi is out of this world! It's almost one in the morning now. I'm trying to go through spreadsheet after

spreadsheet but it all keeps blurring together. Instead of crunching numbers, I'd rather be writing to you. Ok, that made me sound like a dork. I guess that means I'm both an idiot and a dork. Hmmm, doesn't look good for me. You might not be into idiots who are also dorks.

Moving right along then. I like video games. Dork. I like Sci-Fi books. Dork! I like reading (and own) comic books. DORK! Ok ... so this really isn't looking good for me. Hopefully you're at least having a laugh at my expense. Because, if you're laughing, then you're smiling. And who put that smile on your face? That's right, I did. This big dork that's wide awake after one in the morning, slightly delirious from being up too many hours, writing a letter to a woman who will likely never read it; even though he hopes someday she'll eventually read them, take pity on aforementioned dork, and agree to go out to the movies with.

−K (aka, big dork)

Since Anna works from home on Friday and is spending Saturday with Tim, I don't get to see her until Sunday. We meet up at the diner at the end of her block for the best Challah French toast on the face of the planet.

"So ... then what?"

"Then nothing," Anna shrugs. "We had a long lazy picnic on the beach, went to the Aquarium, and then he drove me home." She sighs. "He walked me to the door and I got a kiss on the cheek. That was it."

"Have you said anything to him about it? Maybe you should." She shakes her head. "Take initiative, woman!"

She laughs. "That's funny coming from you. Why don't you show initiative, cut this mystery man a break, and meet up?"

"So not the same thing. You saw Tim at the hospital on and off, you met Betty long before you agreed to go out with Tim, and we know he's a nice guy even if he's slow with the moves. I don't even know who this mystery man is!"

Our waitress Bobbi comes by with the coffee pot. "Anyone for a top up?" After she refills both our cups, she's off to the next table.

"Well, let's get to know a little more about Mystery Man then," Anna chuckles.

Sitting in the diner we go through three more letters, each one starts with a "Hi Sweetheart". We find out that he likes a variety of music (with the exception of Adult Easy Listening and Elevator Music). His favorite color is black. Spiders creep him out. He graduated in the top 10% of his class in high school and the top 5% in college. He did a semester abroad and took classes at Oxford. He then added "nerd" to the growing list of names he'll respond to. Though he assured me he's never had Army issue black framed Coke-bottle glasses with white tape on them, but would run out and get a pair if I said I was into nerds. He loves being a part of a big family and calls his Gran in Australia at least once every two weeks.

"You're smiling!"

"Am not!" I scowl at Anna.

"How we doing here, ladies?" Bobbi starts clearing our empty plates. "More coffee? Some dessert maybe?"

"Just the check, thanks," I say as I get up to go to the bathroom. I know it's a copout and I don't care. I spend an extra few minutes stalling by brushing my hair and checking my make-up; even though I didn't bother with any this morning. I didn't realize I was smiling until Anna pointed it out. I know she's going to say something about it and I don't know what to tell her.

Resigned, I leave the bathroom and head back to our table when I notice a guy standing there talking to Anna. Oh shit, it's that Coop guy! Turning a one-eighty I trip over a lovely old lady's walker, scramble to get my footing, and run back into the bathroom. Geez, I can't even get within 20 feet of the guy without a minor incident! I pull my phone out and text Anna. *Meet you outside. Alone!*

"What? He remembered me from the party and stopped to ask about your foot," Anna says when we get back to her place.

"Yeah, he's to blame for that, my favorite silk blouse that's now garbage, and ruining a wonderful solo-picnic on the beach. The guy is a friggin menace!"

With a sigh, Anna flops down on the couch. "Fine. You win. Let's change the subject from Mr. Menace to Mr. Mystery."

Evening Sweetheart!

That's right; I'm out of work before the sun goes down. Oh yeah! I'm just sitting here in Calvert Vaux looking out at the water and relaxing. Just sipping a beer, writing to you, wondering what it would be like to sit here with your hand in mine instead of a pen and paper. It's a nice thought. One I'd like to make a reality. I'm placing that reality in your hands though. There's no guarantee you'll bother with my letters. But if you do, the decision to meet is up to you. I've already learned my lesson after the sending you the gladiolas.

-K

~*~

"All I'm saying is I feel bad for the guy. You should cut him some slack and send a note back." I seriously cannot believe those words just came out of my brother Marco's mouth.

"Well I think it's really romantic," adds Oliver.

"Why did I even show these to you two?" I ask with a sigh and put my head down on the kitchen table.

"Because you need some help from your fairy godmothers, of course!"

I shake my head and laugh. I adore Oliver. He's the polar opposite of my brother Marco. I think that's why they're perfect for each other.

"I can hear the wheels in your mind spinning. No makeovers. You can stop undressing slash dressing me in your mind. And be glad I know you love my brother because otherwise that would be really creepy."

"Party pooper," he mumbles as he walks away from the table.

"Seriously Donna, why won't you give the guy a chance? He's funny, smart, loves to travel, and he's obviously into you. That's a checkbox in every square on the straight woman's list for an ideal guy!"

He's right, I know he is. He's also my brother, so I'll never admit it. "I don't know, Marco. What if he turns out to be a sleaze or a psycho or something?"

"And what if he isn't? Do you want to throw away a chance at something that could be good because you're afraid?"

"You should listen to your brother just this once," Oliver says putting a glass of wine in front of me before walking over to my brother's chair and putting an arm around his shoulders. "He knows what he's talking about."

After promising to at least consider sending a note when I get to the end of the stack, I head home. It's been a while since I've spent time with Marco and Oliver without being part of a massive group of people. I've missed it.

That night I toss and turn and have some of the weirdest Alice in Wonderland style dreams involving a disembodied voice telling me "I'm a nice guy. Gimme a chance." So I'm not a happy camper when I get to work. I sneer at my computer screen when I boot it up and open up the Shayna Lorayna book.

"Ok, break time!" Anna chimes as she slides into my cubicle. Reaching into my briefcase, I grab the pile of letters.

"There are no more. We've read them all," I say half disappointed. "In the mood for a cup of coffee?"

We head to the corner for coffee and are rewarded with two more letters. Back at my desk, I take out the lobotomizer and open up the first letter.

Hi Sweetheart. How are you? Got out of work a few hours late and came home to a burst pipe from the apartment upstairs. After calling the insurance company, taking pictures, and cleaning up the mess I was going to head to the bar but went for a jog instead. It was a great night for it. Not too many people on the street to have to maneuver around. Not too many cars on the side streets either. Just me, some music, and the night. By the time I got home and got a quick shower, I ended up with scrambled eggs and a bagel for dinner. You're still thinking of me in the shower aren't you, haha. That's ok, I won't hold it against you. On second thought, maybe I will ;) But, we'll never know, now will we. Well, sweetheart, it's now 2 in the morning. I should get some sleep. (Though thinking of you thinking of me in the shower, it'll be a rather restless sleep) –K

"Don't even go there."

"I wasn't going to say a thing! I know you're already thinking it anyway." Anna tips her head back and laughs.

Well hellooooo there, Sweetheart! When I dropped off the last letter, the sweet couple told me they gave you the bag of letters. Of course, this caused a bit of an argument between them, but I'm ecstatic. I don't know what you did with the bag once they gave it to you. But I really hope that you've read them. The unfortunate flipside is, sweetheart, that after I drop this letter off I'm headed to Australia for work for a few weeks. Of all the rotten luck!! I could write while I'm there, but have no way of getting the letters to the coffee cart. Well, shit! I'll think of something. It might take a while to figure out, but I will. I always do when I go after something I want ;) Take care of yourself, sweetheart. I'll be missing you. Try not to forget about me while I'm gone, ok? –K

Well, shit, indeed.

"Hey, you made it!"

"Of course! It's Wednesday, right?" I say handing Leo a bag of goodies.

"Whoa-ho-ho! Someone shoot your dog or something?" Leo asks, putting his hands up in self-defense.

"Sorry," I say sitting down next to him. "Just some shit. Work, etc."

"Doctor Leo is here to help," he says in a fake Freud accent, looking at me over the rim of his glasses. "Tell me about your mother".

I burst out laughing and it echoes through the station. "I needed that, thanks".

"Anytime, wifey," he says with an exaggerated wink.

~*~

"Helloooh, my sweetheart! Coffee?"

"Morning, Dada ji! Better make it a large this morning, thanks."

While he's making my coffee, Nani ji comes out from behind the cart and waves me over. "A lady came by today," she whispers nervously. "She told me to give this envelope to the nice lady that gets the letters. But, I don't know who she is and she didn't say. Do you want it?"

"Umm, ok," I hear myself say. Lady? What lady?

With a worried look, Nani ji hands me the letter and pats my hand, then I get my coffee and head into the office.

I put the envelope on the desk and stare at it. I really want to know what it says, but Anna hasn't been coming into the office until 9 o'clock. I check my watch, stare at the envelope, then start that seated leg bounce thing people do when they're nervous or need to pee. I check my watch and stare at the envelope. "Come on, Anna," I whisper. A few more minutes pass and I'm checking my watch again. 9:05. Damnit, Anna, where are you? I resume staring at the envelope. When Anna walks through the door at five minutes later I run straight for her.

"Finally!"

She laughs. "Most people say good morning this early."

As I drag her back to my desk, she laughs and stops at hers to put her purse on the desk and the light weight jacket she's wearing around the back of her chair. She's humming again.

We get to my desk and have a seat. I notice she's idly toying with the ends of her wig and hasn't stopped humming. "Something's different. What's different?"

"Initiative," she says with a twinkle in her eye.

I pick my jaw up off the floor. "And? Come on! Inquiring minds want to know!"

She laughs again and it almost sounds like a purr. "He spent the night." I squeal. Heads turn. We sink down into my cubicle. "Lots and lots of ladybugs!" she says, quoting a line from *Under The Tuscan Sun*.

"So, are you going to buy a villa together?" I wink and nudge her with my elbow.

Reaching over me, she picks up my coffee and takes a sip. "Mmmmmm. Sorry, but I needed that. I, uh, well, heh-hem, didn't have time this morning for coffee," she says as she sets the cup back down. "What's this?"

Taking the envelope from her, I tell her about Nani ji handing it to me this morning. "I was waiting for you," I say and shrug.

I quickly open the envelope. It's a print out of an email. I look at Anna but she just shrugs.

Greetings from South Australia, sweetheart! I told you I'd figure it out! Remember how I told you my wonderful sister said I'm an idiot? This idiot overlooked the obvious. I emailed my amazing sister! She graciously agreed to print out the email and drop it off! (Thanks again, Avery, and I totally know you're reading this before you even print it. Don't try to deny it!)

Ok, where was I? That's right! G'Day, sweetheart! It feels good being able to write to you without having to wait until I get back! I know it sounds strange, but I've missed you! (Right about now I have a feeling my sister is making gag noises. I don't care. Hear that, Avery? I. Don't. Care!) When I got here I spent the first two days visiting Gran. I told her about you. She says hi, by the way. I told her about the letters. She said it's really sweet. Which made me gag, by the way.

Since we have an audience (go away, Avery!), I'll keep this short. Assuming that my sister hasn't scratched out my email address and written something like "jackass@loserville.com" over it, you can now email me any time you like. Or I can have my sister print/drop off a letter.

Thinking of you,

-K

Saturday night I'm sitting in a lawn chair on the roof of Marco and Oliver's building, drinking Malibu Bay Breezes. Marco and I have always been close, but I've never really been 100% open with him about "the feels" because hello, only sister, overbearing Italian brothers.

Anna's on a date with Tim, tonight is Linda's daughter's dance recital, and besides Joan Marie, Marco and Oliver are the only other people that know about Mystery Man. And right now I need a friend.

"Beer me," I say, holding my glass out to Oliver.

"Uh, if you're mistaking my cocktails for beer, maybe you should switch to water," he says with mock distain.

"Funny, Ollie. Shut up and pour".

"Me-ow! Kitten has claws!"

I sigh. "Sorry. I'm just confused and frustrated. Part of me is starting to maybe want to get to know this guy. I'm confused. Then I get frustrated because I'm confused. It's a vicious cycle. Part of me wants to stop accepting his letters. Sure, he seems likeable. He's told me a bunch of different things about himself. But this whole time there's one thing he's never told me ... his name. Don't you think that's a little weird?"

"Hmmm, I never thought of that before." He takes a sip of his drink and waves away what I was going to say next. "It doesn't necessarily mean anything though. He could sign off on all his personal letters and emails with his initial. It doesn't mean there's something wrong with him."

"Yeah, but still ..."

"No! No more over thinking. Last time you were here, what did you promise Marco and I?"

"To suck it up and write back when I got to the end of the pile of letters," I say looking down at my lap like a chastised puppy.

"Well then, start keeping your promises. Your brother is right. Don't throw away a chance at something good because you are afraid. He knows what he's talking about. He was afraid once and he almost lost me." He reaches over and gives my hand a squeeze.

"Thanks Oliver," I say and squeeze back.

Later that night I'm sitting on my couch, logged into my email, and staring at the blinking cursor. I contemplated created a new email address. What if I meet this guy and he's an asshole or a psycho or something?

With a fake email address, I can just chuck the account. Then I spend half an hour berating myself for letting Ralph still have an effect on my life now. "Fuck you, Ralph! Fuck you!" and I begin to type.

~*~

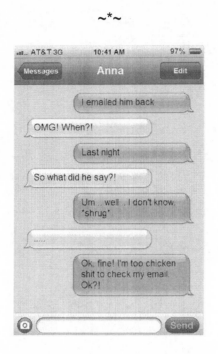

A minute later my phone rings. "Do you need me to come over?"

"Yes? No? I don't know."

"I can be there in about … an hour?"

"Tim stayed again, didn't he?" She giggles. "I'll call you later if there's anything; much later." I laugh and hang up the phone.

After making myself a cup of coffee, I log into my email. Apparently there are a lot of Russian mail order brides interested in me, Prince Tariq Al-Mumbek has money he wants to give me, and I need a bigger penis. Junk, junk, and more junk. Wedged in the midst of all the junk is Re: Hi

Click

Well helloooo there, sweetheart! I've gotta say I was very pleasantly surprised when I checked my email this evening after work. Honestly, I thought I would never hear from you. Well, aside from that first note where you called me crazy and in need of meds, along with a long string of expletives. You kiss your mother with that mouth? (You can kiss me with that mouth any time, hehe)

After the flowers didn't seem to work, I thought I'd try actually writing to you. When I hadn't heard back after the 4th letter I almost gave up. One night I was at my brother Sam's place watching a soccer game. After way too many beers, I told him about you, the flowers, the letters, and how Avery thought I was an idiot. "You are not an idiot, man. You're lame as hell". When the beer fog passed the next morning I thought a lot about it. Maybe it really was lame and I should stop writing to you. It almost seemed like one of those notes you pass in school when you're little. "I like you. Do you like me? Check Yes or No". I'm 30 years old. Had I really reverted to being a 6th grader? What an idiot! What a big lame idiot!

My first thought was to head into Manhattan and go get the bag of letters. By the time I realized the couple with the cart

probably weren't there since it was the weekend, I was already half a block from the train. I headed down to Coney Island and walked the Boardwalk for a while trying to figure it all out. Did I really want to keep writing to someone knowing the letters were just going unread? Was it lame? How lame was it? What if, by the time you ever decided to read them, there were over a hundred? How would that look? But the big question I really needed to answer was "Why?".

As I shuffled along the Boardwalk I realized a few things; one of which was that I didn't care if Avery thought I was an idiot or Sam thought I was lame. I started thinking of each letter as a chance; a chance for you to get to know me, a chance that you might read one or all and say "what the hell" and write back. I didn't want to give up on that chance.

Have you ever seen someone before and thought "I wonder what their story is; who they are, what they're like. I'd really like the chance to get to know them better"? That's what happened the first time I saw you. Before I could come to my senses, you were gone. That pissed me off. Not you. It was the fact that I let the chance go by.

The second time I saw you, I was dumbstruck. I thought I'd never see you again, but there you were. And again, I totally fucked it up. Though the opportunity to say something that second time had passed, desperate times call for desperate measures. That was when I started trying to apologize with flowers. I still feel bad about spooking you with the theatre ticket.

When I moved onto the letters, the more I wrote, the more I started realizing things about myself too. Outside of family and *a few close friends, not many people really know me. Sure, I know a lot of people. But all they see is the suit, the facade. That's because I don't like sharing stuff about myself. Which is kind of ironic with all these letters, huh?*

I also realized a lot of things, especially now that I'm so far away. The first thing being that I work too much. I don't get to see my family and friends as much as I used to. The only time I get to unwind seems to hover around 2am. Only one stamp in my passport over the last 5 years was for fun. I miss you.

When I get back I'm going to work on changing all of that.

11

"Wooooo," Oliver says fanning himself after he reads the email. "Mmmm mm mm! Ooo, I liiiike him," he says with a wink. "No offense, sweetie."

"None taken," Marco says as he bends down to kiss Oliver on his way to the grill.

When I called Marco to tell him that I sucked it up and wrote to Mystery Man, he insisted on an impromptu barbeque at their place and invited Anna. Leave it to these two to pull this together in an hour and a half on a weekday. The table they brought up for the food has a stuffed Koala next to a platter of crudités. Marco has his phone plugged into portable speakers and has a play list queued up with bands like Men At Work and Midnight Oil. I have no idea where they got a surfboard from, but there's one propped up by the door. What really had me laughing was the cooler filled with Fosters and the shrimp they skewered to "throw on the barbie". Oliver insisted on two different cocktails. One is called an Aussie Sunrise. The other is called a "Hell Yeah", which comes from a bar in Sydney (hardy har har).

My cell phone blares out "Trololo Man" and Marco laughs. "Anna's downstairs," I announce as I get up to head down and buzz her in.

"I'll go. You stay here." And with a wave, Oliver heads downstairs.

"I don't know how you two managed it, but this is awesome. Thanks, Marco," I say and give him a hug.

He gives me one big squeeze before flipping over the chicken and toss the shrimp on the grill. "You deserve it," he says and I'm shocked. "No, really, you do. I haven't seen you get this excited about a guy since before …" He waves the tongs to convey things better left unsaid. "I'm happy for you. Not just because of this guy. You took that first step. You broke the hole in the wall you've built up around yourself the past 2 years and took a step out from behind that barrier." He chuckles and bumps my shoulder. "I guess this is your 'coming out' celebration, huh?" He tips back his head and laughs.

When Oliver walks back through the door we're half bent over laughing so hard we're holding each other up. My sides hurt and my eyes are watering, I'm laughing that hard.

"Hey Ollie! Guess what? I just came out!" The look on his face is priceless and sends Marco and me headfirst into another round of laughter.

"That's an interesting way to introduce yourself to your best friend's new beau," he says.

I wave my hand around as if to say I need a minute to catch my breath and try to stand up. "Sorry Anna," I finally manage to say. "It was something Marco said." I explain the wall/coming out analogy then extend my hand to Tim. "Nice to finally meet you."

"Likewise," he says. "And congratulations on your coming out." We all laugh. Oh yeah, Tim will fit in just fine.

I hand Anna the email. After reading it she lets out a slow whistle. "You have to meet him!"

"Makeover time!" Oliver yells. He's typically not overly flamboyant. This is one of the rare moments he's over the top and I can't help but laugh.

"Sorry to disappoint. No makeovers. He already knows what I look like anyway."

"So …. does Mystery Man have an actual name?" Tim asks as we start digging into the barbecue.

"Well, I doubt his parents put 'K' on his birth certificate."

"Funny. Why don't you ask? I mean, think about how awkward it would be," he says. "I take thee, Mystery Man to be my lawfully wedded husband."

I start choking on a piece of pineapple and Anna starts laughing.

~*~

"You look ... different," Leo says.

"Good different or bad different?"

He turns and stares at me. It's weird. It's almost like he's staring through me and into my soul. Looking at him it's like he's this young kid with a wise old man trapped inside; like the kind with the long hair and long beards that you see in old Kung Fu movies. After a minute he shrugs. The wise old man goes back to being hidden, and he's back to being just a kid.

"Just different, that's all," he says as he reaches into the bags to see what there is to snack on. "I finished the second book in the series. Can I swap it for the third?"

"Sure thing. I can bring it next week."

He reaches into his bag takes out the second book from the Septimus Heap series. "I'll try to hang on that long," he laughs. We spend the next half hour talking about the first two books before I head to the train.

~*~

When I stop for coffee on the way into work the next day, Nani ji looks worried. "Everything ok?" I ask.

"I should be the one asking you. I don't know who the lady is. I haven't seen the nice man."

I reach through the window of the cart and give her hand a squeeze. "You are so sweet," I say and smile. "The lady was his sister. He's away on business, so she dropped off the last letter."

"Oh good. He is a very, very, nice man. Perfect for you," she says with a wink.

Taking my coffee, I head into the office and turn on my computer. I immediately log into my email and send off a quick email to Mystery Man. A few minutes later I hear my cell phone "ping" letting me know I have new email. It's more than likely junk mail, but I log back in to check.

Hi sweetheart! I was hoping to hear from you today. It's coming up on 11pm here. That would make it almost 9:30am back home, so I'm guessing you're at work.

First off, you shouldn't feel like you need to say "sorry" for wanting to ask me something. Open book. Ask away. Though there's something to be said for being called "Mystery Man", my name is Killian. Signing off with just a "K" is so second nature that I didn't think anything of it.

Sorry, to keep this one short, but I'm about to nod off with my face in my laptop. I'll be thinking about you.

G'nite, sweetheart.

-K (aka Killian)

12

What a shitty commute home! I stood on the subway platform for 45 minutes. A D train went by, followed by a B, another D, an M but no F train. When the next B train shows up, I give up and jump on that. We're packed in like sardines. After 2 stops, I ended up squashed with my back against the door between cars.

The guy next to me smelled like he bathed in Axe body spray. The music coming out of his headphones is so loud I can't even hear people around me talking. He's also trying to dance in the small space and knocking into me and the girl next to me who barely looks 13. Apparently he doesn't care who gets bumped, he was going to dance. Asshole.

After four more stops I can't take it anymore. When the doors open I give the jackass a shove and get out of the train. I was hoping that the next train would be another B which runs express, but it was a local Q. Well, it's either take this or keep standing here on the platform. Resigned I, hop on the Q and slowly countdown the stops until finally getting off at Newkirk.

As I walk passed PS 217, two kids try to one-up each other with their bikes and I have to jump off the sidewalk to get out of the way.

HOOOOONK!

A truck barrels down the road. It's close enough that I get slapped with a gust of wind. I shake my fist and yell "SLOW DOWN FUCK FACE! IT'S A SCHOOL ZONE!" I step back onto the sidewalk and give the kids a nasty look, then continue walking home.

BOOOOM!

I look up at the rapidly darkening sky. "You have GOT to be kidding me!" I close my eyes as the first big drops of rain pelt me in my upturned face.

By the time I get home, I'm thoroughly soaked to the skin. There's a mini river of water dripping from my hair, down my spine, and into my underwear. I barely get the door to my apartment closed and I'm stripping as I head to the bathroom. I grab two towels. One I use to throw my hair up in a turban like twist. The other I dry the rest of myself off with before tossing on a robe and going to clean up the discarded clothes.

I grab a slice of artichoke pie out of the fridge and toss it on a plate. I don't even bother turning on the oven to warm it up. Knowing my luck, I'd somehow set the sleeve of my robe on fire. Grabbing a can of soda, I head to the living room and flop down on the couch. I snag my laptop off the coffee table. While I wait for it to start up, I dig into my dinner. It's good cold, it's even better hot. I almost give in and get up to toss it in the oven. I log into my email, weed through the crap, and finding one from Killian, I smile for the first time in hours.

Good morning/evening sweetheart! It's about 7:30 in the morning here, so 6 back home. A message from you last night before bed was nice way to end the day, so I thought I'd write this morning and start today "with" you as well.

It's really nice here, even though it's 49F outside this morning. Big change from the 90's you've been getting back home lately. Still, it's gorgeous here. The hotel is in Adelaide right on a lake and has stunning views. I'll attach a few pictures when I'm done typing. Check out the size of the tub! Lots of room ;)

I'm sitting outside on the balcony having my coffee and thinking of you. Not just because of the tub. Well, maybe. Lol! There's a section of town called Brooklyn Park, which makes me think of home, which makes me think of you, which makes me miss you, which makes me write run on sentences (wtf!). Is it weird to miss someone you haven't spent time with? Pfft, so what if it is. I miss you. I don't know how to explain it either.

Well, my coffee is gone and if I don't get out of here soon, I'll be late. I should be in the office by 9 (7:30 your time) and will be checking my email throughout the day.

-K

I click to view the attachments. Holy hell! It's utopia! He included a picture of the outside of the hotel with an arrow pointing to a balcony and the words "you should be here". I laugh. Then I get a view of the bathroom. There's even a window in the bathroom that you can see through the hotel room and straight out to the lake! Of course, then I imagine myself in that tub with it full of bubbles and a glass of wine in my hand. After the day I had, that would be paradise! I check the time. 7:50. He's probably busy at work by now. He said he'd be checking his email throughout the day though. Still, I shouldn't bother him. Screw it, I give in and hit reply.

Evening/Morning! Knowing you're at work, I almost didn't write. I would hate for you to get in trouble with the boss for checking personal email during work hours. I saw the pictures. Wow! The one of the front of balcony with the arrow ... funny. After the day I had though, I could make use of that tub, though I can't promise I'd share. And that view! Is the far side of the tub wide enough for a bottle of wine to sit? Perfect. (I'm definitely jealous!)

I go on to tell him about my shitty day at work. I tell him about the horrible commute - the asshole on the train, having to switch trains, the kids and the truck, and how much it poured. I leave out the part about stripping on the way to dry off.

My two previous emails were maybe 5 sentences combined. This time, once I started writing I just kept going. As weird as it is to tell it all to someone that's still really a stranger, something about it is nice. I think it's kind of refreshing to talk to someone that doesn't know anyone in my family, someone that hasn't known me forever, someone that doesn't know everything about me. When I'm done typing I realize there are eight paragraphs. EIGHT! I'm tempted to click cancel. Then I move the mouse over and click send.

Staring at the computer, I read the line "Your Message Has Been Sent!" The whole thing is kind of cathartic in a way and I think I'm starting to understand why he continued to write all those letters after the flowers.

With a stretch I get up off the couch and realize it's dark outside now. I take my plate and soda can to the kitchen, grab a bottle of wine from the fridge and a glass, and then head to the bathroom. It might not be the same as that huge tub in the hotel, but I turn on the tap. I drop two caps of milk and honey scented bubble bath in and fill the small room with candles. Dropping my robe to the floor, I pile all my still slightly damp hair on top of my head. Glass of wine in hand, I turn off the tap and lower myself into the tub. I take a sip of wine. The contrast between the cold wine and hot water are wonderful. I close my eyes and lean back. Oh yeah, this is the life!

Half an hour later the water is starting to get uncomfortably cool, so I decide it's finally time to get out. After drying off, I slather on lotion that matches the scent of the bubble bath. Pulling the plug on the tub, I toss my robe back on, and after pouring myself one last glass of wine I put the bottle back in the fridge. The clock in the kitchen says 9:30. Yeah, it's a work night, but what the hell. I head over to my DVD's; which are notoriously in alphabetic order, something that drives Anna nuts. Taking *Holiday* with Cary Grant and Katherine Hepburn out of the case, I pop it in the DVD player. To go along with my "what the hell" attitude of the evening I head back into the kitchen and retrieve the bottle of wine. Flopping on the couch I press play on the DVD remote and swap the remote for my phone which I noticed was blinking. Oooo, I've got an email.

Wow, sweetheart. That was some email. With the exception of your "go to hell" note, I've only gotten a line or two from you. It's a surprising (and nice) change. ☺

I'm sorry you had such a shitty day at work. I'm glad I didn't have anything to do with it, but I'm still sorry. The guy on the train sounds like a first-rate dick and deserved more than a shove. I can try to make up for the shitty day though. Say the word and I'll have a plane ticket dropped to the coffee cart by tomorrow morning! The tub is all yours! I'll be sure to have wine, just let me know which one(s). And you won't have to share either unless you want to, I swear! (Would a foot rub make you want to share? Hehe)

Yes. I'm totally serious. No strings attached or anything. And it's the vision of coffee on the balcony, not you in the tub, that makes me want to send you the plane ticket. I have a meeting in 10 minutes. Thankfully, it's not a work through lunch meeting. Take some time and think about it. If you can't make it, no harm, no foul. Hell, I don't even know if you have a valid passport! It's a spur of the moment thing, so don't feel bad if you have to say no either!!

-K

Half an hour later I send Marco a text. *Buzz me in. I'm downstairs. And put on some pants first.* From the moment he was out of diapers, Marco has slept in just his underwear. It was one thing when we were kids. Now that we're older, I could do without seeing him walking around in tighty whities. A minute later the buzzer goes off and I head up to the apartment. When I get there, he pulls open the door just as I raise my hand to knock, and pulls me inside.

"Oh my god, what's wrong?!" he says.

"Is this a coffee, wine, or hard liquor kind of visit?" Oliver calls from the kitchen.

I swipe the screen on my phone and hand it to Marco, the email is already opened. "Not sure," I yell back "This could be one or all three".

We make our way into the kitchen. Marco, who is walking and reading at the same time, knocks his shoulder into the doorframe. There is a bottle of Johnny Walker black and three shot glasses already on the table and Oliver is brewing coffee. I walk over, wrap my arm around his shoulder, and give him a loud kiss on the cheek.

"If you weren't already in love with my brother, I'd ask you to marry me!"

He snorts. "Sorry, sister, wrong equipment. So, what brings you to our door at this hour?"

Eyes locked on mine, Marco hands the phone to Oliver. A minute passes and he still hasn't said anything. It's making me nervous. I pull out a chair and turn it to face him. *"Che ne pensi, Marco?"* I half whisper.

"I don't know about him, but I think you should go." Both our heads whip around to look at Oliver, surprise written all over our faces. "Whaaat?" he says. The way he says it makes me think of Nathan Lane in *The Birdcage*.

Marco walks over to Oliver, puts a hand on either side of his face, and kisses him. "Thank you for that," he says. Standing there in that moment, with their eyes closed and Marco's forehead resting on Oliver's, I envy them.

Twenty minutes later, I've reread the email out loud instead of playing pass the phone, and Oliver has taped two pieces of giant sketch paper to the kitchen wall. We're going over the pros and cons of the trip. The pro side is so small; it could have been written on a bar napkin.

1) Have valid passport

2) Always wanted to see Australia

By comparison, the con side is huge. I even had Oliver write "Drop Bears" on the list. I'm not even sure if I meant it as a joke or if I said it to give the con side more weight. Either way, it doesn't matter. Even without it on the list, the con side is six times the size of the pro list. For some strange reason, I find that disappointing.

"I still think she should go," Oliver says as he's putting the cap back on the marker.

"Are you crazy?!" Marco half shouts as he stands up from the table.

"Only about you, dear," he says as he pushes Marco back into his seat.

"Look, I'm all for her meeting this guy. Here. In New York. On safe neutral ground. I'm not sending her to some country on the other side of the world to meet some total fucking stranger!"

"Uh, helllooo? Standing right here? Yeah, hi. Remember me? If I went, I would be going of my own volition, not being sent like I'm some mail order bride. What the hell?!"

"This isn't a bra burning event, Donna!"

I put my hands under my breasts and shake them up and down. "Good thing, because I forgot my bra!"

"Children, children, children!" Oliver yells. "Sit down and shut the hell up!" He folds his hands on the table in front of him. "Good. Now that I have your attention, let me point out that there are only two things preventing Donna from going. No, shut up the pair of you and listen for once. For starters, you can't call into work tomorrow and say "Sorry I can't come in, I'm off to Australia"; unless of course, you're looking to get your ass fired which I wouldn't recommend, seeing as you have a fantastic job that you love despite the occasional bullshit. The other thing preventing Donna from going isn't a thing, it's a question. What are you afraid of?"

It's well after 1 by the time I make it back to my apartment. The menu for the DVD is still up on the TV screen in the living room. Shuffling my way in, I turn off the DVD player and TV. I grab my laptop off the couch and head to my room, turning off the lights I left on when I headed to Marco's.

Flopping on the bed, I zone out to the fractal screen saver for a minute. I run my fingers over the mouse to wake the laptop and myself up. I squint. Damn that screen is bright with all the lights out! Killian's email is still up on the screen. I hit reply and draw a total blank. I have no idea what to say.

"What are you afraid of?" I hear Oliver say.

Hi. Sorry for the late reply. I just got home from my brother's place. It's after 1am here. I'm too exhausted to calculate the time difference, but I'm pretty sure you're out of your meeting and already back from lunch.

As tempting as it is, there's no way I can fly out in the morning. I'm sorry.

I hit send. Simple as that. I toss the laptop on the other side of the bed, climb under the covers, and start to doze off the second my head hits the pillows.

SPRIONG!

I jump then grumble. Rolling back over, I half open one eye to mute the speakers to make my laptop shut up. I only have a few hours before I have to get up for work and I really don't need to be woken up every time someone posts to my facebook, twitter, et cetera. I open my eye a little wider to attempt to focus as I'm aiming for the tiny speaker icon and missing. That's when I notice the notification was a new email from Killian. Damn, that was fast.

Please stop saying sorry, sweetheart. You shouldn't feel like you have to keep apologizing when there's nothing to be sorry about. After I sent the last email I heard my sister's voice calling me an idiot. I almost thought I'd blown it again. I mean, who flies across the world on a whim to meet their stalker? ;) (That's a joke, btw!!)

Sleep well, sweetheart   -K

Did I just giggle at him saying stalker?! Wow, do I need some sleep! For some reason, instead of lowering the screen, I hit reply and roll over onto my stomach.

Greetings stalker! Lmao! I said "sorry" not as an apology, more as a regret. I've always wanted to see Australia. It's the fear of drop bears that keeps me from visiting ;)

I hit send before realizing what I wrote. I'm awake, but apparently my filter has fallen asleep. But, as my grandmother would say "Oh well!". Probably for the best anyway. It'll give him a chance to "get" my quirks before we meet.

Before? I meant if; IF!

Though if I really think about this whole thing, all the way back to that first silly daisy; none of it would have happened if we hadn't met at some point. If I wasn't awake before, I am now. Killian is someone I've already met. But, I don't know anyone named Killian!!

SPRIONG!

Good one, sweetheart. I actually got a few strange looks because I was sneaking a peek at my email and burst out laughing during a meeting. Whoops. And, no, you shouldn't apologize for that either. Let's just say I'm known around here for being ALL business, so it was funny as hell! I needed the laugh too ;)

Drowning in numbers and flow charts,

-K

Knowing I made him laugh makes me smile. Oh my god, I've reverted to my 13 year old self! Someone save me from myself!

Yeah, well, that's me ... class clown. Haha

So, I was wondering ... how much longer are you going to be over there?

SPRIONG!

I'm leaving Adelaide next Saturday and then flying to Cairns for about a week before heading home. Has my charm finally worn you down enough to want to meet up? Lol ;)

It just may have. I roll back over and fall asleep within seconds.

13

I don't know how I'm even functioning the next morning. Odd thing is, I don't feel worn out. The alarm went off three hours after I finally passed out but I feel like I slept a full eight.

"Helloooh, my sweetheart! You look very, very, happy today! Big, big, smile," Dada ji says flashing a wide grin as he starts making my coffee.

"Even better, I <u>feel</u> happy." He just winks a reply and hands me my coffee.

"Wait! Delivery for you," Nani ji shouts, as she steps around the cart with a small box. "The nice lady brought it this morning."

"Um, ok," I say taking the box and heading into the office.

I put my coffee cup down on my desk far from the box and keyboard. It's post marked the day he left and is addressed to Avery-Wavery Smith. The return address says K.C. & the Sunshine Band. Grabbing a box cutter from my desk drawer, I break the tape and look inside. Laughing, I pull out a small stuffed Koala wearing sunglasses and a funky shirt. There's a note tied to one of his paws. It's a quickly written message on hotel note paper. "Because ... well why not?"

Without thinking, I walk into Max's office. "I'm putting in for vacation time."

~*~

"Wait, what did you say?!"

"I said ... I'm packing for a trip to Australia and need your help."

"Why?" Anna asks.

"Initiative," I say as I hang up the phone.

Half an hour later we're standing in my room. It looks like a bomb went off in here. Clothes are scattered everywhere. The suitcase is empty.

"Staring at it isn't going to make the clothes magically jump in," Anna laughs. "It's winter there right now, right. And you said he told you it was around 50 degrees. I say concentrate on Autumn type clothes." Clearing a spot on the bed, she tosses my jeans down. "Let's start with these and take it from there."

We sort through the jeans; discarding my old worn out ones and picking four pairs that make my butt look good. Next we move on to tops that can be layered but are also mix and match. I toss two dresses on the pile that are casual, but also nice enough that they can look dressy with the right accessories.

"Can you grab my brown knee high boots, black boots, and tan flats out of the closet while I go through this drawer?" I ask Anna.

She manages to unearth the shoes from the now disorganized bottom of my closet and brings them over to the bed. "Oh, hell no!" she says and tosses the pile of pjs on the floor. "You are not bringing those!"

I reach down and grab an old concert T-shirt for Bauhaus and a pair of black boxers. "What's wrong with this?" I argue back.

She throws her hands up in the air and with a sound of disgust heads over to my dresser. While her back is turned, I quickly roll up the boxers in the T-shirt and shove them under everything in the suitcase. I do the same with my Dead Can Dance T-shirt and another pair of pajama boxers.

Anna walks back and hands me two sets of skimpy lacey cami tops with barely-there shorty shorts.

"Where's the rest of it?" I say.

"Trust me, you may end up thanking me when you get back," she says with a wink.

"Um, hello? I don't even know the guy yet," I argue back.

"So?"

"It just looks a little, I don't know, desperate."

"No. It's called initiative."

I take the frilly stuff and toss it in my suitcase.

~*~

"No. You are NOT going," Marco demands. Oliver let's out an exasperated sigh. "And don't you start!" he spins and points his finger. "This is all your fault!"

"My fault? Who was it that told her she shouldn't be afraid? Hmm? I think it's fantastic that she's going. And she'll be more than fine, she'll be fierce."

"Sheeee, is standing right heeere," I point out. I walk over to Marco and wrap my arm around his waist. "There were only two things stopping me, right? Work and fear. I squared my vacation time with Max. The only thing left standing in my way was me. So, I channeled my inner diva and bought my own ticket. Ollie is right. I'll be more than fine, I'll be fierce."

"A one-way ticket, Donna!" he shouts as be begins pacing the kitchen.

"Yes, a one-way ticket. That way I can come back on my own terms too. Think about. If I get there and decide it's a mistake, I don't have the hassle of trying to change a ticket. I just buy one and come home. I moved the money over from my "emergency fund" savings account into my regular savings account. Then it's just a matter of transferring the money to my debit account and buying the ticket."

"Sounds like you really thought it through, huh?" he says on a sigh.

"It may be one of the craziest, most spontaneous things I've ever done, but I also thought it through too."

"Send me a post card, eh?"

I launch myself at him and kiss his cheek repeatedly. "Best. Brother. Ever!"

We all laugh. That is, until Marco says "So what are you telling Ma?"

~*~

My flight leaves JFK at 6:45 Monday evening. After a lot of hugs and kisses from Anna, a reassurance that I'll call her when I get to California and email her when I get to Australia; as well as a promise to bring back a jar of Vegemite, I head to security. I don't let myself think about anything until I'm buckled in and the plane is lining up for takeoff because I know if I do I might walk right back out of the airport.

After 6 hours, the plane touches down in Los Angeles and I turn my phone back on. I send a quick text to Anna and Marco saying "just landed – LAX" with a few smoochie emojis. I have about two hours before my next flight. First stop is the ladies room. I've needed to pee for the last hour but would rather use a spacious airport stall compared to the cramped bathroom on the plane. I check out the little overpriced trinket shops and grab a few postcards before going in search of the biggest cup of coffee I can find. I've been running on nervous excitement since I booked my flight on Friday after talking to Max but now I'm winding down. I pull up a chair at the coffee bar and order a large coffee, regular; which confuses the guy pouring the coffee. Toto, I don't think we're in Kansas anymore.

Once I finally have my coffee in hand, I take my phone out of my pocket. I snag one of the postcards out of the bag, lean it up against the cup of coffee, and snap a picture. I email it to my mother with a quick message about taking a much deserved break and doing something for once that's about my own happiness.

My parents have always had my back. I've never doubted that. They're just very old school about a lot of things. I know that mentioning doing something for my own happiness should make my mother smile even if she doesn't understand why I'm on this adventure. Hell, I'm not even 100% sure why I'm on this adventure! But I am going to take each day away as it comes and enjoy the ride.

I start perusing my email, deleting the junk, bookmarking some to check when I get back, and then open the one from Killian from late last night.

Good afternoon, sweetheart! Or should I say late evening seeing as it's 11pm back in New York. It's a little cooler here today. It's nowhere near as cold as it gets back home in the winter, but I'd rather be sitting at the beach with you under the hot sun with a couple of cold beers.

I hit reply.

Or on a balcony overlooking a lake drinking coffee?

A minute later my phone buzzes and I hold my breath as I open his response, worried he'll laugh it off not knowing I'm on my way over.

Beers on a beach or coffee on the balcony, either sounds just perfect!

Didn't hear from you last night and just seems weird not hearing from you until after lunch. Is everything ok? Busy day at work?

I reply that everything is just fine.

Buzz Buzz

Hmmmm, cryptic one liners. Are you sure everything is ok? Plug these numbers into your phone and use them if you need to call. The first is the direct line to my office. The other is the phone number to the hotel. It rings the main desk, just ask for room 303. Oh, and the country code here is 61.

I write back and tell him that everything is, in the words of Oliver, "more than fine". I tell him that it's been a long day and I have another very long day ahead of me tomorrow so I should get some sleep. Before I even get my phone back into my pocket it buzzes.

If you say so, sweetheart. Promise you'll call if you need anything though.

I promise.

14

Technically I wasn't lying when I said I was going to get some sleep. By the time they call boarding for the next flight, I'm thoroughly exhausted. No sooner was the plane up in the air; I was out like a light. I also wasn't lying when I said it was going to be a long day tomorrow either. The flight from LAX to Sydney was almost 15 hours long. Then factor in the time change and holy hell, it's like I missed a whole day!

Seriously! When I left JFK it was Monday early evening and now here in Sydney it's almost 8am on Wednesday! And now I've got a seven and a half hour layover ahead of me.

By the time I get off the plane, find the nearest bathroom, and make my way out of the airport it's almost 9am. I call a budget hotel that's not far from airport. Check in is 11, but they can let me check in at 10. I hail a cab and head for the hotel hoping there's a café or something nearby that I can get some breakfast while I kill an hour.

By 10, I'm checked into the hotel and headed to my room. I don't care that it's super tiny with a bunk bed. I'm only using it for a shower and a place to leave my carry on while I explore for a bit.

My next flight is at three in the afternoon. I want to be back to the airport no later than 2. That doesn't leave me much time to see a city that I've always wanted to see. It's a disappointing thought, but I'm not going to let it bother me. After the world's fastest shower, I head out of the hotel I hail a cab to the Sydney Opera House because you can't go to Sydney and NOT stop there! I apologize to the cabbie for being a hopeless tourist for taking pictures out the window and he laughs it off.

As he gets to the roundabout at the end of Macquarie Street, I'm dumbstruck. I've seen the Opera House a million times in pictures and movies. I just never thought I'd actually ever get to see it up close and personal!

I know that the design is referenced to shells, but to me, it looks like huge boats, standing on end and half buried in the earth, so that their mighty bows still get to gaze at the harbor.

"Be sure to head over to Mrs. Macquarie's Chair. Best place for pictures of the harbor," he says as I'm paying the fare.

"Is it far? I only have two and a half hours before I have to head to the airport. I have to cram everything I want to see in a short amount of time."

"It's only about fifteen minute walk from here along the Cove."

"Would you mind restarting the meter?" I ask. "I just need a few minutes here."

"I don't mind, but if this is your only chance to be here the walk is worth the extra few minutes."

"Ok, I'll walk it. Thanks!" I try to hand him another $5 but he waves it off.

I walk all around the Opera House taking pictures. It's kind of strange seeing the back side of the building. There's something almost ethereal about it. Since I've never seen it in person and every image is always taken from the harbor, from this side is looks like I'm somewhere else.

An older couple asks if I could take their picture for them. After taking a few shots, I hand them my camera and they take my picture.

I start walking along the bend of Farm Cove. I'm so glad I listened to the cabbie. The view of the harbor is stunning! When I get to Mrs. Macquarie's Chair, I realize it's not so much a chair as it is a bench cut out of sandstone. I get a few pictures of the chair/bench and the sign about it. Then I have a seat and take some pictures looking out toward the harbor.

It's 12:30 by the time I walk from the harbor to through the Botanical Garden, and over to the Art Gallery to use their taxi courtesy phone. "281 Bondi Road, please," I say to the driver when he arrives. I only have time for one more stop and I know exactly where I want to go!

Fifteen minutes later, the cab is pulling up in front of The Corner House. "Just give me one minute," I say and jump out of the cab. I snap two pictures of the front of the bar and one selfie before jumping back in the cab.

"Shame it's closed, but at least I got my pictures." I rattle off the address to the hotel and off we go.

Back in my temporary room, I pop the memory card from my camera into my laptop. While I wait for the pictures to upload I wash my face, brush my teeth, and reapply my makeup. When everything finishes uploading I pop the memory card back in the camera. Before shutting down my laptop, I email the pictures from The Corner House to Oliver.

Too bad they're closed! I was going to go in and order the famed Hell Yeah in your honor. Headed back to the airport, then it's off to Adelaide! Nervous as hell, but also excited! All my love to you and Marco! And thanks! I wouldn't be having this awesome life experience without you! Xoxo

Shutting down my laptop, I head down to check out and before I know it I'm back to the airport. By the time I'm through security I've got just over an hour to go before my next flight and then it's off to Adelaide. I've been nervous this whole time but the butterflies are flapping up a storm now; to the point that I feel like I'm going to throw up.

This adventure is so out of my comfort zone that I feel like I'm looking in at someone else's life. And that thought terrifies me. I'm here, but I'm not, and the closer I get to Adelaide, the farther away I want to be from there. It's making my palms sweat and my tongue feel like it's too big for my mouth.

I used to not be like this. I want to be that easy going person again. I really miss her.

On somewhat wobbly legs, I make my way to a little café and order an herbal tea that has some ginger in it. As I sip my cup of tea, I pull out my laptop and log into my email, hoping for a distraction. I send Anna the pictures from the Opera House before flipping through my new messages. Delete. Delete. Delete. Ooo, Free book event for Kindle. I bookmark that one. Delete. Delete.

Hi sweetheart! Would I sound like an ass if I said that it feels weird having gone almost 24 hours without hearing from you? If it would, then forget I said anything ;) Nah, who cares. Think what you want. I miss you! I know, I know, it seems weird missing someone you don't know; outside of the few chance encounters and letters/emails, but I still do. The time difference sucks, too. I've got three and a half hours left before I can leave work and you'll still be asleep. I'll try not to think too much about you in bed while I have my lonely solitary dinner. That's ok. You'll just have to make up for it when I get back to NY ;)

I laugh and it helps calm the butterflies a bit.

Hmmm, so you want me to make it up to you? I can always try to call wherever you're having dinner and hire the Australian equivalent of a mariachi band to come serenade your table? ;)

SPRIONG

As hilarious as that would be, I'll have to pass. It's great hearing from you. I thought for sure your long day made you forget all about me! Sometimes absence doesn't make the heart go fonder, it makes it forgetful ;)

And the butterflies are gone.

Did you seriously just misquote Disney's animated Robin Hood? Lmao! I might already be halfway in like with you ;)

SPROING

Damn! Here I thought you'd think I was some kind of smooth Casanova, but you saw right through me! Halfway in like, huh? So, what's a guy like me have to do to get an upgrade? ;)

Shit! They've started boarding! Once I'm in my seat, I lift the screen back up.

Maybe I'll tell you. Maybe I won't. ;) But right now I have to go see about a mariachi band ;)

~*~

The flight to Adelaide is just over two and a half hours. It's now 4:40pm in Adelaide, making it 3:10am back in NY. At least it's the same day in both places.

I shuffle along with the crowd to the baggage carousel and get my suitcase. Finding the nearest electrical outlet, I dig out my adapter and plug in my laptop. Killian will be getting out of work in the next twenty minutes. I don't know how long the trip is from the office to the hotel, so I need to work fast.

Ten minutes later I've tracked down a florist that will deliver a dozen daisies to Killian's room along with a note saying he has a reservation in the hotel's restaurant at 6:15 and that I'm sorry I couldn't get a mariachi band. That leaves me just over an hour to head to the airport bathroom to change into one of my dresses, do something with my hair and makeup, and hail a cab to the liquor store in the shopping plaza near the hotel.

After purchasing a bottle of red, a bottle of white, and trying not to get Billy Joel stuck in my head, I stow them in my suitcase and walk over to the hotel. I sit in the lounge, turn on my laptop, and go straight to my email.

There are two emails from Killian. The first one is just a sad little face in response to my last email. The second was to say that he was surprised to get a knock on his hotel door and be handed a bunch of daisies. He couldn't help but laugh. He's half fearing the reservation though because if it's not a mariachi band it could be ANYTHING.

You'll be pleasantly surprised! Oh, come on. Live a little! Or are you chicken? Buck buck buck! Lol I triple dog dare you!

SPRIONG

Ooo, damn you! You just HAD to throw a triple dog dare at me, didn't you? Fine! You win! I concede the battle! I'll get changed and head downstairs. It's a fairly nice restaurant, so I don't think they'd let in whatever the Australian version is of mariachi or a harem of belly dancers or whatever crazy idea you've come up with.

I send a quick email to Anna saying that I just got to the hotel and I'm going to meet Killian at dinner. Nervous as hell, I close my laptop, toss it back in my backpack, and make my way to the restaurant's hostess. I tell her that I'm meeting someone for dinner and was wondering if they could hold my luggage. She calls the front desk and has someone come get my suitcase and backpack; offering to have a bell boy run it up to the room, but I tell her it won't be necessary and I can just get it after dinner.

Giving her Killian's room number, she leads me to a table. Sitting with my back to the hostess stand, I look over the menu while I wait. When the waiter comes over I order a Scotch sour on the rocks. I could use the liquid courage. With any luck, my drink will get here before Killian does.

It seems like I blinked and the waiter is back. Hooray for a fast pouring bartender! I take a sip, close my eyes, and sigh. All nerves vanish as the alcohol smoothly sides down to become a warm pool in my stomach.

"Here we are sir," the hostess says. I turn to say "surprise" and almost drop my drink.

"YOU?!?!"

15

"I am definitely pleasantly surprised," he says as he takes the seat across from me. "You, however, seem quite the opposite."

It takes me a minute to pick my jaw up off the floor. This can't be happening! This so Cannot. Be. Happening! This has got to be some weird half nightmare brought on by lack of sleep and too many time zone changes. I pinch my arm. Nope, I'm not still on the plane asleep.

"Are you ok?" he asks concerned.

"Coop?" It comes out more as a squeak.

With a twinkle in his eye, he smirks. He has a dimple. I never noticed that before. Any other time, any other person; and I might think it was adorable. If we weren't in a posh restaurant, I'd toss my drink at him and slap the dimple right off his face.

My breath hitches and my arms break out in goose bumps. It feels like someone's got their icy hands around my lungs and is trying to squeeze them. My hands start to shake. I need to get out of here. I need to get my suitcase and backpack and get the hell out of here! I'll head back towards the airport and find a hotel. Then tomorrow I'll book the first available flight east. Maybe I'll head to

Hawaii for a few days before heading back to New York. Or I could ...

"Donna? Donna, look at me?" Twenty steps ahead of the present I almost forgot he was sitting across from me. "Sweetheart, please ..."

I flinch as if someone slapped me across the face; only I feel the slap where my heart should be. Killian calls me sweetheart, not Coop. Killian's the one I'm halfway in like with. Coop is my arch nemesis that manages to cause me bodily harm each time I have the misfortune of seeing him. Killian and Coop are the same person! I can't even process it! All I know is, it's time to cut and run. I start to get up to leave; to walk away from whoever this man is and forget all this ever happened. The waiter comes over and I slip back down into my seat.

"Bottle of Moet Chandon Dom Perignon. Kalamata olives and the Ciabatta to start," this stranger across from me says without looking at the menu or taking his eyes off of me.

As soon as the waiter leaves, he comes around the table. He turns my chair, crouches down in front of me, and lacing my cold fingers in his, places them in my lap. "Donna?" he whispers "Please? Give me a chance to explain."

"Eat shit and die," I ground out through my teeth.

"If that's what it takes to get you to listen to me? Gladly."

"How could you?" I swallow the lump in my throat.

His thumbs start to make lazy circles on the backs of my hands. I try not to think about how it feels comforting. I close my eyes, tip my head back, and let out a slow breath. He stands up slowly, not letting go of my hands until we're both standing. Then he wraps me in his arms and whispers "Please".

The restaurant breaks out into a round of applause and cheering. Still in his arms, I take a step back and look up. He tries to suppress a chuckle. Leaning in, he whispers in my ears. "I think they are under the impression that I just proposed and you said yes." Despite everything that just happened, I burst out laughing.

As we sit back down the manager herself brings over the bottle of champagne. "With our compliments," she says as she pops the cork and fills two champagne flutes.

"That's very kind of you, but ..." I start to say before I'm interrupted.

"Yes, that's very kind of you, thank you. But we wouldn't feel right accepting such a gift," Killian says.

"As you wish, sir," the manager says as she winks and leaves.

"I notice you didn't tell her that we can't accept because you didn't just propose," I say, picking up my champagne flute.

"The night is still young," he replies and clinks his glass on mine.

"Has anyone ever told you what a horrible, horrible person you are?" I ask as I take a sip of my wine.

"Two, to be exact. But seeing as they are both my sisters, I don't think they count."

"Wow, this champagne is amazing. What's it called again?"

"It's Moet Chandon Dom Perignon." He twirls the bottle to check the label. "2004. And it better be good at $600 a bottle."

I choke on my wine. "$600 a bottle?!"

"Sorry, $600 Australian. It averages $450 back home." If it was physically possible, this would be the moment my eyeballs would pop out of my head and roll across the table. "Well, YOU were the one that said to live a little if I remember correctly, right? I also believe you called me a chicken and then clucked at me! Drink up, Henny Penny! Let's not let this champagne go to waste!"

16

Taking my own advice (or possibly against my better judgment), I decided to live it up. The food was out of this world. I've had every kind of pasta there is in my almost 30 years of living, or at least I thought I had. Whoever came up with the roasted beetroot fettuccini I had is an absolute genius!

After we finish dinner, the waiter asks if we would care for dessert or coffee but we decline and he clears our plates. A minute later he comes back with the check and before I can even get my wallet out of my small bag, he's gone.

"You shouldn't have done that. At least let me leave the tip."

"Already taken care of. Ready to go?" he asks. I don't move a muscle and he sighs. "All I did was sign my name to the check and it gets billed to the room. Tipping isn't the same here as it is at home. And yes, I left what would be considered a generous tip here."

I sigh and push my chair back. As we leave the restaurant, he starts leading me outside. "But what about my bags that are at the front desk?" I ask trying to turn around.

"While you were in the ladies' room, I had them sent up."

We start walking down the path along the lake. "What makes you so sure I'm staying at the hotel?" I say matter-of-factly, wrapping my shawl around my shoulders.

For a split second I notice a change in his eyes. If I hadn't been glancing in his direction I would have missed it. He almost seemed sad, or lost. And then it's gone.

"Ha! You wouldn't turn down having a turn in that tub!" We make our way over to a small dock. "G'day," he says with a nod to the old man untying his boat.

"Bit cold tonight," says the old man, as he steps on board.

"Better than mozzies."

Both men laugh. Maybe it's the champagne talking but wow! I'll admit he has a great voice, but his full blown accent is drool worthy.

"Well, time to shoot through. Better get your Shelia inside before she's an icy pole," he says as he starts up the boat.

"Reckon! No drama, mate, I'll just give her a hottie."

The old man laughs and I have a feeling I should be mildly insulted, but I'm not sure why. "Hooroo," he calls with a wave as he pulls away from the dock and we wave back.

"Lucy, you gots some 'esplaining to do," I say, ala Ricky Ricardo, once the old man is out of earshot.

He laughs. "Open book, remember. Ask away!"

"Open book, my ass! You lied to me!"

"When?"

"When?! You're joking, right? You knew I'd be pissed off when I found out who you were so you made up the name Killian to throw me off!"

"I didn't make the name Killian up! That's actually my name!"

I fold my hands over my chest and tilt my head as if to say "yeah right, buddy".

"Honest! I'll even show you my driver's license and passport," he says and starts heading towards the path back to the hotel.

Instead of following him, I sit down on the dock. Holy shit that's freezing! But I stand, or rather, sit my ground and bite down on my back teeth to keep them from chattering. I'm not going anywhere until I get an explanation! Realizing I'm not behind him, he turns around.

"Really? Ok, fine!" He walks back and sits down next to me with a sigh. "My name really is Killian."

"And Siberia is a tropical paradise."

"It is! My full name is Killian Holsten Cooper. My parents ... how can I put this? Well, let's just say that I'm one of six kids and we're all named after beers."

I snicker.

"Yeah, I know. Hardy har har. You won't be able to hear the story if you don't stop laughing."

"Sorry," I reply with a snicker.

"Done? Ok. So the long and the short of it is, back in the 1860's a man named Thomas Cooper started brewing beers not too far from here. He was married twice and had a LOT of children. One of those children was my great grandfather, Christopher. When my parents starting having kids they thought it would be a fun thing to name us all after beers. Yeah, they're warped like that. The brewery is still in operation and still family owned and run; but by my distant cousins. Since my firm does business with the brewery, I'm here about once a year for meetings and I get a chance to keep in touch with family and visit Gran."

"So, Coop is short for Cooper; which is your last name, not your first name."

"Imagine being a guy who's first and middle names are beers. Then imagine going through high school and college with those names. My brothers and sisters have names that aren't as easily recognized as beers. I guess when it came to names; you could say I got the short straw. Freshman year of high school was a real riot. Besides being called "Killian's Irish Red", people would say things like "big red", "Hey Irish", "kill joy", it went on and on. So, Matt suggested Coop and it stuck."

"So, six kids, all named after beers? Your parents must be a trip. Your dad isn't named after a hard liquor or something is he?" I ask with a laugh.

"Funny. But no. He's actually named after my great grandfather; which may be why we all got stuck with beers for names." He goes on to tell me that his brother Sam is named for Samuel Smith, not Sam Adams as most people assume. Next is his sister Sierra, named for Sierra Nevada. Then comes Murphy; named for Murphy's Irish Stout. After Murphy is Killian. Next is his brother John Thatcher, who like Killian, has a two beer name; John, for John "JW" Lees and Thatcher for Thatcher's Gold; which is owned by Coopers. The baby of the family Avery, who turns twenty two this year, is named after the craft brewery that opened up a few months before she was born. "A few months ago she got married to her high school sweetheart Tommy, and now her last name is Smith. It's kind of creepy that she's now a Smith seeing as Sam is named after Samuel Smith. Weirder still, if she had hyphenated her last name, she'd be Cooper-Smith; which is the name of a brewery in Colorado. The totally insane thing is … Coopersmith brewery is only about an hour drive from the Avery Brewery! Shit you not! Couldn't even make this stuff up if I tried!"

"Truth is stranger than fiction," I quote.

"Oooo, getting smarty pants with the Mark Twain, huh?" He stands and reaches down for my hand. I take the offered hand because my legs are so cold I don't think I can get off the dock by myself. "Come on; let's get you out of the cold."

"I'm fine," I say, trying not to shiver.

"Who's the liar now?"

~*~

Opening the door to his room, I walk in and realize it's an entire suite. It's more than half the size of my apartment; which at 1,200 square feet is pretty large, compared to most 1 bed - 1 bath apartments in the five boroughs. The far wall is nothing but floor to ceiling windows with an expansive view of the lake. I let out a slow whistle. "Ho-ly hell."

"Pretty fantastic, isn't it?" I hear him say as I walk closer to the windows.

"It's beautiful," I sigh.

"I'd say stunning." He walks up behind me and wraps his arms around my waist. "But then I'd be talking about you, not the view."

"Very smooth, Casanova," I remark.

I'm a tightly wound ball of nervous energy. I'm alone with a strange man. He's pressed against my back and has his arms around me. I should be screaming in full blown "get me the hell outta here" style terror, but I'm not. And I think that terrifies me even more. Hopefully he won't see through my sarcastic façade.

"What? I didn't just misquote *Robin Hood* or something, did I? You'll have to forgive me; I can't help it. I'm an incurable romantic! Just don't let anyone know, ok?" He laughs as he walks away, leaving me to my view gazing.

"Speaking of incurable romantic," he says walking back a few minutes later. "I've just started running a bubble bath for you. Against my better judgment, I lowered the shade between the bathroom and the living room so I wouldn't be tempted to peek. If I had known ahead of time that you were flying over, I'd have had a bottle of your favorite wine already here."

I may have just gone past the halfway mark of in like. "One step ahead of you," I say, picking up my suitcase and placing it on the coffee table. Unzipping the front pouch, I pull out the bag from the liquor store. "I wasn't sure which you preferred, so I got two bottles. One is a Moscato, the other is a Shiraz."

"Yellow Tail. Cute, sweetheart," he laughs taking both bottles. "Let's put the white in the fridge and I'll open the red."

While he's not looking, I quickly grab some non-frilly pajamas out of the bottom of my bag and toss them on the counter in the bathroom. Sorry, Anna. I'm just closing the zipper on my suitcase when he walks back over with two glasses of the Shiraz. "Mmm, thanks," I say after taking a sip.

"Your bath should be full. Why don't you go get in? Do you want to take the bottle of wine with you? I don't think I'll be able to resist the lure of the tub should you need a refill," he says with a wink.

"Hmmm, maybe I should take the bottle in with me," I retort and he flashes a dopey exaggerated smile. "Funny. But after the last time it was you, me, and a bottle of wine;

the last thing I want is to be in a bubble bath with broken wine bottle everywhere."

Winking, I grab the bottle and make a mad dash of the bathroom. He takes off after me but I manage to get in the bathroom and close the door. "Ha! You'll have to be faster than that, slowpoke!" I tease through the closed door.

"I'll remember that!" He shouts back.

Placing my glass and the bottle of wine by the sink, I raise the blinds a bit. Unable to resist I stick my tongue out at him and then make a bunch of silly faces. He folds his arms across his chest and mock pouts.

"Aww, poor baby," I mock through the glass.

He pouts some more.

That's when my inner diva came out to play. Reaching back, I slowly unzip the back of my dress. His eyes lose their gleam of humor and darken. It's a wonder the room doesn't instantly ignite from the smoldering look I'm getting. Very slowly I pull the back to the dress forward to reveal a shoulder. I lower the dress just enough to show the lace edge at the top of my strapless bra. And with that, I drop the blinds and laugh. After all, serves the bastard right for hiding who he is.

I finish undressing, refill my glass of wine, and slip into the tub. It's even better than I imagine. If it weren't for the bubbles, I'd hit the button on the side of the tub and turn the jets on.

Enjoying the warmth from the wine and the water, I let myself relax. The past few days have been hectic, long, fun, frustrating, and emotionally deflating. And yet in the twenty minutes I'm lounging away in this behemoth of a tub, I've realized something about the past few years. I've lost myself somewhere along the way. It's time for Stella to get her groove back.

I raise my wine glass in salute and then down the rest of it in one sip. Rising from the tub, I raise my arms and stretch; feeling the bubbles slowly slide down my body, relishing in the almost sinful sensation as they make their way over my hip and down my leg. It awakens a long since dormant awareness of my own body. It's empowering.

"She'll be more than fine; she'll be fierce," I hear Oliver say as I towel off. I almost wished I'd grabbed the frilly lingerie Anna put in my suitcase. I could just walk out wrapped in a towel, or wearing nothing at all. But I'm not quite to that level of fierce and I chuckle to myself as I slip into the pajamas I had in the bathroom with me. Hitting the drain on the tub, I gather up all my clothes and walk out into the living room.

Gooooood lord! There's Killian lounging on the couch in nothing but a pair of running shorts. He turns to look at me and raises an eyebrow. Like an animal on the prowl, he slowly gets up off the couch and starts walking towards me. He's built, but not in the grossly over muscular way. My mouth goes dry. Fierce me has already fled and I'm glued to the spot.

Stalking towards me, he stops with barely an inch between us and my eyes close. "Two can play that game, sweetheart," he whispers as he continues walking passed.

The bathroom door clicks shut and my breath comes out as a whoosh.

I put my clothes in my suitcase and take my laptop out of my backpack. I send a quick email to Marco saying that Oliver was right. I'm more than fine. I'm just still working on fierce. Then I send an email to Anna. No words, just a picture I took of Killian at dinner holding up the bottle of champagne. I lower the screen and wonder "what now?"

SPROING

No. Fucking. WAY! Coop is Mystery Man?! I haven't left for the office yet, call me!

I bite my lower lip and glance over my shoulder at the bathroom window. I'm tempted to pick up the phone on the desk. So much has gone on in the past few days I feel like I have a year's worth of things to tell Anna. Instead, I take a slow breath and type back:

Can't right now. Initiative.

17

There's a phone ringing. It sounds far off in the distance. It almost sounds underwater. How is a phone ringing underwater? I try to roll over and answer it, but can't move. The phone stops ringing and I hear a grunt. Next thing I know I'm being dragged into a solid wall. Slowly I being to realize that the wall is Killian, the reason I couldn't roll over was his arm is draped over me, and I'm naked. He snuggles in closer and I'm reminded of just how I got this way.

After emailing Anna last night, I shut down my laptop and put it back in my backpack. On the way to get myself more wine, I stopped in front of the mirror and took a good long look at myself. Leaning in, I stared into my own eyes.

"What are you afraid of?" asks the voice inside my head.

Falling. That's what I'm afraid of. Falling for someone and getting hurt. Been there, done that, and instead of the lousy T-shirt, I got battle scars to prove it.

"Then what are you doing here?" the voice inside my head says.

"I'm here to be fierce and find myself again," I whispered back. I miss the "before" me; before when being around people, especially men, didn't scare the shit out of me, before when I was core-deep happy, before I built up these walls and shut the world out. Straightening, I square my shoulders then strip out of my pajamas and walk into the bathroom.

"I thought you might need some help scrubbing your back," I say as I tap on the glass shower wall.

He makes a sound halfway between a groan and a growl. "You are going to be the death of me, sweetheart," he says gruffly, his accent more pronounced.

"I can always leave you alone if you want," I tease and take a step towards the door.

"Like hell you will!" he shouts.

Reaching around the glass, he grabs me by the wrist and pulls me into the shower; the force of which slams me up against him. Killian's mouth comes crashing down on mine and I feel like I've been struck by lightning. His hand slowly runs down my side and over my hip, reminding me of the bubbles from my bath and it's empowering.

Wrapping my arms around his back, I pull him closer; my breasts pressed into his chest. He makes a guttural sound and says something that I can't quite make out through the pounding in my own ears. He begins kissing down my neck and gives my collar bone a light nip.

My nails dig into the muscles of his back and as he presses himself against me I realize that he just may be the death of me. "Oh shit!" I gasp. Sliding my hands down his back, I pull him against me again and groan.

Spinning us through the water, he slams my back against the tile. He takes both my wrists in one hand; and holding them above my head, takes my breast into his mouth as he slowly slides a finger inside of me. Just when I'm sure I'm about to burst, Killian lifts me off the ground. My legs wrap around his waist and he slams into me. There's an explosion of color behind my closed eyes.

Hands and tongues everywhere, he continues to slam into me. I can feel the pressure building within me and try to hold off as long as I can. With one squeeze of my nipple between his thumb and forefinger, I bite down on his shoulder and shatter. One. Two. Three more thrusts and I feel him convulse. Both gasping for breath, he rests his head on my shoulder. Pulling him closer I wrap my arms around him a little tighter for fear of falling; in more ways than one.

"Mmmm, goooood morning, sweetheart," Killian says as he nuzzles my neck.

"Good morning yourself, ready for round ... um, I lost count!" I laugh, and it feels invigorating.

"I wish," he says and lays his head on my chest to snuggle in. "Unfortunately I have to work today. Although ... cough cough ... I think I may need to call in sick. Will you be my nurse?" he asks, drawing lazy circles on my stomach.

"Tempting," I reply as he begins moving his hand towards my breast. "Very tempting. But you, my dear, need to go to work. No playing hooky on my account."

"Piker," he grumbles as he rolls over to get out of bed.

"Excuse me?!"

Looking back over his shoulder, he flashes his dimple and says "it means party pooper".

I pull the pillow out from under my head throw it at him. He slaps it away and laughs as he stands up. I give a low, slow whistle and say "Nice ass!"; which he then shakes for emphasis, as he heads to the bathroom.

I flop back down on the pillow for a full body stretch. Every bone in my body hurts; but in all the right ways. Rolling onto my side, I look at the view. I take a look at the houses on the other side of the lake and imagine what it would be like to wake up to this view every morning. Lucky bastards.

Reluctantly, I get out of bed and go looking for my discarded clothes. I'm just pulling my T-shirt down when Killian comes out of the bathroom with a towel wrapped low on his waist. "Awwww," he drawls, "I missed the show!"

Popping my hip up, I take one finger and run it up my hip, slowly baring the skin underneath revealing that I've yet to put on underwear. I laugh at his growl. "Better get a move on or you'll be late."

He jerks me into his arms. "Pffft, what are they going to do, fire me?"

"Someone is very sure of himself," I laugh and step out of his embrace. "Go get dressed."

As he walks past, I turn and swat him on the ass because, why the hell not? I toss on my boxers and head to the in-suite coffee pot. A minute later, Killian rounds the corner in his suit pants and is buttoning up his shirt.

"What is that heavenly smell?"

"I got the coffee going. Last night I got to lounge in the tub, which I've wanted to do ever since I saw the picture. So I thought this morning you'd get to sit out on the balcony and have coffee with me.

"For you, I'll make time," he murmurs. "Let me just get my socks and shoes. You may want to put something warmer on since it could be a little chilly outside this morning."

Tip, tip, goes the "like" scale.

When the coffee's done brewing, I add milk and sugar to mine. "Uh, how do you take you coffee?" I shout.

"Regular!" he shouts back.

He comes back around the corner, tosses his tie on the table, and puts his suit jacket around the chair. He picks up his coffee and takes my hand, leading me out the door onto the balcony. It's a little more than just a little chilly. I wrap my hands around my cup of coffee and try not to shiver. Killian puts his coffee down on the little table, goes inside and grabs the quilt off the bed, then wraps it around me.

Tip, tip.

Bundled in the quilt, I look out at the lake, sip my coffee, and smile. "I hope it's thoughts of me that put that smile on your face," he teases.

"In a round-about way," I admit. "I was just thinking that every day should start like this."

"So ... you're saying the people in the restaurant assumed correctly, you've agreed to marry me, and we're moving in here?"

"Ha ha, smart ass," I mock, reaching into my pocket for my camera. I lean over the arm of my chair and snap a picture of the two of us. "I just meant the serenity," I say and sit back down in my chair.

"Aaaah, I get it. I didn't flash you a ring, so you won't say yes until you get one! Gah, another idiot move on my part! You, madam, have my most humblest apologies. We shall rectify that this evening and go ring shopping just as soon as I get out of work!"

I reach over and swat him on the arm. "So sure of yourself, aren't you?"

He lets out an over exaggerated sigh. "Fine. I'll take that as a no. We're too far for me to go on walkabout, get lost, and eaten by dingoes. I'll just have to settle for drowning myself in Gulf St Vincent."

"You are too much," I laugh, shaking my head. It feels good to laugh.

"I didn't hear you complaining last night," he says with a wink. "Come on, walk me out."

We head back inside. I toss the quilt back on the bed. Killian goes into the bathroom to brush his teeth and comb his hair back. When he comes back out he puts on his tie and jacket.

"Well?" he asks.

I take a step closer, straighten his tie a bit, and brush my hands down the lapels of his jacket. He wraps his arms around me and leans his cheek against the top of my head. In that moment, I feel a wave of contentment wash over me. A few days ago, it would have had me running for cover. This morning, it had me taking half a step closer.

Well this is all nice and very domestic.

"I know," he says. "I like it."

Oh shit! Did I say that last thought out loud?

"Maybe you'll reconsider ring shopping while I'm at work?" Wink, dimple, tip, tip. "If you need anything, you have my number at the office. I'll stop at the desk downstairs on the way out, have them make you up a key and also add your name to the room, so if you want anything just sign for it." Picking up his brief case, he heads to the door. "Miss me, will you?" He leans in for one last kiss and then he's gone.

Running back around the partition, I launch myself onto the bed and squeal into a pillow. I roll over and check the time on the clock. 6:30pm back in New York. I reach over, pick up the phone, and on the second attempt get the call through to Anna.

"Hello?" she says.

I squeal.

"Donna?"

I giggle.

"Weeh-he-hell," she says. "Aren't you the cat that caught the canary?"

"Oh, Anna, you have NO idea."

I go on to tell her all about the trip here, about the nerves, the daisies, and setting up the reservations. I tell her about the rage that threatened to engulf me when I realized who he was, the sense of betrayal over the fact that he lied, and the scene at the restaurant with the other patrons applauding.

"Then the manager brought out the bottle of champagne to our table and offered it on the house because she thought we'd just gotten engaged. And get this, Anna! The champagne Killian ordered costs $450 a bottle back home! He didn't even bat an eye! I'm going to get some pictures of this place and email them to you, but holy hell, the pictures are nothing compared to the real thing!"

"So, wait ... which guy is he then?" she asks sounding confused.

"Both," I say and laugh. "Reader's Digest version. His first name is Killian. His last name is Cooper. Coop is a nickname Matt gave him back in high school and it stuck."

"Wait! Killian Cooper? THE Killian Cooper?! Killian. Holsten. COOPER?! Holy fuck balls, Donna!" she screams and it reminds me of some radio contest winner screaming into the phone. "Oh my god! Omigod, omigod, omigod! You're serious, right? You're not just pulling my leg are you?!"

"Uuum, no?" I respond thoroughly confused. She screams again. "I'm missing something here," I say. "What am I missing?"

"Ok, now I KNOW you're pulling my leg! Have you been living under a rock the past few years?"

My happy bubble feels like it's about to pop. Damnit! I am not going to let it!!

"Oh, shit, Donna, I'm sorry. Sweetie, say something," she urges full of concern. I can actually picture the stricken look on her face.

"Up until a few days ago, yes, I was still living under a rock," I begin, my voice sounding small. "Yesterday, I took that finally step out from under it". My voice is getting stronger. "Damnit! I will not let my past hold me back from living my life!"

I take a slow, deep, cleansing breath. Out of nowhere I sing to Anna "Ain't nothin' gonna break my stride. Nobody's gonna slow me down, oh-no! I got to keep on movin'! Ain't nothin' gonna break my stride. I'm running and I won't touch ground. Oh-no, I got to keep on movin'!" By the end of the verse I'm dancing on the bed as we finish singing the song together.

She bursts out laughing. "So ... next we sing *Bitch is Back* by Elton John?"

After hanging up with Anna, I call Oliver.

"The frisbee to the head slash bike debacle, burned you with coffee, shards of glass in your foot guy? And you're still all in one piece? Wooo, sister!"

"I was better than fine, I was fierce. And then I was fierce again. Baby, I was fierce all night long and all over that suite!"

"Woooo!   Somebody fan me!" he exclaims. "Though, you better not let your brother hear you say that."

"Why do you think I called you?"

18

By the time I shower, have some breakfast sent up, and check online to see what there is to do its 10:30. I've got my backpack dumped out on the bed to repack for a day out, when the phone rings.

"Uh, hello?"

"Hey, sweetheart! Miss me yet?" he replies with a chuckle.

"If I said yes, would you chuck a sickie?"

"Woooo! Well I'll be stuffed! Look at Ms Smarty Pants studying up on her Strine!"

I laugh sultrily and in a deep husky voice reply, "Anything for you, baby".

"I can be there in 10!" he intones, his voice dropping a few octaves.

I snort and roll my eyes. "You can't call in sick when you're already there."

"No, but I can take a long lunch."

"Funny, but I'm going to go see the sights. I'll meet you back here when you get out of work. 5:00, right?"

"I've got a better idea. Meet me here and then we'll go out to dinner." I write down the address in my notebook, finish tossing a few things in my backpack, and out the door I go.

My first stop is a cell phone place that rents prepaid phones to international travelers. I figured out how to get my American cell phone to work here. It's just a matter of setting it to International Roaming and then calling my carrier. But it's ridiculously expensive.

Leaving the shopping plaza, I head out onto the main boulevard and wait for the bus. I know it's the 117, but when it arrives I double check with the driver to make sure I'm getting on the one headed in the right direction. Half an hour later I'm in Port Adelaide and climbing up to the lantern room of the Lighthouse. After snapping a few pictures, I head back down to take a tour of the museum. I really enjoy the exhibition on the dolphins. I shudder as I bypass the section on shipwrecks.

After the Maritime Museum, I walk over to Pancakes on the Port for a quick lunch on my way to the Fisherman's Wharf Market. I wander around looking at all the things for sale. I find a vendor selling handmade candles and buy a bunch of tea lights. I also pick up some tapers and a few candle sticks. Next time I climb in that tub, the blinds are going to be opened and I'm going to enjoy the view in style!

With about two and a half hours to kill, I find a Dutch coffee bar, sit down for a hot cup of coffee and take out my notebook. I check the Maritime Museum and Fisherman's Wharf off my list and write a little something about each place. I read through my list of places to visit before deciding what to see next.

After finishing my coffee, I start walking to Calton Street. There's a bit of a cold breeze coming in from water, but the gallery is only around the corner, so it's not too bad. The building looks old, without looking run down. There are a few spots that look like concrete or extra mortar was added and reminds me of exposed brick walls in a lot of the warehouse-turned-apartments back home in Williamsburg. Stepping inside, I come to a short stop. It isn't what I expected at all.

"Afternoon," calls the woman from behind the counter.

I look left, then right, then left again. "Did I just step into a wormhole or something?" I ask, obviously confused.

The gallery is filled with a variety of Native American art and jewelry. There are some Sugar Skulls and some Frida Kahlo art along one wall. And the woman behind the counter has a definite American accent.

"No, no wormholes here," she laughs. "But ... did you click your red ruby slippers together as you walked through the door?"

I can't help but laugh at that. Heading toward the jewelry, my eyes are drawn to a Danan silver necklace. The beads are all handmade. There are two whimsical charms. The pendant is a three dimensional square with a small circle of turquoise in the center. It makes me think of my brother Carmine's fiancé Grace. As I head to the register to pay, out of the corner of my eye, I spot a gorgeous Navajo silver and turquoise necklace. It's one of those if-I-don't-get-it-I'll-regret-it-later kinds of things. I try to talk myself out of it.

"Here," the woman says, moving the mirror on the counter closer.

I know I shouldn't, but I hold it up to my neck. It somehow picks up the tiny green flecks in my cognac colored eyes. Checking the price tag, I bite my lip. I hadn't planned on spending on myself outside of food and travel expenses. I rationalize it by telling myself it's to celebrate the first liberating steps towards finding me again. Sold!

After paying for both necklaces, the woman offers to help me put my new necklace on and then puts Grace's in a small jewelry box; which I stash in my backpack.

Heading back outside, I put my scarf back on and head down the road a bit. Taking out my camera, I hand it to a couple of teenagers and ask them to take my picture. Tossing my arms up in the air, I smile wide, and stand under the shop's sign that reads "Carpe Diem. Seize the day!" Thanking them, I turn and head inside.

The first thing I notice is that it has a definite smell to it. It's calming but somehow invigorating at the same time. It's not sweet like Nag Champa. It's not earthy like Patchouli. It's somewhere in between and is amazing.

"G'day," comes a very smooth, very masculine voice. "If you need help finding anything," he says, emphasizing the word anything, "don't hesitate to ask."

I chuckle to myself and start checking out all the tables and shelves. There's so much to look at! There's a small Buddha statue on one of the shelves. The smile on his face looks part fun part mischief. It's so Oliver! I find a Tibetan Medical Bracelet. It's made of five metals which are supposed to influence and balance the five energies of the body and positively influence the general health and wellbeing of the body. It's perfect for Anna! I also find a stunning hand dyed silk scarf with swirling shades of greens and blues that I pick up for my mother. There's something tranquil about it that reminds me of her; well, when we're not loudly discussing things.

I could seriously get lost in this store for a week and still keep looking, but Killian will be getting out of work soon, so I make my way to the register. "Find everything you needed?" asks the shop guy as he smirks and raises an eyebrow.

Feeling bold I lean over the counter a bit. "Maybe. Maybe not." His smile kicks up a notch. "What's the name of the incense that I'm smelling in here?"

Judging by the look on his face, he obviously thought I meant something else. I can't stop the smile that spreads across my face. There's something freeing about being able to banter with a flirtatious stranger. He points me in the direction of the incense, soaps, and whatnot and as I peruse the section I think about how it's a huge baby step. An oxymoron, I know, but it's true. This whole trip has been an amazing experience; both empowering and terrifying at the same time. For the first time in a very long time, I feel like 'being whole again' is attainable.

I grab about a dozen sticks of incense, and taking another minute I look through all the lotions, soaps, and various organic toiletries before heading back to the register. After paying and stashing my purchases, I head down the road to the train station in search of a cab.

Fifteen minutes later, I'm standing in front of a red metal gate. I grab my camera out and take a few pictures of the entrance sign with its big red Coopers bottle cap. Tossing the camera into my backpack, I take out my cell phone and dial the number for Killian's office.

"This is Killian," he answers distractedly.

"You sound busy. Guess that means you had no time to miss me today, huh?"

"Sweetheart!" I can hear the smile on his face. "I'm just trying to finish up some things that fell by the wayside because I was a bit, uh, preoccupied by wandering thoughts." He laughs. "There's a woman at the front desk named Maggie. I'll ring her and tell her to walk you back to the office."

"Even if I knew which way to go to get to a front desk, I'm standing in front of a closed gate."

"So, walk around it. Just turn left and look for a bright red wall. Can't miss it! See you in a few!" And with that, he hangs up.

Stepping between the gate and a small bush, I make my way to the front door. Once inside, I head in the direction of the front desk. There's a woman sitting at the desk with gorgeous chestnut brown hair and sparkling light green eyes. She's wearing a headset, searching for something on the computer at the desk, going through clipboards, switching phone calls, looking back to her screen; all the while effortlessly handling everything all at once.

I walk up to the desk, and without breaking her rhythm she says "You must be Donna. Give me just one moment." She rattles off some numbers on her screen to the person on the phone, switches to another call to rattle off an address from a clip board, and then stands as she takes off her headset. "If you'll just follow me this way, please."

Walking down a hall, she turns and gives two quick knocks on a door before opening it and motioning for me to walk though. Stepping into the office, I'm brought up short by the sight of a perky blonde with legs up to her ears sitting on the corner of Killian's desk. They're laughing.

"Hey, Donna," Killian says patting his hand on this woman's knee and that's when I saw red. We're not exclusive but that doesn't stop the visions swirling around in my brain; me choking him with his tie and beating her with her own shoe.

The leggy blonde hops off the desk and walks over to me hand extended. "So nice to finally meet you Donna, I've heard so much about you over the past few weeks!" She takes my hand in a firm grip, leans in, and whispers "Relax, I'm one of the cousins."

I blink a time or two. She chuckles and gives me a wink before putting her arm around my shoulders and turning towards Killian. "Ooo, I like her! Take my advice, mate, don't let this one get away." She gives my shoulder a squeeze before breezing out the door.

"You should buy her flowers, or diamonds, or a new Porsche or something for having just saved your life," I deadpan. He looks lost and confused. I can't help but laugh. "So are you just about ready to go?"

While he's finishing up the report he's working on, I grab a piece of paper and write a quick note.

I told him he owes you for saving his life. I suggested flowers, diamonds, and a Porsche. You should try to hit him up for all three!

As we go to leave his office, I tell him we need to stop by his cousin's office. When we get there, I walk in and hand her the note. She raises one eyebrow and after reading the note, offers a wicked smile.

Once Killian and I are outside, he turns to me and asks "What was that all about?"

Laughing, I give him a kiss. "Nothing, dear."

19

"Here we are, Mr. Cooper," the driver says as we pull up in front of a two story white building.

"Thanks, Tony," he says as he slides out of his seat. "And I've told you to quit it with the Mister business."

"Force of habit," he apologizes flashing a smile. "Would you like me to wait or should I come back in about a half hour or so?"

"Nah, that'll be it for tonight. Not sure where we're going on to yet."

"Goodnight, sir," Tony says with a wink and pulls away.

"A chocolate factory?" I ask, turning to look at the building.

"From what I hear, the tour they do is a lot of fun. While I was finishing up my report, I emailed Maggie and told her to call in a reservation for us."

"You have someone make your appointments for you, someone to drive you around; wow, must be a rough life," I tease.

Twenty five minutes later, after hearing the history of the company, watching their chocolates being made, and a chocolate tasting; I'm standing in the Visitors Centre drooling at the display cases filled with an array of chocolates in all shapes and sizes.

"Ready to go?" Killian asks as he walks up next to me.

"Um, no," I respond trying to convey what an idiot question that was to ask any woman in chocolate shop. "I haven't even decided what to buy!"

He holds up a bag at eye level. "I got you a surprise," he says with a twinkle in his eyes. I make a grab for it and he moves the bag behind him then ushers me out the door.

"Stop grinning like a shot fox and give me my prezzie!" I say, stomping my feet, and doing my best impression of a spoiled rotten toddler. We both burst out laughing in the parking lot.

"Come on, brat," he says. We head down the main road and hop on a tram.

"Ooo, trying to fit in with us commoners now? Think you can handle it, or do I need to call Tony before you have a nervous breakdown?" I say teasing him.

"Very funny. You won't be laughing later when I don't share the chocolates!"

"You wouldn't!" I gasp in mock horror. I put my head on his shoulder and blink up at him trying to look innocent. "But, but, I'll be your best friend!" He tosses his arm around my shoulder and we sit in companionable silence.

"This is our stop," he tells me a few minutes later and we hop off the tram.

"Town Hall? Is this where I get my chocolate?" I ask.

"And they say men have one track minds!" He slips his hand in mine and tugs. "Come on, let's go."

I'm too busy over thinking to pay attention to all the buildings we're passing. Here I am walking hand in hand with a funny, gorgeous, successful guy, who has a drool worthy accent and is amazing in bed. This same guy totally gets my odd humor, enjoys my company, and right now we're bopping around Adelaide! If you asked me a week ago what I thought I'd be doing now, it definitely wouldn't be this!

Killian opens the door to one of the shops and let's go of my hand so that I can walk in first. When realization dawns on me, I turn one eighty and walk full force into him; reminding me of when he barreled into me at the coffee cart, burning me with scalding hot coffee and I punched him.

I look down at my feet, shaking my head no, and try to walk around him. He blocks every attempt. "Killian, no," I try to say, but it comes out as a whisper.

I can't seem to get any words past the lump in my throat. Normal women would be excited to be in a place like this. I'm filled with thoughts of dread and despair. I need to get out of this store.

It feels like bile is rising up my throat as long ago words ring in my ears, drowning out all the other noises around me. *"You're mine. You belong to me. You're pathetic, you should be grateful there's someone willing to take care of you. If I can't have you, no one will."* Reflexively I put my hand on my shoulder and shudder. Did I really think I was fierce? I'm not; I'm still broken. Old attitudes that I thought I'd caged up slither out and begin to drag me down. The one that's pulling me down the fastest is that I don't deserve to be happy. It's followed closely the feeling that being here in this shop is a cruel joke at my expense. I know it's not true and it's definitely not fair to Killian for me to even think it, but I can't help thinking it when it was so ingrained for so long.

Placing a hand under my chin, Killian tilts my head back. My eyes are filled with tears I refuse to shed. I may be broken, but at least I have a little pride left ... I think.

"Oh, sweetheart," he says tucking me tightly against him; as if the pressure of his arms could press the shattered bits of me back together. Oh how I wish they could! I just want to be whole again; to fully get back to me, to once and for all slam the door on the past, nail it shut, and wall it up in concrete.

"Hey," he whispers so only I can hear him, "Donna, I didn't mean to upset you. I'm so sorry. I thought it would be a laugh. When I left for the office this morning I joked about ring shopping after I got out of work, so I thought we'd stop here and continue the laugh." He leans back but doesn't let go of me. "Sweetheart? Look at me, please Donna?"

I can't help it, I look up. He gives me a slow smile. "Donna, it's all my fault. I am so, so, sorry."

"This isn't your fault," I say, but don't say more.

"Yes. Yes, it is. I'll prove it to you too. Hand me your phone?"

My phone? I reach back, take it out of my pocket and give it to him. He punches in a bunch of numbers and waits.

"Hi! I was just calling ... yeah, I'm well aware that it's 5:30 in the morning .. uh huh .. doesn't matter ... Avery, shut up! This is important! Good, now that I have your attention I'm calling to tell you that not only do I finally concede and admit to being an idiot, but I am also an inconsiderate asshole and should come with a warning label."

He pauses to listen to Avery say something. "No," he says looking down and locking his eyes on mine. "I made Donna cry. She may or may not hate me. It's still a toss-up if she'll ever forgive me. And, should she decide not to forgive me, I'll grovel every day until she does because I ... I ... I have to go Avery."

And with that, he turns off the phone, puts it in his jacket pocket, and kisses me hard on the mouth. Everything fades away; the jewelry store, the street outside, the whole city, the floor beneath our feet. Time seems to stand still. It's like all those scenes in all those books I read over the years, coming back to point and taunt me. I grab the lapels of his jacket and hang on for dear life as I feel the "like" scale blow up because it can't tip anymore.

And maybe, just maybe, I can be fierce while gluing the pieces back together.

~*~

He-hem

Killian lifts his head. One of the jewelers is standing two feet away trying to discreetly get our attention.

"Sorry to interrupt," he says, leaving the sentence hanging.

"Right, yes, sorry," Killian mumbles "Erh, sorry."

I can't tamp down the tiny giggle that bubbles up. He looks down and flashes a megawatt smile. Tip, tip, goes this new scale. Releasing all but my hand, he leans down and whispers "Let's live it up a little and have a poke around. It's kind of rude to just turn and leave seeing as we've been half blocking his door for the past several minutes."

As we look around, I'm very aware of the fact that my hand is still in Killian's and that he's now lazily running his thumb up and down mine. Whether it's an absent minded thing, or if he thinks it'll keep me from bolting out of the store, I'm not really sure.

"We have a variety of diamonds available in a wide range of weights and cuts," the jeweler begins.

"I don't like diamonds," I say.

I didn't realize I actually said it out loud, until both men turn to look at me like I was off my rocker.

"Diamonds are often called rocks. Rocks are unfeeling and lifeless, something a marriage should never be. Diamonds are also called ice. Ice is cold, sometimes so cold it can burn you. If it's jagged, it can cut you. And over time, it can melt and disappear, something that should never happen in a marriage. Diamonds may be forever, but any man that give a woman a diamond engagement ring is a fool," I explain, quickly followed by "Sorry, no offense. I know it's your line of work and all."

Leaving both men stunned in silence, I walk over to the next case and give everything a glance over. Above the case is a flat screen TV that's been recessed into the wall. Out of the corner of my eye, I catch the flash as the screen changes and glance up. Now I'm the one that's stunned silent.

"Do you like it?" the other jeweler asks walking up next to me.

"It's breath taking. I've never seen anything like it."

"Thanks. It's an original design. I overheard what you said about diamond engagement rings and was curious. What do you think is the ideal stone then?"

"My grandmother always said that pearls bring sadness, so definitely not a pearl. Honestly, I don't think there is any one straight forward answer though. If the guy is going to pick the ring by himself, he should get something that reflects the woman's personality, or is her favorite color; maybe something that matches her eyes or even his eyes so that when she looks at it she's reminded of him. Diamonds are all flash. Nobody cares about the thought that went in to it. They're only impressed by the cut, cost, and how garish it looks. It's sad really. And I'm so sorry if any of your other customers just overheard me and I ruined a sale!"

He laughs. "No worries. I think that's the most honest and profound answer I've ever heard," he says patting me on the arm as he walks away.

"What do you think of this, sweetheart?" Killian says pointing at the case. "I'm thinking maybe I should have something sent to Avery as an apology." I walk over to see what he's pointing at.

It's a watch!

"You really are an idiot, aren't you?"

~*~

It's been a long exhausting few days, physically, mentally, and emotionally, so we hail a cab back to the hotel. Somewhere along the half hour ride back I fell asleep with my head resting on Killian's shoulder.

"Hey, sweetheart? We're here," he says.

I stretch and climb out of the cab then look around trying to get my bearings. I look up at him through half opened eyes and mumble "but the hotel is over there", as I point down the road.

"If you want, we can order take away and head back to our room."

Taking a step closer, I wrap my arms around him, snuggle in and give him a hug. "I'll be fine. Let's go in and have some dinner."

We order some wine and a few appetizers to start. When the food arrives it's the most heavenly smells.

"How is everything?" the waiter asks as he comes by to check on us.

"Outside of Greece, I thought Queens, New York was the only place you could get great Greek food. This is phenomenal!"

When we're done eating, we ask the waiter for the check. The owner comes over to the table with the check and a very large piece of Baklava. Without glancing at the bill, Killian hands the man his credit card. I explain that we didn't order dessert and he said it was on the house, since "phenomenal" was the best compliment he's ever had. He's a second generation Aussie, using the recipes his grandmother would teach him whenever he would visit her in Greece as a kid.

"*Pes sti yiayia sou oti eipa efcharisto!*"

He laughs. "Too right!"

"Bonzer," I reply and he laughs harder. Picking up my fork I dig into the Baklava. It's the perfect bite of flaky, gooey, perfection.

"You should seriously have some of this," I say to Killian. With the next bite halfway to my mouth I notice he hasn't budged and he's giving me a weird look. I put my fork back down on the plate. "What?"

"So you speak Greek."

"Enough to get around, yeah.   But I'm far from fluent."

"And you know some Aussie slang now."

"Uh huh," I reply having no idea where this conversation is going.

"What else?"

"What else, what?"

"Languages. What other languages do you speak?"

"Why? Afraid you'll bad mouth me to someone in another language only to find out I know exactly what you're saying?" I tease.

"No. I just find it interesting."

"Interesting … good? Or interesting, bad?"

"Just interesting. I know you speak English and Italian fluently. Now I find out you speak some Greek and do it well enough that you don't sound like a beginner. Now you're picking up Aussie slang at a hundred words a minute."

"Aaaaaand?" I ask, still at a loss as to where the conversation is going.

"Fine! I think that brains are sexy!"

"Brains are squishy, slimy, and grey. You are sooooo warped."

We both laugh. As we're finishing up our dessert, the waiter comes back with Killian's card and I notice he signs the slip without looking. On the way back to the hotel, we follow the path along the lake. It's the same path we walked last night after dinner; which now feels like weeks ago.

"Ok, so what about you?" I ask.

"What about me?"

"You didn't even look at the check before paying for dinner tonight. Last night when you told me how much the champagne was you didn't even bat an eye. This morning you had my name put on the room so I could order whatever whenever regardless of price. When I talked to Anna this morning and I explained the whole Killian/Coop thing she flipped out and was all 'THE Killian Cooper?' So what gives?"

"Sweetheart, you have no idea how refreshing it is to find someone that has no idea who I am before they get to know me," he says and leans in to kiss me.

"That still doesn't explain anything though."

"Ok. Quick version. When my great grandfather died he left each of his children money. He also left each of his grandchildren money. My dad put the money in the bank. When he and Mom married, they left the money in the bank until they were done having kids. Over the years, the interest grew. After Avery was born, they split the money evenly and invested it. When each of us turned 20, we could do whatever we wanted with our share. Once I turned 20, I took my share and split it. Half went into a regular savings account and sat untouched until I graduated college. The other half I reinvested in various stocks so that I would have a diversified portfolio. The money in the savings account I used to start up a PR/Marketing firm which has been very successful. Part of its success of course was that when I was a little fish in a big pond, I had a big name company, Coopers, on my client list."

"And Anna's reaction?"

"Well, promise not to laugh?" he drops his eyes to the ground and asks.

"I can promise to try not to laugh."

"Good enough. Two months ago Forbes put out a list of the Top 40 entrepreneurs under 40. I was on the list."

"You're kidding?!" I exclaim.

"I was number 8." My jaw drops so low it's like those snakes that can unhinge their bottom jaw so they can ingest large animals. "Trying to catch flies? If you were still hungry we could have gotten more to eat back at the restaurant."

I snap my mouth shut. "I'll remember that!"

"Oh, I know you will," he says with a half laugh as we walk into the hotel. "So, what's on the agenda for tomorrow? More exploring while I'm stuck behind a desk?"

"Only after morning coffee on the balcony, of course. Today I was up in Port Adelaide. Tomorrow I thought I might check out another area of town. I'll check it all out on my laptop and decide before heading out."

"Lucky duck," he says as he opens the door to the suite. He immediately tosses his suit jacket on the desk, unties his tie and unbuttons the top four buttons on his shirt. "Aaah, sweet relief!"

"You know you could have ditched the tie and at least the top two buttons the minute you left the office, right?" I say taking off my scarf.

"I was trying to woo you with charm and sophistication. However, I know the only true way to win you over is right here."

He raises the bag from the chocolate shop and gives it a gentle shake. Taking the bag, he slowly starts walking towards the couch and I follow along like he's the Pied Piper of confectionary! Sitting down he puts the bag on the floor between his feet so I can't peek inside or grab it and take off running.

"Come over here, sweetheart," he says patting the cushion next to him.

Taking my backpack off, I put it on the chair and sit down next to him on the couch.

"Ok. Now close your eyes and put out your hands. And no peeking! You peek, you get nothing."

I scrunch my eyes up super tight to prove a point. I feel him place something in my hand, and the size, shape, and weight have me curious but I don't open my eyes until he tells me too. And there, sitting in my palms is a Chocolate Frog! The scale tips a bit more.

I launch myself at him and plant a lot of loud obnoxious kisses all over his face. "You're the best!" I say when I sit back down.

"The best is yet to come, sweetheart."

20

Two hours later we're lounging in the tub, looking out at the view. The only light in the suite is from all the candles I bought earlier that day. A stick of incense is in a holder on the counter; the scent of it matches the small bottle of massage oil that's now half empty on the table out by the couches. I take the bottle of Moscato out of the plastic bucket of ice on the side of the tub and refill our glasses. Raising my glass, I take a sip, close my eyes, and lean back against Killian.

"Mmmmm, a woman could get used to this," I say lazily.

He reaches into a small white box, takes out a truffle, and feeds it to me. Before he moves his hand away from my mouth, I slowly lick the side of his finger. "Huh, huh. Don't get too used to it, sweetheart. Check out is Saturday at 11."

"Who's the piker now?!"

"Funny," he replies. "I know I have to ask it but ... when do you fly back?"

My stomach does a somersault. "Why? Want to know how soon you can rid of me and move on to the harem of women that are still waiting in the restaurant downstairs?" I say to mask my worry. It's like that feeling of waiting for the other shoe to drop.

"As if! One is more than plenty," he replies and gives my shoulders a squeeze. "No, I just didn't know when you were flying back. If you're here through Sunday or after, then I need to call downstairs and change what day I check out."

Tip, tip, and a few butterflies.

"Well, um, the thing is ..." I start to say as I sit up and turn to face him. "When I booked my ticket, I, um, only booked one way."

"Ooh-kay?" He raises an eyebrow.

"Ok, so, I wasn't sure what was going to happen when I got here. Hell, I almost walked out last night when you came over to the table. I booked the one way because I didn't know if I was going to like you when we finally met face to face. Or what if you couldn't stand me? My brother Marco was worried you were some kind of nut job. Basically I ended up booking a one way in case I was ready to leave before my vacation time was up. It would be easier to book a flight home when it's time to leave, then it is to change an already booked ticket to when I'm ready to go."

"And since you didn't leave last night and you're still here today ... that means that you liiiiiike me?" he teases and takes a sip of his wine.

"No. I'm just using you for the sex." I deadpan.

He chokes on his wine.

"Oh my god, are you ok?"

"Great. Fine. Never better," he wheezes out. "My own fault, really. I should know better than to take a sip when you are about to say something. You never know what's going to come out of that mouth," he says as he takes my bottom lip into his mouth.

By the time we get out of the tub, the water is ice cold and my teeth start chattering. I try to dry off as quickly as possible so I can go put on some clothes and bundle up in the quilt from the bed. Killian is whistling "Good Vibrations" with a smug look on his face.

"Don't flatter yourself," I chide. "It's because I'm freeeeezing."

"You're a real ego booster, aren't you," he says as he holds up a big fluffy white robe.

I slip my arms through and as I'm tying the belt, I notice the scrawling embroidery of the hotel's name. "Where'd this come from?" I ask. I'm sure I would have noticed it hanging in the bathroom.

"It was in the closet. Years ago I realized that if I left the robes in here and took a really hot shower they seemed to soak up all the steam. As I prefer to put on something dry after my shower, I keep them in the closet."

"Makes sense I guess, except for the fact that the closet is nowhere near the bathroom."

"That's because I usually leave it over the back of the couch. I was a bit preoccupied tonight." He winks and his dimple makes an appearance. Walking around the bathroom, I start blowing out the candles.

"It's dark. I'm afraid. Help me! Help me!" he shouts, falsetto. I snort and swat his ass on the way into the living room.

Walking through the living room, I head around the partition and into the bedroom. Unzipping my suitcase and tossing back the lid, I start looking through my clothes in search of pajamas when I wonder why I never unpacked it after I decided I was staying. Lost in the thought, I don't hear Killian walk up behind me. Slowly he wraps his arms around me, reaching for the belt on the robe.

"There's also another reason for giving you the robe," he starts, his voice dropping an octave. Having untied the belt, he slowly pulls the robe away from my shoulder. "Ulterior motive."

The next morning when the phone rings, I roll over onto my stomach and try to burrow into the pillow. Having only slept for 3 hours, it is way too early to be awake. After answering the wakeup call, Killian shifts closer and throws an arm and a leg over me. I sink into the mattress from the extra weight, but it's not uncomfortable.

"Mmmm, a guy could get used to this," he says echoing my sentiment from last night. Softly, he begins trailing his fingers along my side. Making his way up to my back, he starts tracing the outline of the tattoo on my shoulder blade. As his fingers trace over the edge of the flames, it feels as if they've sparked to life; the heat searing into the scars hidden underneath the ink. Propping himself up to get a closer look he reads the words woven between the flames.

"What matters most is how well you walk through the fire."

I shove off the bed and toss on the robe. "Coffee on the balcony?" I ask trying to change the subject.

The last thing I want right now is the poison of the past bleeding into my still fragile bubble of happiness. It's nice inside my bubble. There's wine and chocolate.

After I get the coffee going, I busy myself collecting all the spent candles. Picking up the bottle of massage oil, I take a sniff and thoughts of last night push back the past a little further into the cage I try to keep it locked up in.

Walking over to me, Killian kisses me on the forehead then walks into the bathroom. I quickly toss on a T-shirt and boxers, before shoving one of the big chairs in the living room up to the huge glass windows. After lighting a stick of incense I sit down. If it wasn't for the bars along the balcony I would have sat on the floor, but I don't want them marring the view.

Crossing my legs, I straighten my spine and place my hands on my knees palm side up. I slowly take a deep cleansing breath in through my nose, hold it for a second, and then let it out; as I try to find my center. Slowing breathing in and out, I look out at the water and lose myself in the ripples as they dance in the sunlight.

Rising from the chair, I give myself a wide berth and stretch a little before starting in on the yoga routine Alera helped me create. It took a month of trial and error to come up with a routine that helped me not only find my center, but find some inner peace to deal with what had happened. Not only is Alera a great friend and an amazing yogi, but she has more patience than ten saints.

Kneeling on the floor, I move into Child's pose. With arms stretched out in front of me, I feel the tension leaving the spot between my shoulders. Facing down like this cuts off my view of the world around me and allows me to focus on relaxing. I stay in this pose for a minute or two before moving into Seated Forward Fold and feel the warm sensation of my hamstrings stretching. Standing up, I move into Triangle. "Breathe ..." I hear Alera say. I swear if I had only an ounce of that woman's inner strength, I'd be whole already.

As I move into Revolved Triangle, Killian walks out of the bathroom with a towel wrapped around his waist and a smaller one around the back of his neck.

"Well that explains why you're so *heh-hem* limber," he comments.

What was that he said the other night .... two can play at this game? I switch up the routine and bend backwards moving from Revolved Triangle into Wheel pose. Then, just because I can, I push my hands up off the floor and end with Natarajasana.

Instead of feeling calm and centered, I feel invigorated. Killian starts walking towards me, his intent clear on his face, when there's a knock on the door.

"Uh, could you get that?" he asks, glancing down at his towel before laughing and ducking back into the bathroom.

Rolling my eyes, I head to the door. "Who is it?" I ask and look through the peep hole.

"Room Service," comes the reply through the door.

Holding the door open, a woman dressed in the hotel's signature white dress shirt/navy vest/navy bow tie combination wheels in a cart with a few covered dishes. There's a matching bucket of ice with two carafes of different juices.

"Would you like me to set it up in here," she asks nodding her head towards the living room, "or over at the table?"

"He's still getting dressed, so it's probably better to keep them covered for now."

"Ah, I see," she says with a wink. "I have five sons that had no problem walking around in nothing but a towel or sometimes nothing at all. But the moment someone other than their Gran or I were in the house they'd cover up like a virgin on her wedding night."

Laughing, I hand her a tip and she heads for the door. "You can just leave the trolley in the hall when you're finished."

"Is she gone?" Killian asks as he pops his head out of the bathroom door.

"Yes," I laugh.

"Phew good," he says and walks through the living room stark naked. I raise an eyebrow. "She was the one that mentioned it. I'm just following suit." I pull a face and stick my tongue out at him. "Promises, promises."

I head over to the coffee pot, pour two cups, and stir in milk and sugar. When I turn to head toward the balcony, Killian comes around the partition in sweat pants and an unzipped hoodie. "I think that's taking casual Friday a bit too seriously."

"After ordering breakfast, I called Maggie to get word round that I'd be in a little late. I felt bad about rushing coffee and running out yesterday morning."

I take the coffees outside to the table as he rolls the trolley up to the door. Once everything is set up outside, he pushes the two chairs close and runs back in for the quilt to throw over us.

"To the good life," he chimes, raising his cup of coffee.

"To the good life," I laugh. "Well, before it gets cold, bog in."

He tips his head back and laughs. "You're a real trip, you know that, sweetheart?"

While we make our way through breakfast we talk about little things, like my adventures yesterday, the differences between working in Manhattan versus Adelaide, and who makes the best pirogues on the Lower East Side. There's a lull in the conversion and he gets quiet, too quiet. Turning to look at him I notice he has a very solemn look on his face.

"Is everything alright?" I ask tossing my napkin on the table.

"Yeah, why?" he asks, still looking out at the water.

"You've gone all broody," I say and reach for his hand. He raises our linked hands and kisses my knuckles.

"Just things on my mind; things I want to say, need to say, and don't want to muck it up. I don't want to say something meaning it one way and you taking it another. Let's face it; given my recent track record, I'm very likely to get it wrong." He takes a deep breath and lets it out slowly. "I'm half terrified of getting it wrong." I place my other hand over our linked ones and lightly squeeze.

"Killian?" I start and wait for him to look at me. When he does, he looks like he's about to face a firing squad that wants to play Russian Roulette. "Just tell me. If I start taking it the wrong way, I'll give you the chance to explain it the way you're trying to say it."

"It won't be easy since I'm not even sure how to explain it to myself." He leans forward, picks up his juice, and takes a sip. Placing the glass back on the table he sits back and sighs.

"Promise you'll stop me the second I start sounding like an idiot?" I nod. "Ok. Since I'm not really sure where to start, I'll just dive in. First is the apology, or rather, apologies that I owe you. That Frisbee may not have been aimed at your head, but it was serendipitous. Unfortunately, you getting injured seemed to become the theme each time we met. After the Frisbee, was getting tripped up in the bike, next came the coffee, and then the shattered wine bottle."

"You forgot tripping over the little old lady's walker."

"Sorry. Um, don't remember that one. Refresh my memory."

"The day you ran into Anna at the diner. I was in the bathroom. When I walked out I saw you. Fearing bodily harm, I turned one-eighty to go hide and went flying over the walker."

"So you're blaming me for something that happened and I was nowhere near you?"

"Potential energy."

"I refute your hypothesis!"

"You are such a dork!" I laugh.

"And you love that about me. So what does that say about you?" he inquires and waggles his eyebrows. I sigh and roll my eyes, refusing to be bated into admitting anything.

"Ok, fine, five times you were injured and it was my fault. Thing is, I thought that maybe it was a sign that I should keep my distance. So I sent the flowers and then the letters and stayed away. There were a few times I sat on a bench by your building; wanting to talk to you but worried you'd end up maimed. Stop laughing! I was honestly worried that I'd end up having to call an ambulance. But the more I tried to keep my distance, the more I found myself having a hard time keeping away. So I kept writing the letters. Because I thought they'd never get read, I didn't just let my guard down, I dropped it completely. Then you read the letters and I was terrified. It's one thing to have the confidence to walk across the room naked. It's another thing when it's your soul that's naked. That sounds so cliché and I'm rambling on, but it's all true."

His breath comes out in a rush and he runs his hand through his hair a few times. "The more I wrote, the more I opened up; but not just to you, to myself too. And to be super honest, I didn't like the things I noticed about myself." He stops for a moment to take another sip of juice.

"Wednesday I was sitting in the office feeling pretty low because all I ever do is work. Then I get back to the hotel wishing I could talk to you, when there's a knock on the door and I'm being handed a bunch of silly daisies. It did something to me. When I walked into the restaurant and saw you there, I was floored. It didn't seem real. Then I saw the hurt and anger on your face. When you went to get up and leave, it felt like someone pulled out the rug from under me. I panicked. It was like just as everything seemed to click into place it was slipping out of my grasp because I didn't deserve more than to be a drone tied to a desk; and that's no way to live. There are changes I need to make before I wake up one day and realize I'm married to my job, doing nothing more than going through the motions of everyday life. I don't think I'm going back to New York next week."

21

It was like having a bucket of water thrown on me; a bucket of ice water filled with pointy sharp push pins. I know I promised to give him a chance to explain and I try to remind myself of that. In the back of my mind, I hear Alera telling me to breathe, but it's no use; I'll give him the chance to explain once I stop hyperventilating.

Killian jumps up and runs around the table. Swinging my chair to the side, he crouches down and places his hand on the back of my neck, gently lowering my head between my knees. When I can finally breathe again, I slowly sit up trying not to look at him. Leaning forward, he places his head in my lap. "I am the KING of all asses," he says.

After a few minutes, I give in and run my fingers through his hair. I feel all the tension leave him as his shoulders relax. Lifting his head, he takes my hands in his just as he did in the restaurant the other night. I'm half expecting the big kiss off; instead he says "I'm not brushing you off. Donna, I want you to stay with me."

I'm speechless. So many things swirl through my mind. As I try to grab on to a thought, it slides away.

"I ... I don't know if I can," I whisper. Disappointed, he breaks eye contact. "No, wait," I say, placing my hand on his cheek and turning him to face me again. "It's not what you think. When I put in for vacation I only put in through next Sunday."

He's silent for a moment, his eyes searching my face for what, I don't know. "But if given the choice, you would stay?" he asks, his eyes boring into mine.

"Absolutely!"

Killian jumps up so fast, that if he hadn't pulled me up with him, I'd have gone over along with the chair.

"Hey! Hey!" I yell, slapping at his arms. "Ease up or you're going to break me in two!"

"Sorry," he laughs and loosens his vice grip hug. "Got carried away, didn't I?"

"A bit, yeah. Lucky, the broken ribs didn't puncture anything vital."

"Come on, let's clear this away and get inside, it's a bit cold out here this morning."

Together we gather up the place settings and various plates of food. Setting everything on the trolley, Killian wheels it into the hallway while I put the juice in the fridge.

"So, what's on the agenda for today?" he asks, sitting on the couch. "I'm thinking we still need to warm up, so I vote for a hot shower, followed by some time spent wrapped up in the quilt."

"You, my dear," I say leaning down to kiss him, "still need to go into the office."

"Piece of piss!"

"What did you just call me?!"

"Oh sweetheart," he laughs. "The look on your face ... priceless!"

When Killian heads into the office, I opt to not go with him. Flopping down on the couch, I start up my laptop and take out my phone. While it's ringing, I flip to the next page in my notebook, ready to write down the places I want to explore.

"G'day, mate!" I say cheerfully and Anna bursts out laughing.

"Thanks for that. Glad I took that sip of wine before answering the phone! "

"Wine at 9:00 on a school night?" I ask teasing her.

"I'm celebrating!" she says and I can picture the twinkle in her eyes.

"Do tell! Enquiring minds want to know!"

"Well, Tim and I have decided to move in together. We know it's only been a few months, but well ..."

"Wow! Congrats! I'm so happy for you I'm ecstatic! When's the move?

"We're going apartment hunting this weekend. After talking it over we decided that a brand new place would make for a better start. There's more," she says and pauses. It's only about a minute silence but it's killing me. "We're talking about more than just apartments."

"Are you trying to tell me what I think you're trying to tell me?"

"Depends," she giggles. She actually giggles. "Does what you're thinking involve me asking you to be my maid of honor?"

I can't help it, I scream. Then I put my hand over my mouth and laugh. "Yes, it does. And if you're asking, yes I will! Oh my god! I wish I was there to take you out and celebrate!"

"It's not official yet. We're not sitting down and creating the registry or addressing the invitations." She says before sobering. "There's a reason we haven't made it official and got down to planning." She sighs. "I didn't want to tell you over the phone, Donna. But my doctor wants to run more tests. He doesn't think it's anything; he just wants to be absolutely sure. If, and it's the smallest chance ever, I need to go through more chemo, I don't want to be scheduling my wedding around appointments and being sick. And I already know what you're thinking. You don't need to come rushing home. I haven't even gone for the tests yet, so the results wouldn't be in until after you got back. Until we know for sure, I'm not letting it get to me. Do me a big favor? Don't let it get to you either."

I try not to let it get to me. I know she's right, but I can't help the worry that creeps in and have a good cry in the shower so no one can see me.

After I get dressed, I toss my laptop and notebook in my backpack, and head out for the bus. As it makes its way towards Victory Square it goes through the area Brooklyn Park that Killian had mentioned and makes me smile a little. Getting off the bus just before King William

Street, I make my way down to the Central Market to get some lunch.

It's a vast hodgepodge of little markets, restaurants, and cafes. I could easily spend the entire day walking around. The smells coming from one of the shops has my feet turning towards a bakery. Not only do the loaves of fresh bread look delicious, but the fragrance of fresh baked bread has me drooling. I can't stop myself buying one of the loaves of sourdough. As tempting as the fig and walnut loaf looked, this was my first stop so I couldn't be sure whatever else I bought as I walked around would pair well with it.

Walking around with a loaf of bread, the first thing any decent Italian does is buy some cheese; and I couldn't resist stopping at a place called The Smelly Cheese Shop for the name alone. Stopping by one of the fruit vendors on my way out of the Market, I make my way to Victory Square. Finding an empty bench near the fountain, I unpack my makeshift picnic of bread, provolone, olives, and grapes. Something about it makes me think of my parents, so I take out my cell phone. It's about 10:30 at night back home, but chances are they're still awake.

After a few rings, my father picks up the phone. "Ciao, Pops!"

"*Ragazza mia!*" he booms into the phone, and I can tell he's smiling. "Everything ok? You comin' over? You needa me to come over?"

"I know it's a late call, but I was just thinking of you and Ma and thought I'd call"

"Something'za wrong! I know something'za wrong! What'za wrong?" I can hear my mother yelling in the background.

"Tell Ma to calm down," I say on a laugh. "Everything is fine. It's actually really good!" My father tells my mother what I said then he covers the mouth piece on the phone. I can hear them go back and forth for a minute before my mother picks up the other phone and I repeat what I had just said.

"But you call so late? You only call late when something'za wrong!" I can hear the worry in her voice.

"It's only late in New York," I say.

"Aaah," my father says as if that explains it all.

"So you still in California, eh?" my mother asks. I bite my lips.

"Uh, well, about that. Los Angeles was only a pit stop. Don't freak out ok? I'm not in California. I'm actually in Australia."

"*Le Austria*?! *Ma, perché*?" my father asks.

My mother corrects him and explains that you don't go from New York to Austria via LAX. This causes a mild argument. I sit nibbling bread and wait them out.

"Ok," my father says on a big sigh. "Why you gonna go so far? Who you with?"

"A boy-a-frend?!" my mother gasps.

I hate to burst her bubble, but I don't know how to even explain Killian to them. So, as always, I weave around answering by telling them that I needed a break, have vacation time, and since I always wanted to see Australia, I bought a ticket and flew over.

"Alone?" my father asks full of doubt.

"Yes I came out here alone, Pops."

After a few more minutes of reassuring them that I'm fine, no I haven't lost my mind, and that I'd be back soon, we hang up the phone. Sitting on the bench I take out my laptop to see what's nearby to do and realize I can't get a WiFi connection. I debate using the aircard because of the roaming charges and end up giving in.

A few minutes later I realize that the more I look for things to do, my list keeps getting bigger and I'll never get to see it all. So, I toss my laptop in my backpack and decide to just wing it. I need to stop trying to plan every minute and every step.

When I walk down the street and spot St. Francis Xavier Cathedral, I stop and take a few pictures. The building is beautiful. The huge round window above the front doors is absolutely gorgeous.

As I meander around I realize just how nice it is to not have a plan. It makes me feel free in a way. I almost head into the Rundle Mall. I hear it's really nice, but it's a mall. There are malls back home. I want to see things that I can't see back home. I'm not getting ready to plan a trip to the Outback, but I don't want to get home and say "I went all the way to Australia to go to the mall". Lame!

I'm walking along the river when my cell phone rings. "Hello, dear."

"Heya, sweetheart. I'm cutting out early. Where are you?"

"Um, uh." I stop to look around, "standing next to some tree somewhere along the River Torrens?"

"You mean to tell me that you're not at a museum, café, shop, or in route to one or the other?" he asks, trying to sound aghast.

"Uh, huh," I reply.

"Ok, who is this and what have you done with my Donna?"

Back it up! Did he just imply I'm his?

"Uh, hello? Earth to Donna. Still there?"

"Yeah. Yeah, I'm here," I say giving myself a mental shake.

"Are you sure?" he asks on a laugh. "I'm heading out now. Meet me at the Botanic Garden by the Main Gate. Ok?"

"Race you there!" I answer as I make my way back to the main road so I can hop on the bus.

22

I'm admiring the big iron entrance gate when Killian pulls up on a scooter.

"I didn't think you knew how to drive," I smirk.

"Always the comedian!" he barks as he's parking it by the bikes. "Come on let's go in," he says, taking hold of my hand and practically dragging me through the gate.

He's walking so fast; I'm having a hard time keeping up. The top of my body is moving faster than my lower and I feel like I'm losing my balance. "Hey! Stop!" I yell.

He stops and turns, but the momentum from being half dragged doesn't stop with him. I take a header dead center of his chest and we topple over.

"Hooly dooly! Are you alright?!" yells a middle aged as he comes running over.

"Never better," Killian says laying his head back on the ground and laughing up to the sky. I attempt to untangle myself and get up but he pulls me back down. "Oh no! Gravity!" The man smiles and walks away shaking his head.

Leaning down, I lightly touch my lips to his. "Come on, Newton. We're attracting a crowd." He pouts and won't let go. I try to wiggle out of his reach.

"If you don't stop doing that," he groans, "I won't be able to stand up without having to hide."

I laugh and push his arms away before standing up. Getting himself up off the ground he turns to the crowd and says "Sorry, the lady says the show is over."

He laces our fingers together and brings them up to kiss my knuckles. Despite myself, I shiver and he raises an eyebrow. A smile slowly spreads across his face. Reaching up, his hand wraps behind my neck and he pulls me in slowly. His gunmetal blue eyes lock onto mine and I can see the emotions swirling in their depths. Just before his lips come crashing down on mine, his pupils go so wide his eyes almost look black.

In that one moment, it feels like my world flips upside down. I pour every emotion, even the ones I don't understand, into the kiss. I feel as if I'm losing part of myself and yet somehow becoming whole. I try not to overanalyze it.

Killian eases back and places his forehead on mine. He looks just as moved and just as confused as I am. "We have to go," he whispers and kisses me on the forehead.

Heading down the path, we turn and walk over a small bridge. "This way," he says turning left after the bridge. "There's something I want you to see and there isn't much time because the building closes at four."

Hurrying along the path, there's a unique looking building ahead of us. It's completely made of what looks like a lightly tinted green glass. As we walk into the building I notice there's a huge structure that looks like a big red pool in the center. Floating on the top of the water are the biggest lily pads I've ever seen! They look big enough to sit on! Making our way around the pool, he stops and points.

"Just there. See the pinkish purple lily?"

My eyes follow the direction he's pointing and there's a big pale magenta colored water lily with a vibrant yellow center. Compared to the lily pads the lily looks so delicate; almost as if it's been painted in place with soft water colors.

We walk a few more feet around the pool before he points again. "And there's a white one over here. See it? I know you love lilies so I wanted you to get the chance to see them before we leave," he says with a smile.

We make our way out of the building, around the botany museum, and continue down the path to a gorgeous wisteria arbor. As we step inside, it's like being in a secret garden. It cuts off the outside world in a cocoon of solitude, but doesn't feel lonely.

Stopping at a bench, we take a seat. Killian swings his legs up and lays on his back with his head on my lap. Light shines through the twisted branches, casting a mercurial pattern on the ground.

"I know we had to rush through because it was closing, but what did you think of the lilies?" he asks.

"They were gorgeous! And those lily pads, they were amazing!"

"Gorgeous and amazing; kind of like you."

I roll my eyes and slap his chest.

"I'm serious. Earlier at the office I was thinking of places to take you. When I thought about the Gardens, I thought of the lilies. They reminded me of you. Amazon Water Lilies are, as you said, amazing. Though the lily pads look delicate on the surface of the water, underneath they are strong and resilient. The flowers are night bloomers, so if you want to see its inner beauty you have to be patient. They generally are only around for 48 hours, so getting to see it change from white to pinkish purple is a rare find; and that is something to behold." He places both of his hands on my hand that is still on his chest and gives a gentle squeeze. "You are gorgeous and amazing. Underneath it all you are strong and resilient. I've been lucky enough to see that inner beauty. And I know I'm one of the rare few you've let get close enough to see it. You haven't even been here a full two days yet and I've felt more alive since you got here than I have in a really long time. Thank you."

He gently squeezes my hand again. Turning my head away, I squeeze back. I can feel the scale tipping. It started with the kiss by the gate and the only thing keeping it from tipping all the way is my past that I haven't shared with him.

Even though the setting is serene and I feel peaceful, now is not the time or place. I don't want to ruin the beauty of the moment. It's quiet, tranquil, and the feel of my hand in his, rising and falling with each breath he takes, makes the broken pieces start to fit back together.

"Hey," he says and I turn to look down at him. "You ok?"

"Never better," I reply and smile.

~*~

"Tell me if you get too cold," Killian says as he hands me a helmet and starts up the scooter.

Looping my arm through the chin strap, I place my hands on either side of his face and lean in to kiss him. When I step back to put on my helmet, he's beaming. So am I.

We head towards Victory Square and take a ride towards China Town; stopping to take pictures in front of the South Gate. Killian suggests the night tour of Adelaide Gaol, but I pass with a definite "Oh Hell No!" Making our way back to the hotel, we stop off at a Vietnamese restaurant in Brooklyn Park for dinner. It's a cool little place without that hipster vibe back home. Halfway through dinner, Killian excuses himself to go to the bathroom and I flag down the waitress. I hand her $40 and ask her to put it towards our bill so he can't fight me about putting money towards it later.

"Men!" she laughs. "I'll go take care of this before he comes back.

After we finish dinner, Killian asks for the check. When the waitress comes back she winks at me, I wink at her, and we laugh.

"What was that all about?" he asks when she walks away with his credit card.

"Oh nothing." He gives me a skeptical look.

"Now where to?" he asks, waggling his eyebrows, as we get back on the scooter.

I lean in real close and whisper seductively "I know exactly what we need." His eyelids lower a fraction. As his eyes begin to darken, I yell "Ice Cream!!"

"You are such a dork!" he chuckles and pulls away from the curb.

~*~

It's winter. I'm walking along the beach with the most fascinating man I've ever met and eating the most amazing ice cream. It's so surreal, I feel as if I'm watching a movie or a day in someone else's life.

Taking a bite of my ice cream, I moan softly.

"If you don't stop making those noises, we're going to be arrested for indecency."

I laugh out an apology. "I can't help it; this is out of this world!"

It really is. It's called Rose Turkish Delight and I've never had anything like it before. If there was such a thing as a list of orgasmic foods, this would be on the list.

"You know what they say ... everything's better Down Under," he teases.

When I take another bite of ice cream, I flip the spoon upside down before putting it in my mouth. On a moan, I close my eyes and slowly pull the spoon down and out of my mouth.

"If you don't stop, I'm chucking your ice cream in the bin and tossing you on the scooter!"

I call his bluff.

He wasn't bluffing.

23

"But Marco, what do I do?" The second I heard Killian turn on the shower, I seized the opportunity to call my brother. I tell him all about the last two days. Well, maybe not ALL of it. Some things a brother just doesn't need to know!

"I can't tell you what to do, Donna. Before you left I asked you what were you afraid of. So now answer this, what are you still afraid of?"

When I hear Killian turn the water off, I switch from English to Italian. Stepping out of the bathroom he asks if everything is ok.

"*Uno memento, per piacere*," I say into the phone. "Yeah, everything is fine. Why?"

"You're pacing, waving your hands all over, and talking faster than the speed of light," he says, a look of concern on his face. Laughing, I place a hand on his cheek and touch my lips to his as I tuck his hair behind his ear.

"It's how Italians communicate, you better get used to it, *caro mio*," I laugh.

"He's *caro mio*?!" Marco's surprised voice comes through the phone. Just as surprised, I answer with a yes. "Donna, take my advice. Don't put off telling him. Not so much so that he knows, but for yourself. You need to share it and then get passed it. If you don't, the longer you wait, the more it will eat away at you."

"*Lo so, ma ...*"

"Do you trust this guy?"

"Yes," I whisper.

"Then you have your answer."

After we say our goodbyes, I head towards the fridge and take out a bottle of wine. I pour half a glass and down it like a shot for a bit of liquid courage. Just as I finish filling two glasses, Killian comes around the partition and sits down on the couch next to me.

"Setting the scene for seduction, sweetheart?" he asks and flashes his dimple.

"Actually," I say and sigh, my shoulders slumping. "I need to tell you something."

I try to find the words. There's a lump in my throat that's a combination of the tears I'm trying to swallow and the bile that's rising up to meet them.

It feels like I'm standing in front of a painting of the most beautiful sunrise I've ever seen and trying to stop myself from flinging a bucket of mud on it. I take a deep cleansing breath to calm my nerves, but the exhale is shaky. I take a sip of wine to try to wash the bad taste in my mouth away. It doesn't work. Marco is right; the only way is to just tell him.

"You know the tattoo on my shoulder?" Even though I want to turn away, I need to face him when I tell him.

"Hidden underneath the scrolling letters and swirling flames are five scars, each about an inch and a half in length. It's a reminder that I've walked through the fire; and even though I was burned, I survived being stabbed repeatedly by my boyfriend that was trying to kill me."

As I say the words, I'm transported back to that night.

When the adrenaline kicks in, all your senses heighten. I'd always heard that fear has a scent, but never smelled it until that night. Mixed with the stench of blood, my own blood, it was a pungent smell that to this day still makes me want to vomit just thinking about it.

Even though I kept thinking that if I stopped trying to get away it would be over soon, I kept fighting. The more I thought of giving in, the harder I fought.

The story of that night comes tumbling out. I tell Killian about the fight Ralph and I had because I told him I was leaving. I had finally come to my senses and was done being a kicked dog that kept coming back for more.

As I went to leave, Ralph walked up behind me and hit me hard on the head. When I hit the ground I rolled over onto my back. As I fell, Ralph pulled a knife out of his pocket and dropped down to stab me. Instinctively, I brought my knees up. With my feet on his chest, I was able to toss him off, the knife just grazing my collar bone. Shocked by what's happening, my brain didn't even register the sting. I try to stand and run, but the pain in my head from the blow is almost blinding.

As I try to crawl to the door, he drives the knife into my shoulder blade. He tries to pull the knife free. For a second it's stuck in good, so he gives it a twist and yanks it out before stabbing me again. Somehow I manage to avoid the next strike and get close to the door. With one hand on my shoulder to try to stop the bleeding, I reach for the door knob with the other and he stabs me again. I try to put my hands out in front of me, but the force of the blow sends me pitching forward and my temple bashes up against the door knob.

The world starts to go black.

He reaches down and pulls my head back by my hair and every follicle burns. "You're mine. You belong to me. You're pathetic, you should be grateful there's someone willing to take care of you. If I can't have you, no one will," he whispers leaning so close that the feel of his mouth touching my ear makes me cringe.

He licks my ear before pulling away and stabs my shoulder two more times. The blood is soaking through my shirt, creating sticky rivers down my back.

Dazed, I can see my own bloody handprint streaked down the door. I barely have the strength hold myself up. I feel myself slipping and struggle to fight against it.

"Not like this; not today," I tell myself.

With what feels like my last bit of strength, I twist around as he stabs down and my foot makes contact with his nose. The crunching sound of his nose breaking seems to echo in the moment and the force snaps his head back. Seizing what is likely the last chance I have at escape, I'm up on my feet and out the door; banging on every door in his building as I ran blood soaked and screaming down the hall.

"I came to two days later in Mount Sinai," I say half shocked at how matter-of-fact I sound. "I was there almost two weeks. I had my Uncle Nino track down the little old lady that opened her door and half dragged me into her apartment. He arranged to pick her up and bring her to the hospital before I left. I wanted to meet her and thank her for saving my life, but I didn't know her name or which apartment was hers; and I sure as hell wasn't going back to that building. When she came into the room I couldn't believe that this tiny old lady with frail looking hands and kind eyes could get me to safety. 'Never underestimate the roaring force of your own inner strength, child,' she told me. There are times I've forgotten I have strength, and parts of me are still a little broken, but I'm getting there."

As I finish the story, the curtain of the past is pulled away, and despite the fact that I've been looking at him the whole time, I'm not really seeing him until now. He looks absolutely livid; and although I feel relief at having purged the story, I feel like damaged goods; which is probably how he sees me now that he knows.

He still hasn't said a word. Part of me doesn't want him to say anything. If all he has is angry words, I just might crumble into myself. But what would be so much worse would be words of pity.

I guess there's nothing to do now besides toss the few things that are laying around into my suitcase and leave. A part of me wants to yell "Say something for fuck's sake!" but what would be the point.

Letting out a resigned breath, I'm halfway up off the couch when I'm pulled back and crushed against him. Once I'm over the initial shock I realize he's slightly shaking. I try to pull back but he tightens his grip. There's something strong and reassuring about the way he's holding me, but it's also very stifling. I tap his arm twice, nothing. I try to squirm out from under his arm, nothing. I grab hold of a tiny bit of skin at the back of his arm and squeeze as hard as I can between my forefinger and thumb like my brother Carmine taught me.

"YEOW!"

Instantly he lets go and I feel like I can breathe again. I reach forward and place my hand on his cheek.

"Sorry, but you were starting to make it so I couldn't breathe."

He takes my hand from his cheek, holds it in both of his, close to his chest. I feel the rise and fall as he's taking deep breaths. His heart is pounding so hard I'm surprised I can't hear it.

"And ..." he stops and takes a deep breath, "what happened to him?"

"15 to 20. My uncle made sure to give the lawyer a laundry list of charges to push for. He was charged assault in the first degree, attempted murder, and a few minor offenses. When he's up for parole, I don't see it happening." He lets go of my hand, reaches for his wine, and drains it in one go.

"Sorry," he pants, "I needed that."

I refill his glass, then pick up my own and clank it to his. "To letting go of the past."

24

The next morning I'm standing on the balcony with my hands on the rail. I turn as Killian comes through the door with two cups of coffee.

"I'm going to miss this place."

"We can come back any time you like," he says with a smile as he places one arm around my waist.

I lean my head against his shoulder as we look out at the lake. Whether I get back here or not, it will always have a special place in my heart. I didn't just find myself here, I also found inner peace; something I haven't had in a really long time.

"We need to be making a move soon," Killian says bending down and kissing my forehead, before heading back inside.

After a minute, I turn to head inside too. I do one last walk through to make sure we haven't forgotten anything and then we're heading down to the main desk to check out.

As we step outside, the car pulls up. "Ok, that's kind of eerie timing," I mutter to Killian and he laughs.

Tony gets out and is putting our suitcase in the trunk. Another man gets out of the front and Killian hands him the keys to the scooter. "Thanks, mate."

"Anytime you lob in, give a call," the man tells Killian before slapping him on the back and walking away.

The drive to the airport seems faster than it did a few days ago. Then again, a few days ago feels like years ago. Saying goodbye to Tony, we make our way inside and to the counter.

"Checking in," Killian says to the woman behind the counter.

"Oh, and I'll need a ticket for the same flight," I add.

"Already taken care of," he says still looking at the woman behind the counter.

"Figjam," I grumble, making the woman chuckle.

Once we're checked in and are away from the counter, I put my bag down and cross my arms over my chest. It's a few steps before he realizes I'm not behind him and he comes back.

"What's wrong?" he asks in a semi condescending tone.

"You need to stop doing that," I sigh.

"What did I do?"

"Look, I get that your used to having money and don't blink at the thought of paying for stuff, but you've gotta stop paying for everything!"

"But … I'm the guy," he says confused.

"Oh-ho-ho, those words so did not just come out of your mouth."

"Ok, you buy lunch."

"$40 lunch, $945 plane ticket. Oh yeah, that balances out," I say, every word dripping with sarcasm. "Then what, after I pay for lunch, you'll pat me on the head and give me a gold star for the day?"

"So think of it as our money if it'll make you feel better. Now come on, or we won't have time for lunch before the plane. I'm already half starved. Do you really want to let me loose on a plane full of people when I'm hangry?"

"You are such an asshole."

"So, where should we eat?" he asks once we're through security.

"I don't care as long as it has beer."

He picks the first place we walk by and when I order a beer I get carded. "I thought it was a compliment to get carded," he says.

"In America, yeah, but not somewhere that the drinking age is 18!"

I don't know why, but it seems like the farther away we get from the hotel, the ornerier I get. When lunch arrives, I order a second beer. Maybe it was the amazing burger. Maybe it was the two beers. But after I pay for lunch, I place my hand on his. "I'm sorry. Maybe I was the one in need of food." He smiles. "That still doesn't mean you get to pay for everything though. I don't like feeling like a kept woman. Been there, done that. So if you value my sanity, and your own balls, please tone down the 'But I'm the guy' rant."

"Sometimes I think you say things just to throw me off balance because you get a kick out of it."

"Maybe," I reply and with that we make our way to the plane.

~*~

It's only a five and a half hour trip, but with two flights and a quick 35 minute layover in Brisbane, I feel like I've been on the go all day. I also feel ridiculous flying business class on such a short trip. Don't get me wrong, I'm giving serious consideration to flying business on the way home, but for a short flight, the extra $700 per ticket seems like a waste of money to me. For the cost of just one of our tickets, four people could have flown economy and had lunch at the airport! Hell, for the price of both of our tickets, Leo and the guys could get a room plus groceries for almost 2 months! After explaining to Killian that just because you have money to burn doesn't mean you should start up the bonfire, he looked at me like I had two heads. But it was him telling me that I was being a drama queen that put me on edge.

"If what we've got going here is going to have a snowball's chance in hell of surviving after this trip, we're really going to need to have a sit down chat about a lot of things," I say as I grab my bag off the carousel. Without looking around, Killian takes two steps back and sits down on the floor. "See, this is part of what I'm talking about! There are other people trying to get their bags and you just plop yourself down and expect them to go around you!"

Pulling the handle out of the top of my bag, I wheel my suitcase over to a bench and sit. Eventually he gets up and walks over, but stands in front of me rather than sit. "That intimidation bullshit isn't going to work with me. Sit down."

"I don't take orders," he tosses back.

"I know. You only give them! It's what your elitist douchery demands. Well, this time, you're being given an order and for once you're going to follow it."

He folds his arms over his chest and tries to look sterner. I scowl right back, refusing to budge. Eventually he concedes with a sigh and sits down.

"What is your problem, Donna?" he asks snidely.

"My problem is your attitude. You told me that it was refreshing to find someone that has no idea who you are before they get to know you. And yet, here you are acting like a spoiled rich snob. You toss cash around like its crumbs you're graciously scattering for the masses. From time to time you treat people like you're royalty and they are commoners there to do your bidding. Hell, you just plopped yourself down and blocked people from getting their luggage because that's where you wanted to sit. You didn't even notice that woman carrying a baby trying to get to the carousel that almost tripped over you when you sat down! The first night at the restaurant you didn't even acknowledge the waiter's presence, you just blurted out an order. Don't even get me started on what an ass you were to the flight attendant! I swear, sometimes your ego is so big it's like a whole extra person. And sorry, but I'm not into threesomes. The world doesn't revolve around you Killian Holsten Cooper! You had better learn that real quick." And with that, I stand up and start wheeling my bags away.

I get about five steps before he spins me around and crushes his lips to mine. His hands are like vice grips on my arms. "Damnit, Donna! I won't let you walk away like that! I won't!"

"Oh-ho-ho! Excuse me, your Royal Highness!" I say and curtsey.

"It's not funny!"

"The only part that's funny is that you think I'm going to hop to when you order me about. I've lived through that hell and I refuse to go back to it!!"

He releases his grip on my arms and I bend down to get the handle of my fallen suitcase before walking away.

"For someone that took a look at himself and didn't like what he saw," I turn and say when I'm a good two feet away, "you're doing a shit job of doing anything about it. And I'm sorry, but I just can't be with someone whose ego gets in the way.

~*~

"Hi. One-way ticket on your next flight to the U.S., please. I don't care where, I just want to go home," I say.

Even to my own ears I sound defeated. Leaving my pummeled heart on the floor by the bench, I somehow made it back upstairs and to the ticket counter on legs that feel like jelly. When I get back home, I'll take a day to deal with jetlag before going back to work even though my time off isn't over. Or maybe I'll just sell all my belongings and join a nunnery.

"There's a flight leaving for Honolulu tomorrow morning at 6am for $419 Economy or at 7am Premium Economy for $3580. There's one to Juno, Alaska leaving tomorrow at 7am for $6,800 and one at 4:30pm for $1,890. Here's one for Los Angeles, California leaving at 6:30am for $2405 Premium Economy. Regular Economy is sold out. I have one at 6:30am to Seattle that's $984 for Economy and $1950 for Premium Economy."

"But nothing leaving tonight?"

"No, love, sorry."

"I'll take the one to Seattle. Premium Economy."

"I'll just need to see your passport first."

I hand over my passport, then hand her my debit card as well.

"This message is for Donna Giannino. Donna Giannino, your party is waiting for you by Gate 17. Donna Giannino your party is ..." There's the squealing sound of feedback followed by Killian's voice over the PA system.

"Donna, I'm begging you! Please don't leave! Donna, please, I ... hey! Get off of me! Stop! Donnnnna!"

His voice fades as if the microphone is taken away. The last thing I hear is some man saying "Sir, you need to come with us" before there's another squeal of feedback and then silence.

I close my eyes and let out a slow breath. All I need is my ticket now and I can put all this behind me.

"Donna Giannino. Donna Giannino to the security office on the first floor, please."

Well fuck. The ticket agent hands me back my passport and debit card. I'm half tempted to walk out and hail a cab when I get back downstairs, but I head down to security instead.

"Hi. I'm Donna Giannino," I sigh.

25

Three hours after we land in Cairns, I'm finally leaving the airport. I make a beeline for the taxi dispatch and climb in.

"Nearest hotel," I say to the driver as I close the door.

"Can you be a little more specific, dear?" he turns and asks.

The cab door opens. Killian slides in and says "Tropical Queenslander on Lake Street, please."

"Sorry, mate, but as you can see, I've already got a passenger."

"I'm with her."

"Miss?" says the cab driver.

"Yeah, Queenslander, fine. After we drop him, you can drop me somewhere else." With a shrug, the cab driver pulls away and I lean my head back on the seat closing my eyes.

"Sweetheart, please," Killian pleads as he tries to take my hand. I turn away and look out the window. "I'll get down on my hands and knees and grovel if I have to,

Donna. Please, just hear me out. After that, if you want to leave I won't try to stop you. I promise."

"I told you I'm done with pretty words. I just want to go home," I explain wearily.

Having basically shut myself off from the world for the past few years, I'm so far out of my comfort zone that I can't make heads or tails out of anything. Instead of slowly letting the walls I've built up come down brick by brick, I let the whole damn thing get blown open. And worst of all, I'm hating myself for letting it happen and for being unable to control my reactions to it all. I feel like I've been run over by a steam roller. Out of the corner of my eye I see Killian sliding to the edge of the seat. He tries to squash down onto the floorboard of the cab but doesn't quite fit.

"This is the closest I can get to hands and knees at the moment, sorry. And I'm sorry about you having to spend hours in airport security because I grabbed the microphone from the info booth lady. But, damn it, I knew if you were just paged, you wouldn't show up. The thought of you getting on a plane back to America terrified me because I knew the second you did; I'd lose every chance at happiness. Donna, it wasn't pretty words when I told you that you're gorgeous and amazing. It wasn't pretty words when I said I've never felt so alive. And it definitely wasn't pretty words when I called myself the King of all Asses. Five times you ended up hurt because of me, and now I think I've just fucked up so bad that this can be counted as the sixth and probably the seventh. I don't know what I can do to show you how sorry I am. But, if you're willing to stay, I'll spend the whole of this week trying to make it up to you. Hell, I'll spend every day of the rest of my life trying to get you to realize that even though

I'm a lame, idiot, dorky, sorry, asshole, I love you, Donna. I know this isn't the most romantic way to tell you that, but I need you to know before you leave." The cab rolls to a stop in front of the hotel and he sighs. "Please Donna, say something, anything!"

A minute passes and I'm still looking out the window. What can I say? Sorry I have issues? Sorry I'm a broken wreck? Sorry you have to deal with the fallout from an abusive relationship that almost got me killed and the emotional baggage that goes with it?

He sighs again. "I'm really, truly sorry."

There's a slight crack in his voice before handing the cab driver $20 and getting out. He circles the back of the cab and I watch as he walks towards the hotel. Stopping, he turns to look at the cab. His shoulders slump and he bows his head slightly before turning and walking into the hotel.

"Well love, are we headed elsewhere or are you going to go after him?" the cabbie asks.

"Is it cowardice to stay or to leave?" I wonder out loud.

"Depends," the cabbie says. "What are you afraid of?"

~*~

"Room 115. Down the hall on your right, just passed the vending machine."

"Thanks," says Killian sounding deflated.

I watch him turn and slowly head down the hall. His shoulders are still slumped and his usual swagger is replaced by a slow gait. As he shuffles down the hall, I realize maybe what I'm afraid of most isn't men, or relationships, or even getting hurt; maybe it's my own feelings and the sense of not having total control over them. I hear the door to his room softly close before I'm able to unglue my feet from the lobby floor.

As I make my way down the hall, I find I'm more nervous now than I was sitting in the restaurant on that first night. Somehow this one moment seems infinitely more important. When I get to the door, I take a slow breath and try to think of what to say. I draw a total blank. Before I realize it, my hand is knocking on the door. Oh shit, oh shit! What do I say?! What can I say?!

I hear him approach the door and the click of the knob turning. I can feel the fear creeping in, making me want to run. My arms and legs break out in goose bumps, and my brain feels like it's on fire. I don't think I can do this! I can't handle another confrontation. I keep telling my legs to move, but they won't listen. His room is only two doors before the hall turns to the right; if I can just get my legs to move, I can be out of sight before he opens the door. I can hide and be safe. I loathe myself for wanting to run, but I can't help it.

The door slowly swings open and when he looks up all I see is the hurt in his eyes. My feet move of their own volition; and as I take that first step, all the fear and self-loathing evaporate. Wrapping my arms around him, I lay my head on his shoulder.

"I'm sorry," I whisper, half as an apology to him for the fight and half as an apology to myself.

After a moment, he lets go of the door and his arms close around me. "I'm sorry too," he admits on a shaky breath.

"Come on," he says a few minutes later, "I think I need to sit down". His hand runs down my arm to take my hand and we walk over to a small couch.

As I take a seat I look around the small room. It can't be more than 300 square feet. It's decorated in various shades of blues and creams. In addition to the couch, there's a coffee table, bed, small kitchenette, desk, and a bathroom. It looks nice and clean, and more suited to my budget than his; which makes me wonder how the hell he even knew about this place. He sits down next to me and as I open my mouth to ask, he puts two fingers up to my lips.

"I don't care about the argument. I'm just glad you're here."

"I was actually going to ask how you even knew about this place. It's not something I expected."

"Family vacations. With six kids, it could get a bit pricey. When we'd come over from the States to visit family, my parents would book joining rooms so we had space for all of us. I guess after all you said, it made sense to come here. I could have gone to Gran's but I didn't think it was a good idea to knock on the door after midnight."

We sit in a comfortable silence on the couch for a while. Unfortunately, it's the kind of comfortable silence where I find myself dozing off as my head sags down. It's been an exhausting day with such a range of emotions; it sapped my energy more than the travelling.

Everything seems to go kind of floaty for a minute and then I realize I'm lying on the bed and Killian is taking off my boots. I'm no more than a rag doll as he takes off my jeans and sweater before he pulls up the covers. Climbing into bed from the other side, he moves in close. His fingers are feather light as he moves them across my temple and down the edge of my ear to my jaw.

"Thank you for coming back," he whispers. "I love you, Donna."

The next morning, I wake up half sprawled across Killian and drooling on his chest. Opening one bleary eye, I can see the sun is just starting to turn the sky from an inky black to navy blue. I have no idea what time it is, but it is definitely too early to be awake. I roll off of Killian, onto my other side, and start to nod off again. In his sleep, he groans out a protest and rolls towards me. His arm comes around my side and he pulls my back closer against his chest. The feel of his breath against my ear each time he exhales should be sending me into a panic, but it's somehow comforting. The rhythmic rise and fall of his chest makes me feel drowsy; a slow lazy smile spreads across my face as I start to drift.

Through the fog of sleep, I hear a faint groan just as I feel Killian's left hand slide up to cup my right breast. His thumb begins to draw lazy circles and the sensation through the silk of my cami has me straining against his hand. As his thumb runs over my nipple, the heady combination of slumber and arousal has me pressing my hips back in a circular motion wanting more. With his other hand he brushes my hair away from my neck and begins kissing and nibbling. Instead of it sending the usual lightning flash response coursing through my body, it feels like the slow warm burn of whisky and it's just as intoxicating.

Reaching back, I slide my hand inside the front of his boxers. I can feel the guttural sound that escapes him rumble in his chest and it sends a tingle down my spine. Lost in desire, I press my hips back again and begin moving them in time to the rhythm of my hand. Slowly his hand slides down my stomach to toy with the lace edge of my silk boy shorts and I feel every nerve ending in my body come alive. Ever so slowly, his hand makes its way below the lace and silk. As he slides a finger between my folds, he snakes his right arms between my head and the pillow pulling me even closer. Wrapped up in passion, I almost come undone when his one hand gently squeezes my nipple as he slowly slides his finger in me. I try to hold back, wanting to revel in sensations and feelings I've never felt before, but the need for release rockets through me so fast I gasp out his name as I tighten around his finger.

As I shudder, he slowly moves my boy shorts down and with one silken stroke he's sliding inside me. Wrapping my leg back around him, I press my hips back taking him deeper inside me. His fingers dig into my hip and he groans as I move his other hand from my breast so I can lick the side of his thumb. With each slow thrust of our hips I feel myself begin to spiral out of control. Reaching back, I run my hand along his shoulder, up his neck, and into his hair. His hand slides down my stomach to between my thighs and he rubs my most sensitive spot between the side of his forefinger and thumb.

"I ... I ... I can't ..."

"Just let go, sweetheart, he whispers, his voice harsh against my ear. Another thrust and I cry out as the orgasm sends me over the edge. My fingers tighten in his hair and as my whole body spasms I feel him lose control as he moans out my name.

26

"Coffee, how I love thee. Let me count the ways. One sip! Two sips! Three ..."

"Smart ass," I chuckle; though I can't help but agreeing with the sentiment. As delicious as the buffet style breakfast smells, I'm not moving from the table to get any until I've at least got my second cup of coffee in front of me.

"Reckon!" he exclaims with an exaggerated wink. "Dunno about you, but I'm famished! Hell, I'm so hungry I could eat a whole drop bear by myself!"

"You did that intentionally, didn't you," I say after I finish choking on my coffee.

"Mmm, perhaps," he laughs. "If we're going to have more than coffee though, we better go get something to eat before they clear away breakfast. And seeing as I worked up one appetite by satisfying the other; I need food, woman!" With that, he gets up and heads to the buffet.

"Are you sure you're not still hungry?" I ask, twenty minutes later.

"Nah, if I go up a fourth time I'll be too full up and I'm really looking forward to a home cooked meal tonight. Are you ready to go?"

"Sure. Let me just find out about a wheelbarrow for you first."

"Always a comedian," he whines as we make our way to check out.

In the lobby there's a rack of postcards so I pick up the silliest ones I can find. The one with the duck, beaver, and platypus makes me snort. The little boy next to me looks up and asks what's so funny, but I'm not sure his parents would appreciate it if I shared PG 13 humor with their son who looked no more than 6 years old.

"I thought you said it was winter in Australia," I say as we step outside. It's so muggy out; it's like the humidity latches on to your skin.

"It is. We're just in a tropical part of the country now," he informs me as he looks me up and down before heading back into the hotel lobby. "Ok, all settled," he says a minute later as he walks back out.

"Settled. Why do I have the sneaky suspicion that I'm not going to like what you just did?" A few minutes later a cab pulls up and after a short drive we pull up to a shopping center.

"I figured you'd want something to wear that's a bit cooler than a light weight sweater and jeans. And I didn't think you'd be too happy if we went to some boutique, so ...." he says as he points to the corner of the plaza. I turn around and there's the big red bull's eye of the Target logo.

"It definitely earned you some brownie points," I chuckle. Grabbing the handle of my suitcase, I start to walk towards the store when he stops me and pulls me in close for a kiss that leaves my legs feeling unsteady.

"Going for bonus points," he grins and flashes his dimple.

Once inside the store I make him promise that he won't try to pay for anything and then make quick work of picking up two pairs of shorts and a few T-shirts before heading to the shoe section for a pair of sandals.

"That's it? You're done?" he asks sounding shocked.

"That'll be $92.85," the cashier says. I quickly do the math and realizing that it's only about $65 or so US, I don't feel like I spent as much as I thought. After paying, I head for the bathroom to at least change into a T-shirt before leaving the store.

"Much better," I sigh as we start walking out to the main road.

"Good. The bus is just up here. It's only about a twenty minute ride. Gran's house is a few minutes walk from the bus stop."

I've known since I said I'd stay the week that I'd be meeting his grandmother, but it isn't until we get off the bus that I start to feel nervous. I don't even know why, seeing as I've already met his cousin. Then again, at first I didn't know that Kate was family.

As we turn the corner onto Fleming Street, Killian stops. "Look, a house for sale. Should we buy it?" I just roll my eyes at him. "Ok, fine," he laughs. "Gran is just up here on the right."

The house is painted a creamy beige with burgundy trim and has a hunter green staircase leading up to a small porch. Taking my suitcase, he heads up the stairs and sets our luggage down on the porch. Without stopping to knock, he opens the door and I follow him inside.

"Your favorite grandson is here!" he shouts as we walk into the kitchen.

A petite woman with short blonde hair turns from the sink. She has an infectious smile. "Killian! Where have you been?" she shouts, giving him a tight hug before backing up a few inches and slapping his arm with her dish towel.

"Uh, sorry Gran. Bit of an issue at the airport with the luggage." Taking my hand, he moves me forward to try to change the subject. "Gran, this is my girlfriend Donna. Donna, this is my grandmother Laura."

Girlfriend?!

"Nice to meet you," I say as I try to pick my jaw up off the floor hoping the drop wasn't noticed.

"Nice to finally meet you dear," she says giving me a bone crushing hug. "Just call me Gran, everyone does. Did the airport lose your bags?" she asks turning to Killian.

"Nah Gran, they're out on the porch. I'll just go and get them," he replies and he's off like a shot.

"Hmmm," she hums to his retreating back. "Now that he's gone, you'll tell me what really happened, right?" she asks and I can't help but notice that Killian has her eyes, even down to the mischievous twinkle.

An hour later, I'm standing in the kitchen wearing a borrowed apron, gutting small pumpkins and laughing with Laura as she peels and quarters parsnips.

"Sounds like a rip snorter of a rage in here" "says a blonde woman as she walks into the kitchen and gives me a curious look.

"Hello, love! This is Donna, Killian's girlfriend," she intones drawing out the word girlfriend. "Donna, this is my daughter Annette."

"Hi, nice to meet you," I say holding my sticky pumpkin hands up to show that I'd shake her hand but they're gross.

"Well, hello Donna!" she exclaims, her bright blue eyes light up and twinkle as if she knows something I don't. "I see my mother wasted no time tossing you an apron and putting you to work."

She turns to Laura and winks. Maybe it's an Aussie thing all the twinkly eyes and winking. All I know is I'm missing something here.

"I'm more than willing to help out in the kitchen. It's been a lot of fun."

"I could tell before I walked in the door," she says and smiles brightly.

"Donna was just informing me of why Killian was late last night. Seems he decided to take over the PA system at the airport and got in trouble with security. They'd had a bit of an argument. She spit the dummy, told him he was a whacker, and was in the middle of buying her ticket home when he grabbed the microphone and started shouting for her."

"Good onya!" says Annette on a laugh.

"Speaking of, where's he got off to? He's supposed to be setting up outside but I don't see him back there. Doesn't even look like he's set up the barbie yet," she grumbles looking out the window. "KILLIAN!" she yells.

I'm shocked such a booming voice could come out of someone so small. When he doesn't respond, she tosses her dish towel on the table and heads out of the kitchen muttering about men being deaf. Annette and I laugh.

"I really like her," I say.

"I think she really likes you too," she smiles and pats my arm before leaving the kitchen.

Finishing up sorting the last bit of pumpkin seeds, I head over to the sink to get rid of the gooey mess that's stuck to my hands.

"Yeah, Gran?" Killian inquires as he walks into the kitchen.

"Nope, just me. She went looking for you," I respond as I dry my hands. Hanging the towel back up, I turn around and he's standing by the table looking a bit punch-drunk. "Hey, are you alright? Here, sit down," I say as I pull out a chair.

"No. No. I'm fine," he says as he sits down.

"G'Day gorgeous!" Annette says, walking into the kitchen and kissing Killian on the head.

"Uh, heya, Aunt Annette," he responds distracted.

"Aaah, you've noticed it to then, eh?" She walks over to the counter, picks up a folded pile of table clothes, and walks back out of the kitchen humming.

Confused I turn back and forth looking around the kitchen expecting to see a chair nailed to the ceiling or the fridge turned backwards or something. Noticing nothing out of the ordinary, I turn and look at Killian but he seems to be staring out into the great unknown.

"I'll be stuffed," he mumbles to himself.

Snap! Snap!

"Oh, right, heya sweetheart. Sorry, just feeling a bit gobsmacked is all." After a moment's pause, he gives his head a shake. "Um, so, Gran let you borrow her apron and then put you to work?"

"Yeah, and I'm still a gloppy mess. But it's been very entertaining." I smile so wide my cheeks begin to hurt. "Your grandmother is a lot of fun. I really like her. I'm glad I decided to stay for the week and tag along; and I'm *really* glad that I didn't head home last night." I crouch down in front of him and place my hand on his cheek. "I know I was beyond angry last night about having to deal with security for hours and not being able to book a flight home. I'm sorry for the words I said afterwards, and some of the ones I didn't say."

Moving closer, I kiss him before inching back. When his eyes meet mine, everything seems to fall into place and I'm filled with an encompassing sense of contentment. Part of my brain is screaming "cliché!

cliché!", but it's true. I can feel some of the broken pieces fitting back together.

"I love you too, Killian." Leaning in, I softly touch my lips to his.

In a flash, he stands up, pulls me closer, and deepens the kiss. My hand slips from his cheek to his chest and I can feel his heart beating as wildly as mine. I can also feel that he's now covered in pumpkin guts and I can't hold back the laugh that bubbles up.

"Well, look at that," he says taking half a step back. A large part of his shirt is glued to the apron. "I guess that means you're stuck with me now."

I groan and roll my eyes. "You are such a dork! I'm going to go get changed. Where'd you put the suitcases?"

"Right this way madam," he says and next thing I know he's flung me over his shoulder, reminding me that I once nicknamed him Mr. Neanderthal. He spins around and marches out of the kitchen just as his grandmother is coming down the hall. "Sorry Gran, bit of a mess. Need to get us cleaned up!" he calls as he starts to jog down the hall. Instead of heading to whatever room our suitcases are in, he heads out the back door.

"What in the hell are you doing?!" I yell as he picks up speed. "Put me down, Killian!"

"If you say so, sweetheart!" he shouts over his shoulder and next thing I know we're underwater.

My feet touch the bottom of the pool and I kick off hard, trying to get out of the cold water as fast as I can. As my head breaks the surface I can hear people around us laughing. I see Killian rise above the level of the water and slap the water towards him. The small wave hits him in the face and the ensuing splash fight doesn't stop until he manages to get a hold of my wrist and pull me through the water towards him. He wraps his arms around me, and with a kiss flings himself backwards into the water taking me with him. As we come back up he starts laughing.

"Don't know Christmas from Bourke Street, do you?" Laura chastises. "Get out of that water before she freezes!"

My teeth are chattering before I'm halfway up the ladder and she tosses a blanket over my shoulders. As Killian climbs out of the pool, she slaps him hard on the top of his head and people start laughing again.

"Give me your worst, Gran! I don't care!" he shouts. He picks her up, and spins her in a circle, soaking her with freezing cold water.

"What has gotten into you?" she splutters as he sets her back down.

Leaning down, he gives her a loud kiss on the cheek and shouts "Donna said she loves me!"

"Did she now?" she turns and smiles at me before turning back to Killian. "Good onya! Now, before she turns into a block of ice, get her inside so she can get some dry clothes. I'll go get the coffee going."

27

My teeth don't stop chattering until I've been standing in a nice hot shower for a few minutes. When I step out to dry off I realize that the nice dry clothes I was planning to put are still in my suitcase and I have no idea which room it's in. Wrapped in a towel I walk out into Laura's bedroom and poke my head out into the hall.

"Well, if I'd known Gran was keeping gorgeous half naked Sheila's in her room, I'd come by more often." *Twinkle, twinkle, go the eyes. Around the Coopers it's no surprise.* "I'm Den by the way," he says extending his hand. He's classic Hollywood gorgeous and has a slow easy smile and chocolate brown eyes.

"Hi. Donna. I'm not Laura's concubine though. I'm here with Killian. I seem to have lost him and my suitcase though," I smile back and shake his hand.

"Lucky guy," he says. "He's down the hall, second door on the left. Oh, word of advice though," he offers turning back, "don't let Gran hear you call her Laura. Everyone calls her Gran, including her own doctor." With a chuckle, he walks off towards the kitchen and I make my way quickly down the hall.

"Yep. I know," I hear Killian say as I come up to the door. "It's just …. Yeah, exactly!"

Stopping in the doorway I realize he's on the phone. Having no idea if I should walk in or head back down the hall, I just stand there for a minute until he looks up. Something flashes in his eyes, and I can see a full range of emotions run through them just before his pupils dilate.

"Yes. I promise. Well, on second thought, maybe not *every* detail," he says and laughs. "Love you too. Bye Mom." Rising from the bed he walks over, reaches behind me, and pushes the door closed.

"Oh no, you don't," I say trying to give him a shove as I back up. He tries to make a grab for the towel, but I'm holding on tight to the top. "I need to go help out in the kitchen and I don't need more people seeing me wandering in a towel, so I need to get dressed. Hands to yourself," I reprimand as I attempt to swat his hands away. "I also need to see about getting your grandmother's apron and blanket into the washing machine before they dry."

I sidle passed him, grab a new pair of shorts and T-shirt from the shopping bags and start getting dressed. I can feel his eyes on me; just the same as if they were his hands, and try to ignore the need building up inside me.

"Hey root rat!" comes a voice through the door. "Gran's said to let her favorite concubine know the coffee is up!"

Killian's eyebrow goes up a notch as I burst out laughing. Opening the door, he punches Den on the shoulder before slamming it shut again.

"Do I even want to know?" he asks as he turns around shaking his head.

He sits back down on the edge of the bed and pats the spot next to him. When I sit down next to him, he reaches down to grab both my legs and tosses them across his lap. "Did you mean what you said back in the kitchen?" There's the slightest hint of insecurity in his voice, something very out of character for him.

"I wouldn't have said it if I didn't mean it," I tell him as I lace our fingers together. "Though I'm not sure how Gran is going to feel about losing her favorite concubine to her grandson."

The look on his face is so funny I wish I'd had my camera handy. Chuckling, I explain to him about poking my head out of her bedroom and meeting Den.

"He's right you know. Not about the concubine part, and although I agree with the gorgeous part, I owe him another punch for it. He's right about me being a lucky guy; a very lucky guy. That first day on the beach, I can't even put it into words, but I knew that moment would be a life changer. All the letters I wrote, and then the emails back and forth; it felt like I was writing home. And, I don't care if it sounds cliché, but when I saw you in the restaurant everything clicked into place. I can't imagine not being with you every day when we get back to New York. I know it can't be like this all the time because we both have to work and there will be times I need to travel; but I want you in my life, Donna. I need you in my life."

I'm knocked speechless. At a loss for words, I pull him close and bring his lips to mine. A million things race through my head. Did he mean he wants to move in together? And if he does, is he talking about my place or his place? I realize that other than close to Asia King, I have no idea where he lives! I just told a guy that I love him and I don't even know where he lives! How many other things don't I know about him?

"Has anyone ever told you that you think too much?" Killian says on a sigh. "I know what I said is a lot to take in, especially seeing as we haven't known each other that long. But it doesn't matter if I say them now, a year from now, or ten years from now, sweetheart."

He leans his forehead against mine and slowly lets out his breath before looking into my eyes. "Donna, I love you. Make me the happiest man alive and say you'll marry me?"

He reaches back and pulls a small box from under the quilt folded at the end of the bed. Slowly he opens the box and inside is the split halo ring set I was admiring at Everett-Brookes in Adelaide. The center stone of the engagement ring is a grayish blue like his eyes. The stones in the halo are the lightest blue I've ever seen; they almost look clear. Along the sides of the halo bands, the stones start with the gray blue stone of the engagement ring and get lighter in color as they go down, ending on the light blue that's along the top of the halo. It's breath taking.

I open my mouth to say something but all that comes out is a terrified squeak. I only just admitted to both of us that I love him less than an hour ago. I don't even know his parents, where he lives, if he had a pet as a kid, what he likes on his pizza, and a whole slew of other things that you should know before you decide to live with someone let alone marry them! I open my mouth again and nothing comes out.

I wish there was some cosmic pause button I could hit so that I could step off to the side and call Anna! I need a friendly voice, someone that won't judge me while I talk it all out; every question, every doubt, every fear. *What are you afraid of?* That's an easy one – failure. My whole life I've known that if I got married, it was a one shot deal. You shouldn't go into a marriage promising forever when in the back of your mind there's the thought that if it doesn't work out you can always get a divorce. All the unanswered questions about him run through my mind again and I realize just how trivial they are. I could meet his parents tomorrow and whether I liked them or not wouldn't change anything. Again I try to say something but all that comes out is air.

"Uh, maybe I jumped the gun on this one," he chuckles in an attempt to lighten the mood. He's smiling, but it doesn't reach his eyes. "I really am an idiot sometimes, huh?"

"Yes," I hear myself say. His jaw drops. "No. I mean ..." What the hell is wrong with me?! I've gone from silent to sputtering!

"So, no, I'm not an idiot? And, yes that I jumped the gun?" he asks sounding just as confused as I feel.

"No, you are definitely an idiot." He opens his mouth to say something and I hold my hand up to stop him. "But, you're my idiot ... for better or for worse."

"The ... what? Did ... just ... did you?"

"Yes, the answer is yes."

28

"*Che cazzo!*" Marco shouts into the phone. "Are you friggin' serious?! What the hell is going on over there, Donna?"

"You know bro, most people say congratulations."

"Yeah, but that's because people are happy to hear the news! We don't even know this guy, and more to the point sis, neither do you!" I can hear some muffled voices as if he's trying to cover the phone and talk to someone else.

"What's this news that seems to have Marco's knickers in a twist?" Oliver says as he takes the phone away from my brother. I fill him in on the news that Killian proposed and I said yes.

"Are you being fierce?"

"Um, I guess so," I respond.

"Are you afraid?" he asks and I tell him no. "Well congratulations, sweetie! I, for one, am very happy for you! Now, when do we get to meet him and when should I expect an email with the delicious details of how he asked and a picture of the ring?" I laugh as the tension bubble bursts.

"Thanks, doll face. I really needed that! I'll try to email soon, ok? Love you both!"

I hang up and quickly send a text to Anna with a picture of the ring before calling her. Her reaction is closer to Oliver's; which is good because I could use the boost before calling my parents. Thankfully I waited until eleven at night here to call Marco. By the time I call my parents, its 10am in New York. A part of me wishes they'll be out and I can get away with leaving a "hey, just checking in" voice mail and tell them the news when I get home. I'm not that lucky. The second my father picks up, I reach over and grab Killian's hand. That in itself is strange but I try not to read too much into it.

"How'sa your trip?" my father asks. "Havin'a nice time?"

I can picture him sitting there in their kitchen, newspaper opened on the table, the empty bowl from his cereal off to the side. I'd bet money that when he answered the phone, he leaned all the way back in the kitchen chair, stretched out his back, and has one of his hands on top of his head.

"Having a wonderful time, Pops! That's what I wanted to talk to you about, actually. Um, well ..."

"You're not movin'a there, right?" Even though he's half teasing, I can hear the slight drop in his voice.

"No," I laugh. "As gorgeous as it is here, I'll still be home by next weekend."

I hear my mother gasp in the background and start rambling. I can't make out what she's saying, but I have a good idea since she can only hear my father's end of the conversation.

"Pops? Pops! Tell Ma to get on the other line!" After a bit of bickering, my mother picks up the other line and starts going off about moving far away. "Ma? Ma?! MA!!" I yell into the phone. "I'm not moving to Australia!"

"Oh, ok," she says all traces of motherly mania gone.

"Now that you're both on the phone and I have your attention, I'm not moving here. Though, I'm sure I'll be visiting here from time to time. But that's not the reason I called." I let out a slow breath and give Killian's hand a squeeze. "When I get back to New York, there's someone I want you to meet."

This of course leads to both my parents in a flurry of voices that switch back and forth between English and Italian. As they rattle on they get louder and louder as well as faster and it's hard to make out anything either of them as saying; though I do catch a few key things.

"Are you done yet?" I say loudly hoping they can hear me over each other.

"Hey! You no yell at your mother like that!"

"Pops, I'm not yelling AT anyone, I just wanted to make sure you could hear me. To answer the few things I could make out; no, I'm not pregnant. I haven't been abducted. Seriously, how would I be calling if I was abducted? The person I want you to meet isn't a girlfriend, it's a man. His name is Killian. He's a really great guy. I flew here to see him. And before you go off on a tangent again, no he's not someone I met on 'da scary intoor-a-net'. He lives in Brooklyn and is here for his job."

"So, he'sa you boy-a-frend?" my mother asks and I can hear the smile in her voice.

"Well, about that," I start. Killian gives my hand a gentle squeeze of encouragement. "He's kinda sorta my fiancé."

An hour later, I'm finally able to hang up with my parents. I've got a wicked headache that's two more screams away from migraine city and I'm thoroughly exhausted. I toss the phone across the bed as I flop down and close my eyes.

"Wow," marvels Killian as he lies down next to me.

"I feel like all I did was talk in a circle; over and over again."

"Is it always like that?"

I half open one eye and turn towards him. "Having second thoughts?" I ask, only half joking.

He slides closer and puts his arm across me. "Absolutely not. I may be marrying *into* your family, but I'm not marrying them."

"True enough, I suppose."

I close my eye and try to will away the headache. Killian shifts and I can tell he's sitting up now. He takes my hand in his and starts massaging my hand between my thumb and pointer finger. After a few minutes he switches hands and soon I no longer feel like my eyes are going to burst out of their sockets. "I don't know what you just did, but it seems to be working."

"Pressure points. Mom is prone to migraines and has learned a few tricks to try to ward them off, or at least attempt to take the edge off if she doesn't do something in time. Let's see about getting you some aspirin and then head back to the kitchen."

"I can't believe more than half of the people are still here," I mumble slowly sitting up.

"I swear Gran used looking for me before as an excuse to sneak off and call more people to come over," he laughs. I give him a look of disbelief. "I wouldn't put it passed her, sweetheart. She likes you; a lot. She even let you borrow her special apron."

I must have had a confused look on my face, so he went on to explain how his grandparents, oddly enough, met because of an apron.

When Gran was 17, she had gone into a department store to buy an apron. When she went to pay for it, the price on the tag was different than the price of the display and she was a few shillings short. The man in line behind her walked up to the clerk and gave him the extra shillings. Gran only agreed to accept the man's generosity when he agreed to meet the next day in front of the store so she could pay him back.

She showed up with the money, and he showed up with flowers. A few months later they were married and spent fifty three years together before he passed away.

"The original apron she retired before I was even born. In the 60's just before the Aussie currency changed from quid to dollar, Grandpa bought a second special apron saying it was the right thing to spend the last of his shillings on. Gran tucked that one away until she retired the first one. He bought a third for their 50th anniversary, which is the one you were wearing. She has another still in the box that he bought when he got sick so that when it came time to retire the third, she would have another. Because they have a special meaning, she only lets special people wear them."

"But, she only just met me."

"Yep. That's all it takes apparently. I always thought it was a fluke thing. The story goes that apparently Gran can tell instantly if she meets the soul mate for each of her children and grandchildren."

"So, you proposed because your grandmother thinks I'm your soul mate?" I ask letting go of his hand.

"No. I already had the ring; I was waiting for the right moment."

"Which was when you saw me wearing the apron?"

"You don't think I brought you to Gran's to see if she'd lend you her apron before proposing, do you?" He sighs. "Donna, as sweet as the apron story is, it has nothing to do with how I feel about you. I already had the ring ordered before you said you'd come to Cairns with me. I had Tony stop by the jewelers on the way to pick us up at hotel and he slipped the box into my carry on when he put our luggage in the trunk. Listen, I love Gran. But I wasn't waiting for her approval. I was waiting for a sign from you that you felt the same way I did."

"Promise?"

"May I live a thousand years and never hunt again!"

I tip my head back and roar with laughter, then wince as it echoes in my head. "How can I resist a man that can quote *The Princess Bride*?" I say as we head out of the room in search of aspirin.

"Mawwage. Mawwage is what bwings us togevah today."

"Um, about that," I say as we walk into his grandmother's bathroom. "You're not thinking of a wedding the minute we get back, right?"

"Nah, I figured at least two weeks. Joking! Joking!" he grins putting his hands in front of himself as if to ward off an attack. It's a bit eerie that he knew I was going to slap his shoulder and I hadn't even moved my hand.

"Bit déjà vu, isn't it sweetheart. Here you are sitting on the edge of the tub, I'm going through the medicine cabinet, and you want to slap me," he says all smiles and dimple. I stick out my tongue. "Mmmmm, maybe later. Here, take these and let's get back to the kitchen."

Using my hand as a cup, I scoop up some water then tip my head back and swallow the pills.

"Aindee-aemo!" he says in an attempt to say let's go in Italian and I chuckle.

29

"Wakey wakey, Sleeping Beauty."

I roll over with a groan and try to go back to sleep. My brain feels fuzzy and my tonsils feel like cotton balls. He tries to tickle the back of my neck and I growl.

"I'm not the Princess, I'm the Dragon. I will roast you and eat you whole," I grumble.

"Come on," he laughs. "Breakfast is already on the table."

"How?!"

The last of the party goers didn't leave until after two in the morning. Then there was a bit of clean up to be done and the leftovers to be put away. It was almost three by the time I flopped onto the bed. The thought of Gran, a woman in her 70's, running circles around me, has me pushing myself to get out of bed.

"Sure you don't mean you're draggin' instead of the Dragon?"

"Dick," I toss back as I grab a change of clothes out of my suitcase. Ten minutes later I'm sighing as I take my first sip of coffee. The second sip has me feeling a little more human.

"You didn't have to do all this," I say to Gran as she sits down at the table.

There's enough food to feed a small army. There's a small platter of bacon, sausage, and fried ham. Another platter is filled with grilled halved tomatoes, mushrooms, and roasted potatoes. There's a plate with fried eggs and another piled high with toast slathered with butter and a smear of Vegemite. She's even put out a large bowl of beans.

"Nonsense," she chuckles.

"Gran doesn't believe in having a dingo's brekkie," Killian says with a smile and she laughs.

With that, the door opens and his aunts Annette and Dottie walk in, along with his cousins Den, Mac, and Tammie. "Dingo's brekkie means no breakfast; just a yawn, a leak, and a good look around," Killian leans in and whispers.

"Seriously, did she sneak back into the kitchen after we all went to sleep and started making breakfast?"

"She only got up about 7," he shrugs.

"She's amazing."

Breakfast is as entertaining as it is delicious. Killian's cousins take full advantage of the small gathering to tell me stories about funny and embarrassing things he did as a kid; most of which he laughs at too.

"Hey Donna, bet you can't make your way through a full piece of toast with Vegemite," Mac says.

"Bet I can. Name your price," I counter. Having three brothers I know this game well.

"Alright," he smirks leaning back in his chair with a grin. "$20"

"Pfft, that's it? Not worth my time," I reply with a shrug and take a sip of my coffee. This solicits a chorus of "ooooooo"s from around the table.

"Ok. Fifty!" he shouts.

"So the bet is $50 that I can't make it through a full piece of toast with Vegemite. Is that correct?"

"Yeah, and no sips of coffee either!" he adds.

"Ok, full piece, no coffee, fifty bucks?"

He smiles wide and nods. Poor sucker, I almost feel bad for him. I take a piece of toast and cut it in half before running one Vegemite smeared side through my egg yolk and smooshing the two halves together like a sandwich. It's gone in under a minute.

Extending my hand, I grin and say "one pineapple, mate." Gran slaps the table and laughs so hard that for a second I think she's going to fall off her chair.

"Doesn't count! You put egg on your toast!" he fires back.

"Aaaah, but you only agreed to no coffee. You didn't say no about anything else."

"Wooo, she's got you, mate," chuckles Tammie as she slaps Mac on the shoulder.

"Gorgeous *and* smart! Any way I can convince you to dump my cousin and run off with me?" Den asks folding his hands together as if he's pleading.

Without even looking at him, I know Killian's opened his mouth to say something and I hold up my hand.

"Let's see," I say and start counting on my fingers. "You're very handsome. You're funny. You're charming. You're self-confident. All are traits many women go for. However, your cousin has all of those same traits in addition to knowing many of my strengths, my weaknesses, and my fondness for chocolate and old movies. But most importantly, he has my heart; which wasn't easily given. So, sorry but no, there's nothing you could say or do to convince me to run off with you."

"Strewth!" exclaims Tammie. "She's bested both of you at your own games!"

~*~

"Need anything while we're out?" Killian calls to his grandmother Tuesday early afternoon.

"No thanks," she calls back, followed by a chorus of goodbyes from her friends.

They meet up at her house once a week to get together for knitting, but I think it's more about the wine and gossip than it is about the yarn.

"Let's go," he says and takes my hand as we head out the door.

It's a gorgeous day outside; perfect to just go for a walk. It's around 80 degrees and sunny, and I can't get over the fact that it's winter!

"You sure?" he asks with a grin as we pass the house with the For Sale sign.

I just laugh at him and give his hand a tug to keep him from stopping. When we get to the next corner, he turns us to the right. It's an odd feeling not knowing where we're going and not getting anxious about not knowing. Even when I go out for a nice relaxing day, I still know where I'm going, how I'm getting there, how long it will take to get there, and an idea of how long I plan to stay. The shrink I saw after getting out of the hospital said it was my subconscious trying to gain a sense of control after going through trauma; a fancy way of saying trying to cope with PTSD. I told her that I didn't have PTSD, that I was just trying to get my life back to normal, and to save the diagnosis for people that actually had it ad needed help. Needless to say, I never went back.

"Hey, you alright?" Killian asks when we stop at the next corner.

"Yeah, fine, why?" I reply absentmindedly.

"You look pissed off and your hand has gone all clammy."

"Sorry, brain wandered off," I say, not offering more of an explanation.

He looks into my eyes as if he's trying to see just where my mind wandered off to. "Ok," he says after a moment, "nearly there."

Before I know it, we're stepping off the sidewalk into the parking lot of a strip mall. There's a café down the end. The sign above the building looks like someone slapped pressboard up, painted it white, and wrote espresso and gelati on it. There's graffiti on the building, but it looks like it's intentional. I'm not really sure what to make of the place, but when I step inside, it's not at all what I was expecting. The first thing I notice is the heavenly smell of coffee. My eyes close and I smile as I inhale the aromatic bliss. It's like aromatherapy that you can also sip.

"Better?" he asks on a laugh. My response is more like a purr than actual words.

There's something about the place that makes me think of Coney Island. It's a cool little neighborhood spot to hang out without the pretentiousness of a lot of hipster places. There are adorable characters painted along the white brick wall that have swirls of gelato for hair as well as mini replicas of famous paintings, like the Mona Lisa, holding ice cream cones. There's a variety of amazing looking gelati up at the counter and they have a wide range of coffees. I glance up at the large chalkboard menu behind the counter and realize they have a whole range of foods they offer; each one sounds absolutely amazing.

"So, what'll you have?" Killian asks

"One of everything," I reply which gets both him and the group of three behind us to laugh. Not wanting to hold up the line, I tell them to go ahead of us and order. "We are so getting some things to go too. You know that, right?"

"Obviously," twinkle, smile, dimple.

I decide on the smoked salmon sandwich and a Ten120 Raw Salad which is named after the café and has all lovely raw green veggies, shaved pecorino, and preserved lemon. I played it safe and went for the yummy sounding healthy food first that way after when I get some gelato and take pastries with us, I won't feel so guilty. Killian goes for their French toast which has caramelized bananas, a berry coulis, and coconut crystals which is then all topped with coconut caramel sauce and a scoop of vanilla bean gelato.

I go get us a table while he is waiting for our coffees. When he comes over to the table I look down and instead of a swirly design in the foam I saw the group ahead of us get, there's a face that looks a bit like a cartoon version of Killian!

"What the .... ?!" I lean forward and look at his coffee and there's a face that looks like a cartoon version of me!

"They're pretty talented all around in here. Oh, and when we get the order to go, do *not* let me forget a chocolate beetroot cupcake for Gran. If she found out we were here and didn't bring one back for her, she'd skin us both."

"Wait? A what?"

"Chocolate beetroot cupcake; she adores them."

"Beetroot? In a cupcake?" I sputter in total disbelief. I get up and go look in the display and sure enough, he's not pulling my leg! "Don't get me wrong," I say as I sit back down, "I love beetroot, I love chocolate, but together? I dunno about that one."

"I thought the same thing," he admits, leaning back in his chair when they bring over our lunch, "but they are awesome!"

All thoughts of cupcakes, chocolate beetroot or otherwise vanish when I see our plates. Holy hell! It looks almost too good to eat. The first bite of my sandwich has me purring again.

"Hey now, unless you want a repeat of Turkish Delight ice cream on the beach, you'll behave yourself."

I know that he means leaving before I get to finish the food, but that could so be taken in a different context that I can't help the "ooh, really" and wink.

"You take your life in your own hands turning up without that cupcake," he laughs. "So, I've been thinking of different things to do and see over the next few days. Anything you want to see?"

"I haven't looked at anything online to know what's around."

He jumps up and slaps his hand on my forehead. "Hmm, nope, doesn't seem like you have a fever."

"Hardy har har, wise ass. I've just been enjoying the relaxation that's all. We can take a look when we get back and decide then."

"Going to need to book plane tickets too," he says and the bite of salad I was chewing doesn't go down as smoothly. I don't want to think about how close the end of my vacation is, but I really don't want to think about flying back and leaving him here.

"What's with the face?" he asks.

"It's the one I always have," I tell him. "Ok, fine. It's just, well, I don't want to get home and not see you for however long you're here for. Even to my own ears it sounds a bit clingy, but I've kind of gotten used to you around. I'm thinking of calling Max and seeing if I can get a few more days off if he sends me something to work on."

"That's really nice, sweetheart. But I've kind of been thinking the same thing and I've decided that I'm flying back with you. I don't want to be here without you, and you shouldn't have to explain it all again to your parents while I'm here with my toes in the sand."

"If we weren't already engaged, I'd ask you to marry me!" I chuckle.

"We should also figure out living arrangements too."

"Funny, the other night I was thinking about how here I was saying yes and I don't even know where you live or any of that. I mean, I know it can't be too far from Asia King, but that doesn't quite narrow it down."

"I didn't realize that you didn't know. I'm on 9th Street just west of 7th Avenue, right by the F. I'm only 5 stops from you. You're building is co-op, right? Do you rent or own?"

"Own."

"I own too. So the choice is yours. We can live at your place and I'll rent mine out. Or we can live at my place and rent yours out. We could also find a new place, and either sell or rent out where we are now."

"Honestly, I hadn't thought about any of that because I thought it would be a week or two before you got back," I say with a shrug.

"Fair enough, I suppose. Ok, so no decisions on housing until we get back."

"Good. Now that that's sorted out, how about some gelato?"

~*~

We try to cram in as much as we can over the next two days. We even took Gran with us on the trip to Kuranda. The scenic train ride is like stepping back in time. While we were there we also went to the Butterfly Sanctuary and Kuranda Market. Killian tried to convince me that if I was marrying someone that's part Australian I needed to buy a didgeridoo and know how to play at least one tune before we can have the wedding because it's customary.

"And I'm guessing it's also customary that the groom needs to be full of shit first too, right?" I toss back.

"He can't help it dear," Gran laughs, "his Grandpa was the same way; always thinking of funny things to say to tease me. I swear it's written in the Cooper DNA."

"Ah, come on, Gran! Whose side are you on, anyway?"

"Donna's of course," she replies.

Killian goes wide eyed and his jaw drops down in surprise. Gran's chin is tipped up and she's chuckling. I pick up my camera and snap a few pictures.

30

Friday morning we're up with the sun and Gran sets out another feast for breakfast claiming it's a long flight and airport food is horrible so we need to fill up now. She's even bagged up some pastries for us to take with us.

"You come back any time you want, with or without him," she says as Killian is tossing our suitcases into the trunk of his cousin's car.

"Hahaha mate, I think you've been replaced," Den barks as he bumps Killian's shoulder.

"Wow, thanks Gran. I feel the love," he says dejectedly.

"Like recognizes like. We're both old souls that are young at heart; rare breeds need to stick together," she says as she winks at me.

"Not to sound like a conchy bastard, but we do need to get going," says Den. "A few minutes late and I'm sure my patients won't be too put out, but let's not test that theory."

"Ah yes, you know how much everyone *loves* a trip to the fang carpenter."

"Stuff it, kiwi."

"Boys," Gran bellows sternly. Just the one word and they quit bickering. Turning, she takes both my hands and gives them such a squeeze I'm surprised my fingers haven't popped off. "Take care of yourself dear."

"You too, Gran. I'm going to miss you."

When she loosens her grip I try not to shake the feeling back into my hands as I give her a hug.

"Save some love for me!" Killian runs up and tosses his arms around the both of us.

After a round of sad goodbyes, we're off to the airport. As much as I'll miss being here, I'm looking forward to being home; I'm just not looking forward to the almost twenty eight hour trip, five which are waiting during the two layovers. Flying business class should make things a bit more comfortable, well except in my bank account. Thankfully, Killian didn't argue with me putting money towards our tickets though. Don't get me wrong, he did try to pay for both, but I turned the tables by tossing his own line back at him: think of it as our money.

I am, however, just as nervous if not more, headed home. It was one thing to fly to Australia on a whim to finally meet Killian, especially not knowing who exactly I was meeting ahead of time. It's a whole different kind of nervous knowing that I'm going to be flying back from this trip with a fiancé and having to introduce him to my parents.

"Hey, are you ok? You look like you're going to be sick?" Killian asks.

"Need me to pull over?" Den calls from the front seat.

"I don't think it'll be a technicolour yawn, but she has gone a bit grey."

"No, no, I'm fine. Honest. It's just ... well, introducing you to my parents should be a lotta fun. 'Ma, Pops, this is Killian, a man you've never met before and know nothing about, who is going to be your son in law'. You heard the phone conversation the other night. Now think about that in person."

"Ok. And?"

I roll my eyes at him.

"No, seriously. Let them yell it out if they have to. It doesn't change anything, sweetheart. We got engaged. It's not like we ran off and got married before they met me. And, even if we had, this is about you and me, nobody else." He leans down and just before he kisses me, he says "I love you". I feel a slight swerve in the car and then it stops.

"Um, this isn't the airport," I whisper to Killian.

"Oi, mate, what's up?" he asks his cousin.

"Kerbside quiche if I have to listen to you sweet talk and snog the Mrs. much longer!"

"Get stuffed!" Killian counters and shoves the back of Den's seat.

"Piss off, ratbag!"

"Boys!" I shout. They shut up instantly. "Oh, wow, didn't expect that to work so well. Listen, you have patients to get to and we have a plane to catch. So quit it, and let's get a move on!"

"Hoo hoo, caught yourself a true blue cracker, mate!"

"What did he just call me?!" I yell turning to Killian.

I look pissed, Den looks confused, and Killian roars with laughter. As Den pulls back out into traffic, Killian explains what it means and how in Australia it's a compliment and that in America being called a cracker is an insult.

"There are times over the years I've had to translate Italian into English for friends when they're around my family, but I never thought that I'd have to have someone translate English into English for me," I say to Den as we're standing on the curb in front of the airport.

He laughs and gives me a hug. "It's been fun, especially when I first met you," he says with a wicked chuckle and a wink.

"Break it up," Killian interrupts. "Go find your own girl."

"Girl?" I turn and raise an eyebrow.

"Woman, I meant woman. I was, uh, making sure you were paying attention. Yeah, that's it," he quickly says and smirks.

We say our goodbyes to Den and make our way into the airport. Seems strange to think that less than a week ago I was here having to deal with security because of Killian and his antics; it feels like it was weeks and weeks ago.

"What is that odd look all about?"

"Sorry, was just thinking how the last time we were here I was ready to kill you. Promise you won't do anything stupid while we're here, ok?" I ask.

"Stupid?! Trying to prevent you from walking away was stupid?"

"Well, when you say it like that, no. But, the way you went about it was." We check in, get through security, and find a spot for coffee all incident free. "I love it here. I love back home. The one thing I don't love is the traveling from point A to point B. I can't believe you do this all the time."

"Not all the time, sweetheart, just once a year for work. I try to get over for a social visit once every other or every third year. I also break up the flight a bit and fly half way, spend an overnight in a hotel by the airport, and then finish the last leg. It helps with both the jet lag and the travel fatigue."

"Now you tell me," I grumble. He suggests changing the flights so that instead of a layover in San Francisco we just spent the night and fly home the next day. "We haven't even gotten on the first plane yet and I'm already dreaming of my comfy cozy bed. Once I get home I'm dumping my bags in the entrance, flopping on the bed, and not waking up until dinner time."

"I'll make you a deal. When we land at JFK, we get a cab to your place. We'll both flop and when we wake up at dinner time, we order delivery from Asia King."

"If I hadn't already told you I loved you, I'd say it now!"

"So wait a minute, this whole time all I had to do was offer take out? Geez! Here I thought it had something to do with my wit, charm, devilishly good looks, or that you can't get enough of me in bed. But all along it's been my ability to suggest delivery? I'm gobsmacked!" he huffs, but then tosses in a wink at the end.

"Don't forget the accent."

"My accent?" he asks sounding stunned.

"Yeah. It's definitely more pronounced here though than it is at home."

"Ok, let me get this straight, what won you over was take out and my accent?" he asks bewilderedly.

"And you've got a nice butt. You scored bonus points for sense of humor and your dimple." I say straight-faced.

His jaw drops and he gives me a look like he can't believe I just said that. It makes it hard not to laugh. I can feel my eyes start to tear up trying to hold it in. What comes bubbling out ends up being more of a cackle than a laugh and I have to put my head on the table just to catch my breath.

"You numpty!" I finally manage to get out. "Do you really believe that? Or are you fishing for complements? "

"Maybe somewhere in the middle," he admits.

"Flight One-Seven-Four to Auckland, New Zealand, now boarding at Gate 5. Flight One-Seven-Four, now boarding at Gate 5." We toss our empty coffee cups and make our way to the gate.

"Want the window seat?" he asks as we board the plane.

"What's your motive?" I speculate, arching an eyebrow in suspicion.

"No motive. I've just done this flight a million times and thought you'd like the window so you can look for Rivendell or Mordor or something." I roll my eyes at him, but still take the window seat.

"So, we've got over an hour layover in Auckland," I say after I sit down and get situated, "I'm guessing that isn't enough time to leave the airport and see Wellington, huh?"

"Seeing as it's over an eight hour drive away, no," he chuckles.

"Yeah, well, I only did a quick study of Australia's geography before the trip. Just because I was flying to SEE a Kiwi, doesn't mean I'd be setting foot in his homeland."

"Fair enough, I suppose, but since you're going to marry said Kiwi, maybe you should brush up on it," he teases and puts up his arms to preemptively block a slap. I hadn't even gone to slap him, but the minute he drops his arms, on principle I get him with my book and then raspberry at him. "You know, I'm surprised for someone

248

that spends every day at work reading, that you read on your off time."

"I enjoy reading, that's why the job was a perfect fit. I have a list pinned up at my desk of books I've done the editing on that I want to pick up once they've hit the shelves. It doesn't matter that I know the story already."

"Seriously?" he asks, surprised.

"Yeah, it's no different than rereading a book you already have or watching a movie you've seen before."

"So I should expect to see you rereading books and rewatching movies a lot. Ok. What else?"

Over the course of the four and a half hour flight we talk about the usually boring average everyday stuff that we don't know about each other. Unfortunately, I realize just HOW boring my life has become over the past few years. I go to work, I come home, once a week I say hi to Leo, I hang out with Anna, and about once a month we have a get together of friends at my place. Up until recently I only saw my family a couple times a month. There's the commute to and from work, the occasional trips down to the beach, and once every six weeks or so I stop by LaLinda's. I lead a very boring, stunted, sheltered life.

Killian on the other hand, is a rarely-at-home workaholic. Even when he's not at work, he's out. He's either out jogging or at the beach. Sometimes he sees his siblings that live nearby and occasionally hangs out with Matt and Nicole. About every two months or so he heads up to his parents' in Greenwich. Even though they are only an hour away, he can't get up there as often as he likes.

"Well, we'll be seeing my family soon enough since most of them are in Brooklyn. It looks like we'll be driving to Connecticut too. And then I guess we should have our families meet each other."

"What's with the look?" he asks, his eyebrows drawn down in a V.

"Have you ever seen the movie My Big Fat Greek Wedding? Picture the guy meeting the parents for the first time scene and then the scene where the parents meet each other. Then just make the woman's family Italian instead of Greek."

"Lucky for you, my parents are nothing like the groom's parents!"

"Well, that's a little relief at least," I concede with a half shrug.

"Listen, try to relax about it. I know they're your family and you love them. Honestly though, I really don't care what they think of me. Just like I don't care what my parents think of you. There will probably be a bit of 'but you only just met' from both sides; even though technically we met months before you flew out. I love you; you love me, that's all that matters."

He's right. I know he's right. So for the time being, I try to just let it go.

~*~

"Seriously, this is messing with my brain," I sigh as we get off the plane in San Francisco. It was 11:50am when we left Cairns. According to the clock here, it's only an hour later, even though eighteen hours have passed! I need coffee. Or maybe something a little stronger will help."

"We still have 4 hours before the next flight. Are you still sure you don't want to change the tickets?"

"Tempting, however, I'd like to get home and have a longer break before having to go back to work."

"As you wish," he smirks.

"Whatever Westley. Less talky, more coffee," I grumble.

Half a cup of coffee later and I start to feel a little more human, when Killian asks what should we do with the three hours we have left until our flight home. "I've never been here, so I'm not sure what's close by," I tell him.

"Ok, let's wing it," he says, and after a trip on the AirTrain we're at the Rental Car Center.

"A rental car, for a few hours, you can't be serious?"

"Settle down, Mrs. It's not flash, it's actually practical. A cab could run us anywhere from $40 to $80 one way depending on where we want to go, and seeing as we have no game plan, a $45 rental from Dollar Rental makes more sense." Keys in hand, we head out to the car and make our way out of the airport. "I've been here before, you haven't. Is there anything you'd like to see?"

"Well, a tour of Alcatraz is obviously out because we don't have that kind of time. Hmmm," I say as I bite my lip and try to think of things. "Oooo! Lombard Street! That's in San Fran! Can we go there?"

"Lombard Street, it is then," he grins.

About half an hour later, we've reached the twisty part of Lombard Street. "Whoa," I say in awe. "Pictures don't even come close to how crazy this is! Pull over. I want to drive down it!" He laughs. After swapping seats and fastening seat belts, we're off. "Can you take my phone out of my bag and snap a picture? Anna's never going to believe this!"

31

"I'm glad we picked my apartment," I slur as we wheel our bags into the lobby of my building. "Closer to the airport," I explain when he gives me an odd look.

As we step into the elevator I grab my phone from my pocket, snap a selfie with my eyes closed and head resting against the wall of the elevator before sending it to Anna and Marco saying that I'm home and thoroughly exhausted.

After Lombard Street the rest of our time in San Francisco seemed rushed even though it wasn't. We hit Fisherman's Wharf and from there snapped pictures of the Golden Gate Bridge, the Bay Bridge, and Alcatraz before heading back to the airport. The flight home seemed to take forever, but I chalked that up to a lot of time zones that both seemed to shoot us back in time and then tossed us forward. When we left Australia, it was just before noon on Friday, and even though we traveled almost 28 hours, it's only an hour and a half into Saturday.

With my eyes barely opened I manage to get the key in the door and then stumble over the threshold. "I vote for dumping the luggage right here," I mumble as I lock the door behind us and manage to hang my keys on the hook after three tries. "So this is the apartment. Living room is that way, kitchen is …" That's when it hits me that he's been here before. Looking over my shoulder, I realize he's smirking at me. "Shut up or you get to sleep on the couch."

Kicking my shoes off as I walk into the bedroom, I go to flop down on the bed. I'm pretty sure I was out cold before I landed because the next morning I don't even remember hitting the pillow.

~*~

"Morning. Rise and shine, coffee is ready." Killian's voice barely breaks through the sleepy haze. If it wasn't for my brain picking up on the word coffee, I'd still be drooling on my pillow.

"What time is it?" I mumble without opening my eyes.

"Just passed 10."

"So, it's just passed midnight back in Cairns, and instead of waking up I should be going to sleep. Oh, it's going to be an interesting day," I groan as I sit up in bed and take the offered cup of coffee from Killian.

"You've already missed a call from Anna, one from Marco, and 2 from your parents. Anna called again a few minutes ago, so I thought I should probably wake you up."

"How are you up, wide awake, and cheery?" I grumble and toss a pillow at him.

"So I shouldn't mention that I've already unpacked the suitcases and would have taken the laundry to the laundromat; but as I don't know where you usually go, or have a key to get back in, I figured I'd just make coffee and watch some TV for a bit."

Taking a sip of coffee, I feel the magic elixir work its way down my throat and begin to feel a little more alive. As I go to take another sip I realize there's something about the coffee that doesn't make sense.

"How is there milk in my coffee? I dumped it, and the eggs I had in the fridge before I left. So, if you didn't go out, what did you put in this?"

"Calm down Poirot, I found a small milk pitcher in the cupboard, so I left the front door cracked in case it locked behind me, and knocked on the door next door. Sweet old lady, by the way."

"Mrs. Lukashenko doesn't speak more than a few words in English. How'd you manage to get milk?"

"I speak Russian."

"Oh really," I say dragging the words out slowly to show I don't believe him. "*Ya ne znayu, vy govorili po-russki.*"

"Fine," he chuckles, "you got me! I have no idea what you just said." His eyes go from laughing to something more primal in a flash. "But, it sounded sexy as hell." Just as he takes a step towards the bed, the Tarantella comes blaring from the kitchen."

"I should answer that before they decide to show up in force," I sigh. Getting out of bed, I make it to the kitchen just as my phone stops ringing. Two seconds later it starts up again.

"Hey Ma. No, I wasn't ignoring you, I was sleeping. Yes, I realize what time it is, but I'm still on Australia time and it's after midnight there now." Killian walks back into the kitchen with my now cooled coffee. Dumping it in the sink, he refills it and sets the fresh cup down on the table in front of me. "I dunno, Ma. There's still the unpacking," I tell her as I wink at Killian, "then the laundry, and I really need to hit the grocery store since I'm out of milk, bread, and eggs. We're not even showered and dressed for the day yet, I said I only just woke up. Yes, he stayed here last night. No, I don't see why that's a problem." Pinching my bridge of my nose I left out a long, slow, sigh. "Ok Ma, fine, we'll be there around 5. Love you too. Ciao."

"I take it that means we have around 6 hours to get the laundry going, run to the grocery store, and be able to function like normal non jet lagged adults, right?" Killian smirks.

"Give the man a prize, Bob!"

~*~

"There is no way I'm going to remember all those names!" Killian exclaims, leaning his head on the back of the couch and closing his eyes.

"Sure you can! It's mostly the same five names over and over!" I can't help but laugh at Oliver's 'helpful' advice. "Besides, they know they're a large crowd and it'll take a while. You'll get the hang of it eventually."

"Please tell me you've written a manual and you're willing to share."

"Trust me, you won't need it," laughs Oliver. "But I can give you a few pointers though. Until you get used to the noise, always pop a few ibuprofen before showing up, never ever eat before showing up, and always greet whoever's house it is within the first 15 minutes of being there; as well as the future in laws, the grandparents, and the godparents. It's always a bonus when one of those three are also the one's hosting the party. Don't attempt any of the dancing or drinking of the homemade wine and/or grappa until you've gotten some practice in. I think that just about covers everything. Now it's time for cocktails," he announces as he gets up and saunters into the kitchen.

"More drinks?" Killian half whimpers, opening his eyes wide.

"Welcome to the family, Bruce," Marco chuckles. As exhausted as we are, I'm glad we decided on this little detour to Marco and Oliver's place on the way home.

"So, I guess this means you don't think I'm some nut bar that's going to kidnap your sister and drag her into the heart of the Outback."

"Oh please, he never thought that," I say. Two heads swivel in my direction, before they look back at each other and burst out laughing. "What's so funny?"

"He totally thought that, sweetheart," Killian says the same time as Marco says "I totally did". And they both burst out laughing again.

32

"Welcome back!" Joan Marie shouts as she jumps up from her desk to give me a hug. "You look wonderful! How was the trip?"

"Amazing!" I set my bag down on the low wall of her cubicle. "I have something for you". Reaching into my bag, I pull out a silk scarf like the one I got for my mother, only this one is decorated in vibrant streaks of red, orange, and gold.

"Oh my, that's lovely dear!" she exclaims as I hand her the scarf. Taking my hand, she gives it a squeeze. "Thank You! And may I say; what a lovely new ring I see sparkling on your finger."

"Nothing gets passed you," I laugh. "Yes, it's a new ring, an engagement ring to be exact."

The next half hour is spent standing by Joan Marie's desk explaining to my co-workers that I went to Australia, came back engaged, his name is Killian, and that he's a really great guy. I also seize the opportunity to hand everyone the various little stuffed animals I brought back for them. As each Koala, Kangaroo, and Kookaburra, comes out of my bag I'm glad to do this all in one shot, rather than go desk by desk and have to repeatedly talk about my vacation and new relationship status.

"Why didn't I get an invite to this party?" Max says trying to sound stern.

"That's a wonderful idea, Max! We should have an impromptu engagement party!" Joan Marie suggests.

"Engagement party? Here? Who?" he asks confused. I raise my hand and wish I'd had my phone out to get a picture of his face.

~*~

"Seriously though, the look on his face, totally priceless," I say as I run the last of my egg roll through some duck sauce.

"You still never explained how you got out of the whole party idea," Killian says as he leans back in his chair.

"I told Joan Marie that on such short notice you couldn't just waltz out of the office for a party, impromptu or otherwise. She said we'd have to plan something soon, and the subject was dropped," I shrug.

"How does Wednesday work for you?" he asks. With a clank, my chopsticks rattle on my plate. "No good. Hmmm, perhaps next week then? I'll check my calendar later and you can pick when."

"Ooh-kay? Who are you and what have you done with Killian?"

"I told you while we were away that when I got back I was going to make some changes. I need to be less of a workaholic. There are still going to be days that I'll get stuck in the office. But unless I absolutely need to stay late, once 5 o'clock rolls around I need to disconnect. Not only that, I'm sure that leaving one day early will shake things up enough in the office that people will realize more changes are coming."

"That was so not what I expected to hear you say. If you're sure, I'll find out tomorrow about Wednesday. Although, if you're not into the idea, I'm okay with that too."

"Nah, it's fine," he says as the waiter clears our plates.

Over dessert we discuss how having a little something at the office is the closest we'll get to an actual engagement party as we both feel it's a bit antiquated. As it turns out, neither of us is really into the whole "must have" bachelor/bachelorette party either.

"I wonder if I can get away with bypassing the bridal shower too," I ponder out loud which causes Killian to laugh.

"I wouldn't claim to know your mother well, but from what I know of her, sorry sweetheart there's just no way around it. You're her only daughter, her only chance to help plan something girlie like a bridal shower, her only chance at being mother of the bride. As long as she doesn't try to take over every detail of the wedding planning, there's no harm in having a shower."

There's silence at the table for about half a beat before we both burst out laughing.

~*~

"I've gotta tell you, I was a bit worried that party was going to be something almost pantomime. But it was low key and more like a meet and greet with champagne and cake. It was nice," I say to Killian as we leave my office on Wednesday.

"It was nice to be able to put faces with names and stories I've heard. Though I'm sure that was all a one sided thing as before your trip you had no stories to tell about me. Well, except that I was *the flower guy*, as Joan Marie kept calling me."

"Better that, than *creepy stalker guy* which is what you were called for a while. Sorry", I apologize even though I can't help but smile and laugh.

"Helloooh, my sweetheart! And helloooh, mister nice man!"

"Hi Dada ji, hi Nani ji! Two coffees, regular; and this guy here isn't allowed to pay," I tell them as I point to Killian. "Oh and before I forget," I say as I dig into my briefcase and pull out a small box, "this is for you."

Opening the box, Nani ji lifts out a wad of red tissue paper with gold spots on it. Inside the wrapping is a wooden figurine of two elephants sitting on their butts, trunks in the air, and laughing. Placing the figurine back in the box, she runs around the cart and gives me a bone crushing hug.

"Thank you sweetheart, thank you mister nice man," she exclaims and after letting go of me, gives Killian the same bone crushing hug, though I swear I hear a small giggle escape her as she does.

Coffees in hand, we make our way to the Subway. "Why did we just get on a D train instead of an F train?" Killian asks, a look of confusion on his face.

"There's a friend I'd like you to meet. It's only one stop so we can hop an F train home easily. Though, we should probably figure out an official home soon instead of going back and forth between the two apartments."

"I told you, sweetheart, I'm fine with either place or finding a whole new place if that's what you want."

"Yeah, I know, but a little input would be helpful. Where you live now has always been your space, with your things. If I moved in there, things will need to be rearranged and I'm not sure how you'd feel about it. Same goes if you move into my place. I don't want you thinking that once you move in, it would still be my place instead of our place. Plus, it adds to your commute," I say as we step off the train at Herald Square. "This isn't one of those 'whatever you like, dear' things. It's something that we both need to agree on and be happy with the decision."

"Ok, how about I move into your place then? We decide which furniture we want in that apartment, the rest we can put in the other apartment and rent it out as a fully furnished, or as an air bnb," he suggests.

"I never considered a fully furnished or air bnb. That would solve the issue of what to do with the doubles of everything. Smart, very smart."

"See.   I'm more than just a pretty face," he proclaims as he flashes a big smile. "So, how far is your friend's place from here?"

"Actually, he's just up ahead."

Not even twenty feet away, Leo is sitting off to the side reading a book. To the casual onlooker, he just looks like some scruffy kid lost in a book, but I can tell the way his head is tilted that although he has his eyes on the book, his ears are picking up all the sounds around him.

"What's shakin' bacon?" I say as we approach.

"Hey wifey!" he shouts as he jumps up from his spot on the floor. "I'd give you a hug, but, well, it's been a while since we got a room."

I hug him anyway.

"Here," I say as I hand him a bag. "Special delivery this time; some of it is all the way from Australia."

"No shit! That's where you've been? Your friend, the pretty blonde, she came by to say you'd be out of town for a bit, but wow! Australia! What's it like?" he asks as he starts digging into the bag.

"I'll tell you about it, but first I want you to meet someone. Leo, this is Killian. Killian, this is Leo." Lost in the excitement, Leo looks up from the bag a bit surprised to see someone with me.

"Hi, how are you?" Killian says as he puts his hand out to shake Leo's.

It's almost comical the way Leo looks from me, to Killian, to Killian's outstretched hand and then back to me;

his eyes getting wider and wider with each glance. "No. Friggin. Way!" he finally stammers as he reaches out and shakes Killian's hand. "The guys are never going to believe this! Dude!" he shouts looking back at me, "that's some souvenir you brought back with you!"

"So I've gone from wifey to dude have I?" I chuckle as I sit down on the floor.

Both guys follow suit. And although I've gotten to know a lot of the ins and outs of my new fiancé, it's still surprising to see him casually sit down on the subway floor in a suit that I know cost a small fortune.

"Well, yeah," Leo says with a one shoulder shrug. "With you and me, 'wifey' was in name only, but this guy, whoa, he's the real deal. I can tell by the way he looks at you. Well, and by the ring that's on your hand that you never wore before."

"Don't sell yourself short, man," Killian tells him. "You never know what will happen today, tomorrow, even a month or a year from now.

On a resigned sigh, Leo bows his head. I notice his shoulders begin to shake and for a second I'm worried he's trying to hold back tears until he begins to chuckle. "This is one of the most surreal days I've had in a long time! I mean, I'm sitting here on the floor in the Subway, homeless, hungry, and funky; and I'm hanging out with a guy that's wearing a suit that costs more money than I've seen in the past year, and who was on a Top 40 list of a financial magazine. Can't get much more polar opposite than that! And somehow it's not weird and doesn't feel forced; which in itself makes it weird." Reaching into the bag, he pulls out an apple, smiles, and takes a large bite.

"So, what will it take to get you up on your feet?" Killian asks.

"Mike's made about half of what we need to rent a place for a month. It would have been more, but we had to dip into the money he gets from his sorta-job because we weren't getting much panhandling and really needed to eat. Minor setback, but we're getting there."

"What if I told you that I know a place that will be available in about 2 weeks that's $450 a month, fully furnished, no pets, and the price includes electric, gas, hot water, and cable?"

Leo raises an eyebrow and looks at Killian over the rim of his glasses. "What's the catch?"

"No catch, but it's only a three month lease. You're expected to keep it clean and be respectful of the neighbours. No crazy parties or anything like that. It's in Brooklyn though, not Manhattan. So if your friend works around here, he'll have to commute. Think about it," Killian says as he gets to his feet and holds out his hand to help me up. "Like I said, it won't be available for another 2 weeks, so that should give you and your friends plenty of time to talk it over. Just let Donna know when you decide."

As we head to the train, I glance back and wave goodbye to a very stunned looking Leo.

266

33

By Sunday night I feel like I've been hit by a Mac truck. Even with calling in the available cavalry of siblings; shuffling and combining our apartments was backbreaking, sweaty work.

"How about I stop and pick up take out on the way back from dropping the U-haul?"

"Have I told you how wonderful you are recently?" I manage to ask from where I flopped on the couch.

"Hmm, not yet today I don't think. You can make up for it when I get back." He winks as he puts on his shoes. "Pizza and antipasto from Cosenza's work for you?" I grunt in reply. "I'll take that as a yes," he chuckles as he leans over to kiss me. "Love you, be back in a bit."

And with that, he's out the door before I can even respond. As I attempt to push myself up off the couch, I wonder how the hell he has the energy to be up and moving. I get as far as lifting myself up onto my elbows before giving up and flopping back down.

I'm woken up to the sound of pounding on the door that matches the pounding in my head. Ugh, sometimes catnaps are the worst! Bleary eyed, I glance at the clock on the wall and wonder how busy Cosenza's was for Killian to be gone two and a half hours. It's only a ten minute drive to the U-haul place on New Utrecht and a half hour bus ride back. How did he manage to unlock the front door, but couldn't open ours, I think to myself as I turn the knob.

Expecting to see Killian, it takes a few seconds to register that what I'm seeing is my brother Carmine and his girlfriend Grace. "Oh my god, I've been worried sick!" Grace yells as she throws her arms around me, quickly followed by "where the hell have you been?!"

"I must have dosed off. Why? What's going on? What's wrong?" The pitch in my voice gets higher with each question as I look back and forth between the two of them. Carmine reaches for my hand and tries to lead me into the living room, but I dig my heels in.

"We've been trying to call you for the past half hour. Avery has been trying to text and call you." Carmine lets out a slow breath and for a moment it seems like everything stands still. "Donna, Killian's at the hospital. I think maybe we better sit down."

Sit down? Sit down is bad. Sit down is very bad. I don't want to sit down, I want to go get my shoes and go to the hospital. Hell, I don't care about the shoes, I'll go barefoot! Why aren't we heading to the hospital?! Why won't my feet just head out the fucking door?!

Grace brings a chair from the kitchen into the hallway. When did she walk away? I didn't even see her move. Carmine gives me a gentle nudge into the chair, crouches down in front of me, and takes both of my hands in his.

"Donna. Listen. We'll head over to the hospital in a few minutes, but there are a few things I need to tell you first." My stomach drops to my feet, then comes flying back up and gets lodged in my throat. "We don't know all the details yet. But what we do know is he was on 18th Avenue when someone shot ... mugging maybe ... C-Town ... tackled him ... 911."

"Wait, what?" I whisper, having missed half of what my brother said because I couldn't hear him over the pounding in my ears.

"Carmine, go get her shoes," Grace suggests before she sits down on the floor in front of me. "Sweetie listen. Killian's in surgery right now. Until he's out and wakes up, all we know is there was some sort of confrontation and he was shot. He managed to knock the guy over or trip him or something. A guy came running out of C-Town, tackled the shooter and shouted for someone to call 911. The police have statements from the guy that tackled the shooter and from a few people that were nearby when it happened." Standing, she tells my brother to help me with my shoes while she goes and gets my purse, phone, and keys.

Sitting there by the door with my brother kneeling on the floor in front of me, reminds me of how right after he learned to tie his shoes, he had Marco and I sit on the bench by my parents' front door while he kneeled in front of us and tried to teach us how to tie our own shoes. Instinctively I swing my feet back and forth a few times before he looks up at me. The sadness in his eyes chases away the happy memory and I burst into tears.

~*~

I don't know how I got my legs to move, but flanked by Grace and my brother I made my way from the parking lot into Maimonides. The ER waiting room is absolute chaos which would regularly be an assault on the senses, but I'm too numb to notice.

Through the chaos, Carmine spots Avery and steers us in her direction. Her eyes, though teary, look relieved as she sees us through the crowd. Dropping the magazine, she was holding, she quickly comes over to us and throws her arms around me. My arms encircle her and at that point I'm not sure who is holding up whom.

"Have there been any updates?" Carmine asks over my head.

"Nothing yet. Everybody else is this way." As we head down the hall with Avery, she links her arm through mine. "Murphy got here not long after Tommy and I did. Sam and Monica got here not too long ago. John and Aveline agreed that he'd wait until after the kids went to bed to head in so that they weren't up all night with a million questions. By then the traffic getting in from Jersey shouldn't be too bad. When I came down to wait for you, Murphy was pacing the hall trying to get a hold of Mom and Dad."

None of us speak on the elevator up to the 6th floor of the Gellman building. I don't know if it's nerves, or that there's really nothing more to say, but the ride seems to take forever as we stop on every floor on the way up. With each stop, people meander on and off. I just want to yell

"Yo! Move or get the fuck outta the way!" The more agitated I get, the slower the people seem to move. Carmine puts his arm around my shoulder, gives a gentle squeeze, and it helps take the edge off a bit. I really can't afford to go ballistic and be escorted out of the building.

As the doors finally open on the 6th floor, my brother gives my shoulder one extra little squeeze before letting go. In a rush, the top half of my body tries to step out of the elevator without the lower half and I take a header into a passing nurse in purple tie-dye scrubs. Carmine tries to suppress a laugh that turns into the snort. It's quickly followed by an "ow" after Grace slaps his arm. The nurse seems unfazed, and after telling me to be more careful, she's back on the move.

Avery leads us down the hall to the visitor's lounge and introduces us to her husband and Sam's girlfriend. "No word yet on anything," Murphy says. "Mom and Dad are on their way. Sierra said she'll be on the earliest flight she could get on tomorrow morning. I told her to stay, but there's no telling Sierra anything. John should be here in another fifteen minutes or so."

"Wait. I thought he lives in Jersey." I look from Murphy to Avery and back again.

Murphy looks at me and his eyes get that twinkle I've seen so often over the past month. "Ah, well, you'll come to learn soon enough that John, hmmm, how do I put this?"

"John is a schemer," Sam finishes for him. "Our slick brother turned the clocks ahead an hour. He and the wife pretended to be surprised that they didn't realize how late it was. Then they told the kids to hurry and get ready for bed since it was past their bedtime."

"His scheming is funny now," adds Avery, "but it wasn't so funny while we were growing up."

"I can only imagine. I'll need to remember that trick for when ..." I let the rest of the sentence fall away. "Excuse me, I should go call Anna and let her know what happened."

Once outside of the lounge, I lean against the wall. With my eyes closed and my head tipped back, I try to take slow calming breaths.

"Hey, do you want me to call Anna for you?"

"Thanks, Grace," I reply as I hand her my phone. "Has anyone called Ma and Pops yet?"

"We called Marco and he went over to their house. We figured it would be better than telling them over the phone." I just nod. "Hey Anna, it's Grace. Yeah, she's right here. Uh-huh. Yeah. Um listen, I really don't know any other way to say this, but we're over at Maimonides, Gellman building, 6th floor lounge. We don't have all the details yet, but Killian was shot and is in surgery. Donna asked me to call you. Yeah, we're here for the long haul. Marco and Oliver will be by later. Then Carmine and I will go home and come back in the morning with my in-laws. Can you do me a favor? Get a hold of Max and tell him Donna won't be in tomorrow. Thanks. I will. Ok, bye." Grace hands me back my phone, takes my hand, and leads me back into the lounge. "Sit here and I'll go get you something to drink. They have soda, juice, coffee, or tea."

"No scotch?" I ask only half joking.

"Did someone say coffee?" In the doorway is a tower of a man holding two dozen doughnuts and a Box O'Joe. If it wasn't for the fact that he looks like Sam but with darker hair and broader shoulders, I'd have thought he was my own personal Fairy Godfather.

"I love you. You're my new best friend," I blurt out. For a split second there's absolute silence before the room erupts in laughter.

34

"Ok, that was Mom. She said that they're just parking the car." Murphy slides his phone back in his pocket as he gets up. "I'll go down and meet up with them."

"How bad is it that I wish I could go hide?" All heads turn in my direction, each with a varied look of confusion. "This isn't how I'd hoped to meet my future in-laws. Now anytime I think about meeting them, I'll be stuck with the memory of this visitor's lounge."

Avery comes over and gives my hand a squeeze. "Don't think of it as nerves, worry, sadness, anger, and all the other emotions. When you look back on it, think of it as a sign of strength, that we're all here for each other, good times and bad. Ok?"

I squeeze her hand back at a loss for words. Grace sits down on my other side and puts her arm around my shoulder. I try to draw strength from both of them, but all the "what ifs" come screaming into my head so fast that they're actually screaming over each other.

Avery gives my hand another squeeze. "Just breathe," she whispers close to my ear as she stands up.

Over the noises inside my head, I hadn't even heard Murphy walk back into the waiting room or the sounds of

Killian's siblings getting up to greet their parents. My legs feel numb from all the adrenaline rushing around in my system. If Grace hadn't pulled me up with her when she stood, I don't think I'd have been able to get out of the chair.

"Hi, I'm Grace, Carmine's fiancé," I hear her say. I blink my eyes a few times and realize that Sam has walked over with his parents.

"Mom, Dad, this is Donna," Sam says, placing his hand on my shoulder and giving it squeeze. "Donna, these are our parents, Connie and Christopher."

I open my mouth and try to say hi, but it can't get passed the lump in my throat. It should be Killian's hand on my shoulder as he introduces me to his parents, not his brother. I can feel my eyes begin to fill with tears, but I refuse to let them fall.

Warm hands envelope mine. "I understand, dear," Connie confesses as she squeezed my hands. "We wish we'd met you under happier circumstances as well. However, we're glad to have finally met you. Christopher and I have been very curious about the woman that was able to trump our son's love of work."

"I was hoping to make a good first impression," I admit as I give myself the once over and realize that although I'm wearing two sneakers, only one of my feet has a sock on it.

"Given the circumstances, you did, dear. You did." I'm pulled into fierce hug. "Don't you think so, Chris?" she asks her husband as she steps back.

"Indeed," he replies before he hugs me too.

As he steps back I notice that he has the same eyes as Gran, only instead of a mischievous twinkle I see a swirl of worry and sadness.

"Oh my god!" I exclaim as my hand flies up to my mouth. "Has anyone called Gran yet??"

I'm pulled back into a bone crushing hug. This time when Killian's father steps back his eyes are brimming with tears. "My son definitely chose well."

~*~

Killian's parents had decided on the car trip in not to call Gran with the news until after he got out of surgery and we knew more about what happened. As we sat there in the waiting room his parents told me stories about him growing up. I told them about myself and my family. Around midnight, Marco and Oliver showed up with a bag full of cold cuts and rolls and another bag full of sodas and fruit.

"You call me the second there's news. *Promessa!*"

"I promise, Carmine. Promise me that you'll bring me two matching socks when you come back, ok? And make sure he remembers," I say as I give Grace a hug goodbye.

"I'll walk out with you guys," Monica offers as she stands up and stretches. "I could use a smoke break and I'm sure we could all use some more coffee. There's a

Dunks right on the corner. Anyone want anything besides coffee?"

"I'll go with you," Sam says as he goes to stand.

"You stay here, hon. If there's news, I know you'd rather be here than somewhere else," she replies and leans down to kiss the top of his head. "I'll also check out what bagels they have so we can get breakfast in the morning."

As soon as she leaves, Sam lets out a long sigh. "Five years she's lived in the City, three and a half with me, and she still thinks fast food bagels are great bagels. The other night she said she'd order pizza for dinner and 15 minutes later knock-knock cardboard delivery. Hell, until we started dating, she thought that spaghetti and meatballs only came in a can!"

"You poor, poor man," Oliver consoles as he pats Sam's arm. "Probably a good thing Mama wasn't here or they'd be rushing in with a crash cart. Though I'm not sure if it would be for her or for Monica."

"Excuse me? Is there a Mrs. Cooper here?" asks a middle aged woman in mint green scrubs and a crisp white lab coat as she walks into the room.

"I'm Mrs. Cooper," replies Connie. As she stands she holds her hand out to her husband.

"Are you our son's doctor?" Chris asks as he takes his wife's hand and stands. "Is he going to be ok? What happened?"

"Yes, I'm Doctor Deshpande. I'm sorry, but I need to know who here is Donna Cooper before I can answer any questions." All eyes turn in my direction.

"Ma's so gonna kill you," Marco mutters. John slaps his knee and laughs.

"I'm Donna Giannino. I'm not officially a Cooper yet, but I'm Killian's fiancé."

"If anyone else comes in asking for Donna Cooper," the doctor says in a stage whisper, "just say that you are and go with it. Ok?" All I can do is nod in response. "Ok, let's all have a seat then."

"I'm not sure if I want to sit. Sitting means bad news," I respond.

Dr. Deshpande takes my hand and gives it a pat. "I think we should sit because there is a lot to go over; that is all. Please have a seat."

"Before you start, we need to know one thing." I swallow hard trying to push down bile. "Is Killian ok?" Connie reaches over and grabs my hand.

"That's difficult to answer I'm afraid. He is ok now, but there is a lot yet for him to still go through. I do not know the whole story of how he was shot, but he was brought in with two gunshot wounds. The EMS said when they arrived on the scene, he was barely conscious. He didn't suffer a head injury, and though he lost a lot of blood, I believe at that point he had reached his threshold for pain. According to the report he was able to tell EMS his name when asked. He kept saying 'Donna' and when asked who Donna was he said 'wife'."

"As good as," Chris added with a firm nod.

"Yes. I can see," the doctor replied with a warm but somber smile. "As I said, there was a lot of blood loss. Judging by the shots, the first was along here," she says as she points to a spot just below her ribs on the right hand side. "It went in and just grazed the ascending colon. There was a small tear in the intestine that we were able to repair. I am a bit concerned with infection given the nature of the injury; however, as long as there is no infection, I expect that to heal nicely with no long lasting effects. The second shot caused the most damage and will likely require more surgery. The skin at the entrance was burned meaning that the gun was either very close to or right against the skin. It went in right here." She raises her hand to her right shoulder along the top. "The collar bone was shattered. The bullet went in at an angle just missing the subclavian artery and became lodged in the scapular spine, which is the bone along the back of the shoulder blade. Given the angle and the course of the second bullet, we have reason to believe that after the first shot, he raised his right arm and may have been trying to strike or tackle his attacker and that's when the gun went off the second time. Killian's collar bone required fifteen pins. We were able to remove the bullet from the scapular spine and repaired it with a cancellous bone graft. There was some repairable damage to ligaments and nerves. He has a long road ahead of him. Physical therapy will be required and more than likely he'll need additional surgery. We won't know the extent of the nerve damage for a while yet though, so I can't say either way if he will lose the feeling in his hand, his arm, or both, if at all. For now, we are keeping him under heavy sedation to make sure he stays immobile."

"I need to see him," I blurt out.

Dr. Deshpande reaches over and pats my knee. "I understand, but it will be a while yet. Once he is moved into a regular room I can let people in two at a time to see him. In the meantime, go home, get some sleep, we're taking good care of him."

"I'm staying," I reply, the tone in my voice letting everyone know that there's no room for argument. Connie gives my hand a squeeze and when I look over, she has a small smile on her face.

"Remember, you can't pour from an empty cup. Take care of yourself, otherwise you won't be able to take care of him," the doctor adds before rising and heading for the door.

Once the doctor is gone, I stand up and face everyone. "Now that we know, Marco, you call Carmine. I'll call Anna. Someone will need to call Gran and Sierra. I'm assuming John that you'll call your wife and let her know. Since our apartment isn't too far, that can be used as a place for people to shower and rest."

"Our place is available too," says Oliver. "Shower, sleep, laundry, food, coffee, whatever anyone needs."

"Thanks Oliver. Anyone that doesn't have my number in their cell phone already its 646-555-0791, text me your numbers. I'll need someone to run to our apartment and bring back a change of clothes for me, toothbrush etcetera, my cell phone charger, my laptop, and some bottled water. Knowing my mother, she'll bring breakfast early. Tomorrow's lunch and dinner we'll figure out when the time comes. We've got a wait ahead of us to see him, but as soon as he's in a room, Connie and Chris can be the first to go in. The rest of us, we'll figure that out based on who is here then. Any question? No? Good. Now where the hell is Monica and the coffee?"

"You. Are. Priceless." laughs John as he claps.

35

The next few days pass by in a blur of sitting with a sleeping Killian, coffee, and attempting to work from the hospital. The nurses have stopped counting me as part of the two visitors at a time rule. Connie and Chris have been using our apartment to shower, cat nap, and come back with more clothes for me. I've gotten to know them a bit better and vice versa while we sit here for hours on end day after day. I know I should go home and get a good night's sleep, rather than attempt to sleep each night on the make shift bed I've created out of two armchairs.

Killian's siblings have been coming by as they can. After we spoke to the doctor, Connie called Sierra and convinced her to wait until the weekend to fly in. Chris had a harder time getting Gran to stay put. My mother brings or sends Nico with lunch every day, claiming that the hospital food "is-a no good-a for you", "prop-ably make-a you sick", and that when Killian wakes she's "gonna make-a him a nice bowl a pasta so he feels-a better".

"Donna? Donna?"

"Oh, sorry!" I reply looking up from my laptop.

"No worries," Chris says with a smile. "Connie and I are going over to that great little Polish deli on New Utrecht that your brother told us about. What would you like for dinner?"

"I'd love a Zywiec, but I don't think beer would go over well with the nurses," I reply, trying to make a joke.

"If it's what you really want," Chris starts placing a hand on my shoulder, "I can make it happen."

The mischievous twinkle in his eyes, the same one I've seen a million times in Killian's eyes, is almost my undoing.   My only response is to pat his hand and slowly shake my head no.

"I know, dear," he adds, crouching so that we're eye level. "He's young and he's strong.   Have faith in the doctors and his body's own ability to heal itself. You're a smart, kind, caring woman.   Our son was lucky to find someone that both compliments and completes him. Remember that, because once he's up and coherent, he's going to be a stubborn impatient ass. You may want to rethink that beer."

I squeeze his hand and nod.   "Thank you," I managed to get out on a quiver.

With a smile and one last glance at Killian, he heads out the door. Slowly exhaling, I set my laptop aside and walk over to the window.   The view is such a stark contrast. It's people, and cars, and noise.   The chaotic rhythm that is Brooklyn is an assault on the senses that both invigorates and centers me.   Twice I've gone outside for a few minutes to recharge my system.   It's actually done more for me than all attempts at sleep combined.

"Hey Momma!" comes a shout from the doorway. "Sorry I couldn't get here sooner. I just dropped the kids at their Dad's for the three day weekend and thought I'd stop by. How are you holding up? How's your man?" The whirlwind of energy that is Linda pulls me into a hug.

"Hey Chica" I reply on a half sob. "I'm attempting to hold it together. This is Killian. I'd do the intro thing, but they've still got him under."

"*¡Ay mamí!* Woooo, fan me! He's a damn fine specimen of man meat! Good for you!" I can't help but laugh. "What? I'm being serious! I mean, look at him! Even unconscious in a hospital gown and in desperate need of a shave he's USDA Prime! Now, show me the ring and then spill the details! Oh, and this is for you."

Taking the bag from her, I open it up to find a container of her homemade empanadas and under that a few 187mL mini wine bottles. Digging in, I give her the short version of the trip and since we've been back.

"Ok, two questions. One, this hunk is Frisbee guy? Seriously?! And two, does he have any single brothers?"

~*~

Around two in the morning on Friday just as I start to nod off, I hear the door to Killian's room open. It's a miracle patient's get any sleep while they are here with the constant flow of nurses coming in to check their vitals. Just as the nurse starts finishing up, I hear him softly talking to someone. Recognizing Dr. Deshpande's voice, I sit up and stretch.

"Morning-ish," I mumble and rub my eyes.

"Sorry, we didn't mean to wake you."

I wave away the apology. "Hard to wake someone up that wasn't completely asleep anyway."

"I just wanted to check in one last time before I left and to add some notes to his file. Everything looks good, so I'm going to have them start weaning him off of the Propofol to bring him out of the sedation. They'll start slowly though so that he doesn't immediately start trying to move around. Once he is conscious, Dr. Brikatz will make the decision regarding fully weaning him or not and then determine what pain medication should be administered. Once he's fully awake we'll run a few tests to check for nerve damage and continue to take blood samples to make sure there's still no infection. We don't want him moving much. Should he wish to be propped up in bed, no more than a twenty degree angle, and not without the assistance of one of the nurses. Strict orders. And nothing to eat or drink until he's given the all clear. I will be back here Sunday evening and will stop by to check in on him. I'll close the door on my way out. Try to get some sleep while you can."

Sleep? Is she serious?

~*~

Apparently my body followed the doctor's orders and I manage to sleep a full five hours. Next thing I know, Connie and Chris walk in with a take-out container from the

Coffee Shop on Fort Hamilton and 45th. It's piled high with chocolate chip pancakes.

"If you want coffee, we'll go back later and get some. But you've been living on way too much caffeine lately so we brought you a cranberry juice," says Connie. "No. I mean it. No coffee until after all your breakfast and juice are gone."

As I dig in, I tell them what the doctor said during the night. While Chris goes out into the hall to call Gran, I send a blast text to Ma, my brothers, Anna, and Killian's siblings.

"Sure you don't want any of these?" I ask, motioning to the pancakes.

"We've already had breakfast. We gave serious consideration to coming here first and dragging you with us. You could use a break from sitting here. And the little trips downstairs for five minutes don't count."

"I'm actually thinking that after I finish breakfast that I should be the one to walk down to the Coffee Shop for the coffee. Knowing that they're bringing him out of the coma makes me feel a bit lighter. Once he's awake I'm not going to want to go far, so this looks like my only opportunity." Popping another bite of pancakes into my mouth I smile for the first time in days.

36

By Friday evening, the family waiting room is full of Coopers and Gianninos. We've been rotating which two are in the room with Killian. Both moms are in the room when I walk in. "The general consensus is 'whatever' for dinner. Any thoughts?"

"I'll call Nico, tell him to bring the lasagna I make-a earlier."

"Not sure one pan will be enough for everyone. What should we have with it?"

"Maccas," comes a faint groan from the bed. I run over to the bed and squeeze Killian's hand.

"Hey, you're awake," I say, calmer than I feel, as I brush his hair off his forehead. "Try not to move too much, ok?"

"See! I toll-a you, macaroni fix-a everything!"

Connie and I burst out laughing as I hit the button for the nurse's station. Once the nurse comes in and we tell her that Killian is awake, it's a flurry of activity. When the doctor comes in, we're sent to the waiting room. There's a cheer from the group as we tell them Killian is awake and everyone starts talking at once. My mother goes into the hallway to go call my brother Nico. Once she's out of the room I tell everybody about what was said in the room and how she thought Killian was asking for pasta.

When Nico shows up, my cousins Susanna and Massimo are with him and between the three of them, they each manage to carry in a tray, one of lasagna, one of meatballs and sausage, and one of salad, as well as 2 huge loaves of bread, a grocery bag full of fruit, a few bottles of soda, and all the plastic ware for our feast.

We're half way through dinner when the doctor comes into the room. My mother automatically jumps up and hands the doctor a full plate of food; followed immediately by questioning him on when she could go bring Killian a plate. She wasn't pleased when the doctor said that it would be a while yet before he could have anything to eat.

"We will keep him on a steady dose of pain killers. Remember, no food or beverages right now. We've already sat him up in bed as far as we're allowing for now. Should he want to lie down, call the nurse's station. The police will be here in the morning to get his statement. We've put off blood work for tonight, but will do two draws tomorrow. If those come back clean, then he can eat. However," he warns making a point to stare at my mother, "he'll only be allowed things like jello and broth, nothing spicy, nothing acidic, and nothing very filling. And still only 2 visitors at a time. I'll be back in a few hours to check in on him and see how he's doing."

I tell Connie and Chris to go first. They try to convince me to go in with them, but it seems only right that they should go in first by themselves. A part of me is stalling, trying to siphon strength from the group so that I can go in there stronger than I feel. Another part of me would rather wait until everyone has had a chance to go in to see Killian because I know that once I go in there, I'm not coming back out of the room.

"Has anyone seen Monica?" Sam asks when it's their turn. "She went out for a cigarette twenty minutes ago."

"Knowing your brother is awake, she probably went into the gift shop when she came back inside," Connie suggests.

"Well, I can't wait," he sighs and walks out of the waiting room.

"Should I go downstairs and see if she's in the gift shop?" I ask.

"She probably went out for a cigarette, wandered off, and is sitting at the Urgent Care on 42nd wondering where we all are," answered Murphy.

"Seriously, she'd get lost in a paper bag. Even one with a giant neon arrow pointing the way out," added Tommy.

When Sam comes out of Killian's room and Monica still isn't back he says his goodbyes and heads home, a look of anger and defeat on his face.

"We should probably head home too," Avery says as she stands up and stretches. "I want to be back here early tomorrow morning. Do you know where you're staying yet, Sierra?"

"If there's room with Mom and Dad, I'll just follow them."

With a round of hugs, Avery and Tommy head out only to have Monica barrel into them in the doorway. Apparently she got off the elevator on the 5th floor and had been sitting in that waiting room down there wondering where everyone was. When she got Sam's text saying he was heading home she realized she was in the wrong waiting room.

Slowly the waiting room empties as people get their chance to see Killian and then leave. Dr. Brikatz has already come back to check on him, and once Connie, Chris, and Sierra leave, I head into the room.

With the exception of him being propped up a bit, he looks the same as he has all week. He's just lying there, eyes closed, paler than usual, and scruffy from not shaving. I quietly make my way into the room and sit down in the chair beside the bed. Elbows on knees, I lean forward so that my forehead is leaning on the mattress and let out a slow breath. It's been a long rough week, and things aren't going to get any easier for a while.

"Donna?" Killian whispers.

"I'm right here," I reply reaching for his hand and giving it a squeeze.

"I'm so sorry."

"There's nothing to apologize for," I insist as I reach up and brush his bangs from his face.

"So, so tired."

"Get some rest, *caro mio*. I'll be right here."

He moves his hand from my grasp and places it on my cheek. "Need … to talk … before tomorrow … it's important."

Every word is an effort for him to get out and he's fighting against exhaustion to get them out. I try to shush him and reassure him that I'm not going anywhere, but he slowly shakes his head no.

"I wasn't mugged," he pleads. "Don't … leave … the hospital. Not safe … sweetheart," he manages to say before passing out.

37

Late the next morning when the cops arrive, I'm asked to leave the room. I'm adamant about staying but Killian says its fine; just not to go further than the waiting room. Any time I've brought up his cryptic message from last night, he brushes it off and changes the subject.

I'm glad that it's a Saturday though because there are more of us sitting here in the waiting room. It makes waiting out here only slightly less nerve racking than it would if I was sitting out here by myself.

Just as I get called back into Killian's room, Marco and Oliver show up with enough sandwich fixings to feed a small army. Figures. I hate not being in Killian's room, but I also don't feel right eating in front of him right now.

When I walk in, I notice that Killian looks like he needs to vomit. He's paler, with a pinched look on his face, and a little sweat on his brow.

"Hey! Are you ok?" I ask rushing over to the bed. "Are you in pain? Should I call the nurse?" He shakes his head no.

"Miss Giannino, I'm Officer Loesche. This is my partner Officer Shaughnessy. If you could have a seat please; we have a few questions, then we'll be on our way."

I slowly lower myself into the chair next to the bed and take Killian's hand. For the next ten minutes I'm asked all manner of questions regarding my whereabouts Sunday night, my relationship with Killian, and if I would any reason to believe someone would want to harm Killian or myself. All pretty standard questions, but when Officer Loesche asks if I've seen anything out of the ordinary recently, something clicks.

I tell her and her partner about the suit in the subway that Leo spotted on more than one occasion. I leave out the part about him being a kid on the streets. I don't want him involved or picked up so I spin it and say he's a friend I meet after I get out of work and he gets out of class and then we ride home together.

"After the second time we saw him, we switched up where we'd meet. We haven't seen him since."

"And how would you describe this guy?" Officer Shaughnessy asks.

"About your height, though not as broad shouldered, he had a shaved head, 5 o'clock shadow, brown eyes, olive complexion. He didn't look like he was used to wearing a suit."

"Why would you think that?" he asks.

"He would mess with his shirt collar and tug at the jacket sleeves. Then again, maybe he was nervous about something or was allergic to the material the suit was made out of. He could have been a well-dressed junkie for all I know."

"Well, the description doesn't match the guy we've got in custody for the stabbing incident, so it may or may not be related. We won't rule it out yet given Mr. Cooper's statement of the incident."

The hair at the back of my neck stands on end. I look from the cops, to Killian, and back again. There's a hint of something in the female officer's eyes, but I can't place it. Apprehension? Warning? Sympathy?

"What are you not telling me?"

Killian gives a slight nod to the officers.

"According to Mr. Coopers' story, there was an altercation and an exchange of words. The assailant drew his gun, shot Mr. Cooper, and said 'and that fucking bitch is next'. At which point Mr. Cooper tried to tackle the assailant and the gun went off a second time."

And that's when the world went black.

~*~

My head feels funny. Like someone cut a hole in my skull and poured in Pop Rocks, or boiling oil, or maybe both. I can hear voices but can't make out quite make out what they are saying. I slowly open my eyes and then squint against the brightness.

"There we go. Easy does it. Let's try to sit you up."

"What happened?" I ask.

"I'd say that you fainted," replies the doctor as he helps me up. "Have you eaten anything today?"

"I think it was something that was said," Officer Loesche answers.

That's when the conversation comes flooding back and slaps me in the face. If the doctor hadn't already been helping me into the chair I had been sitting in, I would have hit the floor again. I feel a cold sweat start to break out on my forehead and the back of my neck. My arms feel like jelly and my fingers like sausages as I reach out for the small garbage can that's just behind the chair. I luck out and get it onto my lap just as I start vomiting.

As I'm heaving all I can think about is that this is all my fault; that Killian got shot because of me. That sets off the crying, which makes me vomit more. Now I'm sitting there a vomitus snotty mess, clinging to a bucket of my own puke, wishing I had never been fierce and gotten on that plane. If I had stayed in my safe little hole, none of this would have ever happened. My past wouldn't have harmed his present or future. I don't know why or how, but I know this has something to do with Ralph, I know it!

"Don't go there, Donna! Don't you dare go there," Killian admonishes as he reaches over and places his hand on my shoulder.

"How can you stand to be near me, this is my fault!" I scream and it feels like a rake being scraped down my already sore throat.

"Look at me," he says. He tries to sit up when I don't look at him but the doctor stops him.

"How is any of this your fault?" Officer Shaughnessy asks.

It's all too much at once, so I tell them to have Marco come in and explain it all. As my brother tells them what happened between Ralph and I, I can feel myself retreating; slowly slinking back and shoring up the walls I'd built up. I can't help it. It makes me sad and at the same time I'm angry with myself. I'm far from fierce. I'm not even close to fine. Most of all, I hate how weak I am and how weak I must seem to everyone else. I've always hated weak female characters in the books I've worked on, and here I am being everything I've ever despised about all of them.

"Are you ok?" Officer Loesche asks, bending down to look me in the eye.

A hollow laugh escapes. "Do I look fine?"

"No. You look like you're in shock. I've seen the look before, way too many times before." She takes my puke bucket and hands it to the nurse. "Come on, let's go for a walk."

I'm surprised that my legs are able to support me when I stand up. I can't even look at Killian as I follow the officer out of the room. With my head hung low, I shuffle alongside her down the hall to the room with all the vending machines. She offers me a cup of coffee, but I shake my head no. Walking over to one of the small tables, she pulls out a chair and has a seat. Seeing no other option, I do the same.

"Listen. This isn't your fault," she says. I just look down at my lap. "Look, I know you don't believe your fiancé; that somehow he's just saying it to make you feel better. But take it from someone outside of all this, he's right. It's going to take you a while to realize the truth of the matter, but don't give up on yourself. Once you give up on yourself, it's almost impossible to dig your way back out. I've seen it happen all too often to too many women. It almost happened to me. Don't let it happen to you."

As she gets up from the table, she places her hand on my shoulder and gives a little squeeze. "Remember, if you continue to blame yourself, he wins all over again. Don't give him that power."

38

I spend the next two weeks thinking about what the officer said. It's almost become the mantra that gets me through the day. And right now, I need all the help I can get. Killian has been more than a handful since being released from the hospital. I'm glad that Connie and Chris have been here to help out, but I'm feeling a bit walled in. With everything going on, Killian doesn't even like the idea of me going downstairs to watch the old Russian guys play chess.

"I'm telling you Ollie, I feel like any minute now and I'm going to start climbing the walls!"

"Just be glad that you have this lovely little courtyard back here."

He reaches down and picks up the pitcher by his feet and refills my glass. To anyone else in the buildings, it just looks like two people sitting on a bench in the courtyard having some iced tea. In reality, we're secretly sipping contraband Long Island iced teas and this is the most I've been outdoors since we left the hospital. And the only reason I'm "allowed" out here is because it's fully enclosed, with the only way in being the locked front doors of the two apartment buildings.

"I guess," I sigh. "It's just frustrating as all get out!"

"That's because you finally knocked down those walls you'd built up and now that you're free, you feel like you've been tossed into a cage. I get it. But it won't be forever."

"What happened to telling me to be fierce?!"

"Stop giving me the hairy eyeball, sweetie. There's a time to be fierce, but there's also a time to watch your back."

I grumble and take a sip of my iced tea. I know he's right but it's driving me insane.

"Donna! Ollie!" I look up and there's my mother leaning out the window yelling down to us. *Vieni di sopra adesso! Andiamo!*

"I feel like I'm twelve years old again being called in for dinner." I chuckle and shake my head.

Oliver grabs the pitcher and we head back upstairs. As we walk in the door, the smell of my mother's marinara slaps us in the face. We turn to look at each other and crack up laughing.

"No time for the jokes. We got people comin-a for dinner."

"Ok, Mama," Oliver says, "what do you need us to do?"

"Such a good boy. You toss the salad while Donna cuts the cheese."

I try to suppress the laughter and snort so hard I end up feeling like my tonsils are going to come flying out of my nostrils. Oliver is wheezing so hard he has to sit down. Hearing the commotion, Killian comes into the kitchen to see what's going on. I pull out the chair I had been using to hold myself up so he could sit and then tell him what my mother said. He tries to turn his face so that she can't see the tears in his eyes from trying to hold back the laugh. As she's reprimanding us for being a "bunch-a the heinies", we completely lose it.

"Sounds like one hell of a party going on in here," Marco calls as he walks in the front door.

Before he can head to the kitchen, I cut him off and turn him towards living room. Clutching my side, I fill him in on what my mother's orders were for Oliver and I and how she then tried to call us hyenas but messed up the word and called us heinies instead.

"It's good to hear laughing around here." Marco throws his arm over my shoulder as we head into the kitchen.

"*Finalmente!*" my mother exclaims as she waves her wooden spoon at Marco, "someone to help! Pull outta the meat and put it on-a the table".

Eventually we all calm down enough to help set up the tables and chairs in the living room and help my mother with the rest of the food. Killian was relegated to folding napkins. In my mother's eyes, just because he's injured and had to take something for the pain in his shoulder from laughing so hard, doesn't excuse him from helping especially since he was one of the "heinies".

"That's an awful lot of plates and silverware for just us," I say as I take in the set-up of the living room.

"Yeah, but with our family, you never know who is going to drop in," Marco shrugs.

He wasn't kidding! Zio Nino and his family show up; followed by Zio Giovanni and Zia Grazia with three of their twelve grandkids, Avery and Tommy, John and Aveline with their kids, Sam, and Anna and Tim.

Dinner is loud and fun, everyone is in small groups all chatting away. It's like boisterous family gatherings, but on a smaller scale. Well, except for the food that is; doesn't matter if it's a small or large group of people, my mother always cooks as if she's feeding an army.

"I got the call from my doctor," Anna says as she reaches for Tim's hand and I have the sinking feeling that my dinner isn't going to stay down. Looking up through her eyelashes she smirks (SMIRKS!) and says "Cancer Free!"

I jump up from my chair, knocking my plate to the floor. In my excitement I throw my arms around her and almost tip us and her chair over. We hug, we laugh, we cry, and then she shares the news with everyone.

After everything settles down and I clean up the mess I made, we go back to eating and chatting. She just finishes filling me in on how she saw Leo and that the guys are going to take the apartment, when there's a knock on the door. Everyone that was coming over is here, and the buzzer from the door downstairs didn't go off. I go to get up but Zio Nino puts up his hand before heading to the door.

"Donna, can you join me in the kitchen for a minute?" he asks, poking his head back into the living room.

Shrugging, I get up and follow him.

"Sorry to barge in on your party," says Officer Loesche as I walk through the kitchen door.

"Um, sure, no problem," I reply.

It's really weird seeing her here. For some reason, it seems even weirder seeing her out of uniform. She gives a small smile as if she feels the same way.

"Late last night we got a call from a lady downstairs that there was someone lurking around by her window. When the officers arrived on scene to check it out, he tried to jump into the front bushes." She laughs and shakes her head. "They brought him in for questioning and he's being held while they see if he has any priors, et cetera. When they put it in the system it cross referenced your case because the addresses match. On a hunch, I thought I'd stop by with his mug shot." Reaching into her shirt pocket, she pulls out a copy of the picture and hands it to me. "Is this the guy you and your friend saw in the subway?"

The hair at the back of my neck stands on end and my eyes go wide. With an unsteady hand, I give her back the picture and nod. "He's a bit scruffier looking, but that's him."

"Would you and your friend be able to come down to the 70th Precinct station and pick him out of a line up?"

"I can see if Anna can get a hold of him for me. He's in the process of moving from Manhattan to Brooklyn and kind of without a phone right now."

"Here's my card. If you'd feel more comfortable, I can meet up with you over there. But try to go sooner rather than later since we can only hold him for another day and a half if he has no priors."

My Uncle volunteers to bring me over to the Precinct tomorrow, and after declining to stay for dinner, Officer Loesche heads out the door.

39

My Uncle and I head over to the Precinct before Anna finds Leo. It's probably better that way anyway.

I'm not exactly sure what to expect when we get there, but I didn't expect it to be over and done in a manner of minutes. We were shown into a small room with a double mirror. As soon as we were seated, they turned off the lights and the suspects were brought into the next room for the line-up. I knew which one he was even before the last guy walked in. I pointed him out, was asked if I was one-hundred percent sure, and then we were leaving.

Instead of heading right back to the apartment, my Uncle drives us over to Green Pavilion and orders us each a chocolate milkshake and a plate of fries to share. It reminds me of so many other times, both good and bad, that he's brought me here over the years. From things like losing my first tooth and getting my driver's license, to losing my first cat and getting dumped by my first boyfriend; it's always the two of us slurping milkshakes over a plate of fries. It makes everything feel right in the world.

"I know it's going to take a while, but I really wish this was all over and done with. I thought I'd already put this behind me, but now it's back and trying to screw up my life again!"

"You've got yourself a good man. So I don't see all of this messing that up," my Uncle insists.

"But it is!" I argue. "We're basically trapped in the apartment until this all blows over. That's not living."

"It's going to take the detectives and then the prosecution a while to get it all wrapped up. Until then, just try not to kill each other, ok. I've already bought a new suit for your wedding."

I tip my head back and laugh so loudly a few heads turn.

~*~

The next month actually flies by incident free. Not long after my Uncle took me over to the Precinct, Connie and Chris head back to Connecticut. Anna has been coming by on Wednesdays and we work from home. On Saturday afternoons we get together to look online at wedding stuff. My mother has decided that every Sunday my kitchen is her kitchen and we have a large family dinner like we did when I was growing up; the only exception being that now I don't wake up to the smell of her sauce cooking like I did as a kid.

We've even left the apartment a few times; twice for Killian's follow up doctor's appointments and once we went over to his old apartment to meet up with Leo and the guys. We had them sign a lease so that they have proof of address and then handed them the keys. All three times we went out, my Uncle has been our chauffer.

The following month Officers Loesche and Shaughnessy come by to let us know that the detectives have been able to connect the guy that shot Killian and the guy that was stalking me with Ralph, along with two others.

"The Prosecution is building a case against all of them. You'll both have to show up to testify," Officer Shaughnessy informs us.

"Be aware though," Officer Loesche says, looking me dead in the eye, "that Ralph will likely be transferred down here to appear in court. And, he could be in the court room at the same time you are. I want to make sure that you know that ahead of time and it doesn't come as a surprise. Will you okay with that?"

"Absolutely," I reply, taking hold of Killian's hand and smiling as I give it a squeeze. "I'll more than fine, I'll be fierce."

Epilogue

8 months later

"Fuckity fuck fucker, where's my other shoe?!"

"Donna! Language!" Anna scolds and points to the other side of the room where the cherub cheeked flower girl is being helped into her dress.

"Shit, sorry! Oh damnit! I mean ... aww hell, I give up! I'm just so nervous. I want this day to be perfect!"

"And it will be, now shut your yap, zip me up, and I'll help you find your shoe."

"How are you so calm?!" I yell.

She just laughs and turns so that I can zip up the back of her dress. Then she goes and checks all the bags along the back table while I look under chairs.

"Found it!" she calls out a few minutes later. "Though how it got behind the fruit basket I have no idea."

Laughing, she hands me the shoe and I wobble a bit as I shove my foot into it. We head over to the mirror for final hair and make-up checks, when there's a knock on the door.

"Everyone decent?" Oliver chimes from the door, "Well, with the exception of Donna who's never been decent. Bah-ha!"

"Thanks!" I laugh and give him a big loud kiss on the cheek. "I needed the tension breaker."

"Glad I could be of service. But I'm really here to give you your five minutes to show time heads up."

After a quick flurry of excitement and a few last minute primps, we line up in order by the door. I reach for Anna's hand and give it a squeeze.

"Ok, breathe."

"I am breathing," she laughs.

"Sorry, that was more for me."

The door to the bridal suite opens and Pachelbel's *Cannon in D* comes drifting into the room. I hand my flowers to Anna, shake out my hands and feet, then slowly take a deep breath and let it out. Opening my eyes, I take back my bouquet and give Anna a quick hug.

"Love you, Anna Banana!" I say before walking out the door.

I slowly make my way down the aisle, concentrating on not falling flat on my face. It's not easy. Up ahead I see Killian's smiling face and I feel myself smiling even more. We've been through a lot over the past year. But no matter what life has thrown at us, it has only made us stronger. He winks as I get to the last few pews and I blow him a kiss as I walk passed and up to the altar.

In keeping with the Ukrainian tradition, Anna and Tim walk down the aisle together. She looks stunning; like a bohemian goddess in her short white shift dress with a slightly longer taupe colored crochet overlay. No longer needing her wig, she has her short hair done up in braids and accented with tiny blue and purple flowers. Gone are the sunken cheeks and dull, pasty complexion. She looks radiant and full of life again.

As they reach the altar and the priest begins to sing, I'm overcome by an overwhelming sense of joy. My vision a bit blurry with unshed tears, I'm deliriously happy for them.

I'm also grateful that I'm here. I'll forever be thankful to the amazing detectives and the team of diligent prosecutors who brought an end to Ralph's ring of former prison buddies wreaking havoc. The guy that shot Killian was charged with attempted murder and conspiring to commit murder. The stalker was charged with stalking in the 3rd degree and trespassing. He was also charged with conspiring to commit murder and accessory to attempted murder; as were the other two guys we hadn't known about. All four were sent to different prisons for no less than fifteen years each and they aren't allowed contact with each other. As for Ralph, being the mastermind of the whole scheme, he spent three weeks in solitary before being transferred out of state. He's now in a maximum security prison down in Louisiana and has had all chances of parole revoked.

After the priest binds Anna and Tim's hands and they begin to walk around the altar three times, I steal a glance over my shoulder at Killian. Who would have thought that being nailed in the head by a rogue Frisbee could lead to the one person that makes you feel whole?

As I turn my head back to the altar, my eyes catch the addition to the tattoo on my shoulder; an intricately detailed phoenix rising from the flames with the words "she'll be fierce" woven across its wingspan. I faced the fire ... and then rose from the ashes.

310

Special Thanks

To my amazing husband and kids - for their patience and understanding. I know it can't be easy dealing with someone who bounces from one creative outlet to another and back again. You are what keeps me grounded and centered. *Anche, a mio marito, senza di te, la vita sarebbe una esistenza noiosa.*

To my parents - for not trying to cram a square peg in a triangular hole; and for being supportive, even when you didn't agree with the various paths I kept jumping on and off of. I guess being the way you are is why you ended up with three really cool daughters, huh? Seriously, ask Gina and Dre, they'll tell you the same thing. A big thanks for giving us the gift of reading, and encouraging us to read often - even if it's the newspaper as a bedtime story.

To my sisters - for all the wacky moments that kept us from becoming dull. "Bonsai!" "Run into my foot!" "Stabilize yourself, MOO!" "Needs more pepper!" "ALMA!" "P&T" "Dinner interlude"

To my Aunt Lu – if a person's wealth was measured in love, I'd already be a millionaire.

To fellow authors Mary Frame & Janet Elizabeth Henderson for their invaluable wealth of knowledge that helped make this journey possible.

To the following people for sharing this journey with me each in your own way. (It's hard to put the feelings into words, but here goes)

Paul Rively - for listening to my babbling and venting; and for being a soundboard that I could bounce ideas off of, in all manner of crafting! 2017 is going to be our year, and we're going to kick Con ass!

Wyelene Davis – for help with San Fran local geography, and for being a ray of sunshine, sass, and sarcasm; which kept me sane(ish) in my 219/5 cubby. Love You!

Eric Lao - for all the crazy nights in a tiny dive bar called The DownTown (thankfully all before camera phones and social media), for lending your artistic talent to both this book and my body art, and for keeping me level before the "s" got a chance to "htf".

Dana Spano – for keeping my 3rd eye opened and tuned into creativity and for pushing me to keep challenging myself.

Raina van Setter, my wonder twin! - for the million and one years of friendship, life would have been greyer without you in it. Your love and support means more than you'll ever know. You are an amazing woman! (I still owe you a sweater!)

Annie Whitaker & Laurel Boxsell – Though it was sadness that brought us together, you've both become more than friends to me, you are family.

Radha Raman – for your vast medical knowledge & your words of wisdom while I was in labor ("push, bitch!").

Melissa Libutti – my soul sista and fellow Norman-drooler, thanks for being the laugh break among the nutters.

Christina Schaefer – for being able to deal with my "oddness" all these years and for feeding me fries while I drive.

Linda Price-Gonzalez – from Warbrick's all the way to now .. it's been one crazy ride! I'll bring the wine, you bring the empanadas, and let's break out the dye! (I miss when we still lived in The County of Kings!)

Steve Spence – for answering oddball questions and letting me pick your brain; repeatedly, and then again.

My 11th grade English Teacher David McTamaney – for kicking my butt into academic shape and reigniting my love of learning.

Robin Gardner, Helene Löfgren, & Georgia Jennings – Three amazing women who I wish I could hug in person! The three of you have been a big support through this whole journey, I couldn't have done it without you! One day we should really all try to get together offline. Perhaps meet up in a café and hit up Java Joe for coffee. (hahaha)

My "HodgePodge Ohana", all 5,000+ of you – A big thank you for all the mental breaks and words of encouragement over the past few years. Trends come and go, the crazies flounce, but YARN & Helena are forever!

To my Beta Testers – thank you, thank you, thank you! And thank you some more! I can't begin to put into words how amazing you all are!

The Rasmus – whose music kept me sane during the 24+ hrs of formatting the paperback layout and during the redo of the redo for the cover wrap. *Suuri kiitos, kaverit! Halauksia!*

To Bree, Tim, and Smitty – I hate that you had to leave us all behind.

314

Notes From The Author

Now that you've made it to the end, I don't have to worry about spoilers so much. I thought I'd add this section to the end so that I can address some questions and "but what about ___?" that I've gotten about the story and tell you a little about myself.

First and foremost, I'm not Donna. We do have some similarities, but we're not the same person. I'm Italian (though only half) and my father is "off the boat". My mother isn't Italian, but makes the best marinara I've ever had. I used to live in Brooklyn and I set Donna up in my old neighbourhood. I also used to work in midtown right around where I set Donna's office. The park that I mention in Tudor City is Ralph Bunche Park and was one of my favorite places to sit and have lunch ... on the rare days I actually left the office to have lunch, that is. I used to love taking the subway down to Coney Island to just sit on the beach and have down time. I love Nathan's fries, but I don't eat hot dogs. I've never been hit in the head with a Frisbee.

Killian isn't based on anyone I know. Though, some of his expressions are what I refer to as "Matt-isms" (things my husband says). There was a time where we were living on opposite sides of the country, so there were a lot of emails and AOL chats back then, like Donna & Killian.

The beers that Killian and his siblings are named after are all real beers. If you haven't tried them (and are of legal age where you live), you should try them.

Besides writing, I also love to knit, crochet, paint, read, doodle, dance in the kitchen while I cook/bake, and I have a SERIOUS love affair with learning. I don't have one favorite subject though, I have many.

Leo does really exist, though that's not his real name. The scene that describes how Donna met Leo is how I met the real life Leo. I did change some of the details about his age, where he came from and his family, and the number of guys that were in the band. I'm not sure what became of him and the guys though as I stopped seeing him around about 8 months before we left NYC.

When I was in my early twenty's, I did have a fiancé that told my friend he was going to kill me after I broke up with him. No, he never attempted it. And, it wasn't an abusive relationship like Donna was in. I didn't base Ralph on of him, but that character got the name specifically because thinking of my ex-fiancé used to make me want to "ralph", aka puke. Teehee!

I haven't been to Australia ... YET! As a result of researching the flights and local info, I've been bitten by the travel bug. Cairns will be part of the itinerary for the trip. However, my passport is both out of date and has my maiden name on it, so it'll be a while yet before I get there. That ... and I need to get over my fear of drop bears before I go – HAHAHA!

I have 2 sisters and no brothers. I'm the oldest.

I don't have a Zio Giovanni, but I based him on my Uncle Carmine who sadly passed away just before I started writing this book. I named Donna's brother

Carmine and his fiancé Grace after my uncle and aunt so that they are together always.

I'm a stay at home mom and we're a home school family.

Oliver's personality is based on a combo of my friends Paul and Arthur. Paul chose the character's name. Anna's based loosely on a combo of my friends Mary and Zoryana (Jerry doesn't exist in real life). Alera is based on my friend Dana and she got to name her own character.

The characters Matt and Nicole are named after my husband and I.

I have boxes and boxes filled with notebooks of various stories, some of which are written in other languages and none of them are close to half finished. My first attempt at a novel started out as a letter I was writing to a friend in Denmark (Hejsa Anders!) while I was on a 6 hour train ride from Plattsburgh, NY to Croton, NY in the late 90's. I got about 15 chapters in and it fizzled. I'm glad it didn't keep me from wanting to try again (and again).

When I fill out paperwork, I check "Other" for race and write in "HUMAN".

If you ever find yourself in Manhattan, the coffee cart in the book really does exist. It's on the NW corner of 42nd and 2nd. It's only there early in the morning though but the coffee is beautiful, there's no other way to describe it. You won't run into Dada ji and Nani ji though, as they are purely fictional, but the guy that runs the cart is a really nice guy.

I don't like vanilla ice cream, which is why the milkshakes Donna and Nino get are chocolate as it's the only kind of milkshake I like.

In the breakfast scene in Gran's kitchen, Donna says "one pineapple, mate". A "pineapple" is slang for a $50 bill in Australia.

There really is a Paddy O'Fadden's in Midtown. Though that's not the real name of the place, if you happen to figure out where I'm talking about, I highly recommend the food there!

Avery's husband Tommy Smith is named after a friend of mine who passed away too soon. I still remember getting that phone call like it was yesterday and how grabbing a hold of the sink kept me from hitting the floor full force.

Tim is named after Tim Walker, who, like my sister in law Bree Hayes, had Pulmonary Hypertension. They are both sorely missed by many.

Stay Tuned for Book 2 of the 5 Boroughs Series!! Keep up to date on Facebook, Instagram, and Goodreads!

***

About your purchase:

For the first 60 days this book is for sale, 20% of the total sales will go to fund Jenny Janzer's lung transplant fund. After the first 60 days, 20% of the total sales will be donated to phaware global in memory of Bree & Tim. We're all in this PHight together!

From Book 2 of The 5 Boroughs Series

(Coming Winter 2016/2017)

"Ladies and gentleman! Please out your hands together for the new Mister and Missus Coooo-peeeerrrr!" the DJ announces to the roar of everyone in the room.

As Killian and Donna enter the room, flashes start going off in all directions and the cheering intensifies. When they reach the center of the dance floor, the music changes. Ed Sheeran's voice starts filling the room and they begin to dance in a swirl of white, purple, and blue lights.

Just as the chorus to the song begins, the DJ tells the wedding party to join the happy couple. Leading Donna's cousin Susanna onto the dance floor, I wonder where my girlfriend is. As the best man, I obviously have to dance with the maid of honor right now, but the last time I saw her was as we were all walking back down the aisle after the ceremony. She was sitting in one of the last rows with some of my brother's friends.

"Take me into your loving arms. Kiss me under the light of a thousand stars. Place your head on my beating heart."

Susanna and I are close enough that I can hear my brother singing along as he's dancing with his new wife. Glancing over I get a look at his grinning face. It puts a smile on my face but at the same time it leaves an empty feeling in my gut, laced with a hint of jealousy. Not that I'd admit that last bit to anyone. Ever. But in the almost five years my girlfriend and I have been together, I don't think I've felt anything that strong.

"Hey," Susanna says quietly as she moves in closer. "Is everything ok?"

Forcing a smile back in place, I tell her I'm fine; that my mind took a short side trip. She just raises an eyebrow and gives me the "nice try, buddy" look and I shake my head and chuckle.

The song ends on a repeat of "we found love right where we are" and I look down at Susanna. In another time, in another life, maybe. She's sweet and has an easy, from the soul kind of laugh. She's also easy on the eyes and has curves that could make a man beg. But seeing as her cousin is now married to my brother, that puts her in the "big book of never" right next to never take advantage of the elderly, never sleep with your boss's daughter or wife, and never harm someone unable to protect themselves; unless they are causing harm to someone you love.

The dance floor starts to clear as people make their way to their tables. Before she has a chance to back away, I lean in and whisper "promise me, if you see me getting melancholy again, you'll come kick me in the shin or something, ok?"

She gives our still joined hands a squeeze and laughs loudly before lightly kicking me in the shin. I snort. She takes my offered arm and we make our way to the head table.

"Anyone see Monica around?" I ask as I pull Susanna's chair for her.

"Last time I saw her, she was over at the bar," answers Tommy.

"Thanks," I respond as I head over towards the bar. On the bright side she hasn't decided to cut out early. A part of me wouldn't be surprised if she did. That part of me also wouldn't really care if she did; which is fairly poignant considering she's my girlfriend.

I can hear her laughter before I pick her out of the crowd. She's at the bar doing shots with the bartender and some of my brother's friends. I'm about ten feet from the bar when the DJ announces that it's time for the toasts; so I'm forced to change directions and head back to the head table.

In contrast to my current mood, I manage to come across upbeat during my toast. Since I'm truly happy for my brother, being jovial hasn't been difficult. I've even made it through the night with Susanna only kicking me three times. Though the last time I think was more for her own amusement than anything else.

It's been a long exhausting day and tomorrow the wedding party is getting back into their wedding attire to head out to Coney Island to take some more pictures. So once the festivities start to wind down, I head over to the table Monica was at.

"She and a few of the others decided to continue the party at a bar down the road," one of her tablemates informs me.

I shrug and go back to the head table to say goodbye to Killian and Donna. I'm really not surprised that she left without a word. It still irritates the shit out of me though. Recently it's more like we're roommates than a couple.

I can't pinpoint when it happened either. I spend the ride home trying to think when it all went wrong, but I can't. So caught up in my own thoughts I almost miss the 169th St stop.

It's a gorgeous night; not a cloud in the sky, and even though it's still summer, there's almost no humidity. There are still people out and about this late at night, but I'm glad it's not insanely congested like a lot of places in Manhattan get on a Saturday night.

I'm also glad it's not a far walk. Usually I don't mind the walk, but my feet are killing me in these goofy looking dress shoes. Killian insisted that we all wear the same shoes, but for the life of me I have no idea why he would pick pointy toed dress shoes! Seriously, who the hell has pointy toes?!

Three blocks later, I'm trudging up the steps to our place across from Saint Stephen's and wondering how painfully Donna would kill me if I made her a widow tomorrow.

I head into the kitchen, grab a beer from the fridge, and flop down at the table. As I kick off my shoes, I make a mental note to wear sneakers down to Coney Island tomorrow and just carry these implements of torture my back pack.

Popping the top off of the Doppelbock, I open up the gift bag from the wedding. Inside there is a small box of chocolates, a magnet with a picture of a didgeridoo that say "I Doo!", and another small box tied with a ribbon.

After sliding the ribbon off the box, I open it to find a golden keychain of a miniature Frisbee. It cracks me up. With a smile on my face, I finish my beer and hobble off to bed.

Made in the USA
Charleston, SC
25 January 2017